The Opposite Of Gravity

A novel

By D. L. Prophet

Acknowledgments

The process of creating doesn't happen in a vacuum for me. As solitary as writing can be, it would never have any meaning without life and the people in it who inspire us. I want to thank my dear friends Jodelia, Nancy, and Sandy for planting the seeds of the idea for this story. I also want to thank my other BFFs Patti Whitfield and Theresa Clarke for your support, feedback and ideas. Theresa, you were the first one to read my lowly little manuscript. Your response to it was beyond encouraging.

You are an amazing group of women who inspire me with your humor, strength and insight. Knowing you all has been a huge blessing to me.

I also want to thank my sons. Eli, thank you for helping me with formatting my book for publication and helping me to put the cover together, (I couldn't have gotten this book out there without your help) and Sky, my go to IT man, thanks for helping me with my technological challenges!

A BIG thank you also, to my sweet man, Ivan, for patiently helping me to get this story into print. You've been my best cheerleader throughout this whole journey!

Last, but for certain not least, I want to thank my mother, Elizabeth, for instilling in me my great love of books. Since I was a little girl you were, and are such a great storyteller, mom!

To…
Eli, Sky and Ivey

Foreword

The idea for writing this novel was born one evening over take-out Thai and many glasses of wine with my besties. I had been divorced for a couple of years and had spent the past few months in the strange world of online dating. I was telling tales of my misadventures to my alternately amused/horrified friends. After hearing how I had negotiated my way around some challenging situations, they suggested that I write a "how to" manual...an *online dating for dummies.* I am so not the manual writing sort and I figured someone out there probably had already done it and better than I ever could. But, a tell-all was a tempting idea...except for the part where I embarrassed the crap out of my two teenage sons, or maybe that was tempting too.

So I started. And something happened. It seemed like everywhere around me people I cared about were experiencing tremendous losses. Two friends lost children, two friends were diagnosed with cancer, and another friend went through a painful divorce. I had gone through my own personal scare with cancer. We had lost pieces of our bodies and pieces of our lives. We had all been rocked by these emotional tsunamis. It changed us. It had changed me.

I found that I needed this story to be about more. I still wanted it to be entertaining. I still wanted to make people laugh, but I also wanted to say I know what you're going through. I wanted it to be a kind of love letter to anyone who had experienced heart-breaking loss.

Life seems to be a strange process of ongoing loss and change. Traveling though it with grace involves learning to let go. This book became an often-humorous look at those losses and how they inevitably change us. It's about how those changes make us grow and become more than we were and the gifts that come with that.

Chapter 1 ~ Happy Birthday to Me, or The
End of the Beginning

I'm coming up on my thirty-eighth birthday.
My husband, Nathan, is taking me out for my
traditional birthday dinner to Flora's, one of my
favorite seafood restaurants. Flora's is an eclectic
little pearl perched right on the edge of the
waterfront overlooking the harbor of the tiny town
of Sandyport, with it's fishing and lobster boats
moving in a seemingly choreographed procession to
and from the sea.

For as long as I've known Nathan he's been
bad at keeping a surprise a secret. He knows this
about himself. As a result, he will pretty much
avoid you if you are the intended recipient as a way
to avoid spilling the beans. The bigger the surprise
the more covert he becomes. When he threw me a
surprise party for my thirtieth birthday he barely
said a word to me for the entire week leading up to
it. Whatever he has in mind for this year, it's going
to be huge. He has hardly spoken to, or looked at
me for the past two weeks. Yesterday morning he
came out of the bathroom after taking his shower
and said good morning without taking his eyes off
the runner on the floor. The past few nights he
didn't come to bed until I was fast asleep.
Controlling my excitement is bordering on painful.

The kids have been left with my mom and
it's just the two of us out for a romantic celebration.
Nathan is pretty quiet during dinner, which isn't
particularly unusual. He's quiet by nature. I happily

chatter away filling up his share of the conversation as I anticipate the big reveal. At the end of our meal the wait-staff and chef, who know us well after our many years of dining here, come to our table and perform a lively, off-key rendition of happy birthday complete with cake and candles. Shortly after they've left, and I've all but licked the last bit of chocolate-raspberry torte off my plate, Nathan hands me the large envelope I had earlier observed him stashing on the floor by his feet.

"What's this?" I ask, smiling coyly, my eyebrows positioned expectantly. He scowls at his napkin as he answers almost in a mumble,

"Something I thought I should give you."

I'm beyond intrigued. He's being so weird and mysterious even by Nathan standards. It obviously isn't the usual little box with earrings, or a necklace. My mind is racing. This has got to be major and I'm hoping it contains brochures and airline tickets for the trip to Santorini we've been talking about taking for years. I open the envelope and slowly remove the contents briefly smiling across the table at Nathan who has an oddly uncomfortable look on his face. It's an official looking document. As I begin reading it the words begin to swim in a blur before my eyes. I feel as though time downshifts and everything around me seems to move in slow motion. The waiters and waitresses swim laboriously past our table as if through a sea of corn syrup. It is without a doubt the most surprising birthday gift I have ever received, and surprising for many reasons. What I am holding in my hands are divorce papers.

I never saw it coming. About six months before, Nathan and I had started couple's therapy not because we had a bad marriage, but because we wanted an even better one. Our therapist was an energetic, New Age practitioner named, Debbie Lane, who prided herself on being a non-traditionalist. She seemed like a good fit for us and in no time at all Nathan and I were moving through our negative stuff and "getting clear" with each other, as Debbie liked to say. We saw her as a couple and also had sessions individually.

A few weeks before my birthday, Nathan had been scheduling his individual appointments in the evening. Sometimes, he wouldn't get home till nine, or nine-thirty. He explained that he was the last patient of the day and that they had lost track of time. I was impressed and touched by how dedicated he was to making things better. I would never have believed those many months of working on my marriage with my husband would have led me to this place.

When I look back up at Nathan he's staring into his water glass. His right hand is sitting on his linen napkin as he nervously fingers the monogrammed "F" like a blind man speed-reading Braille. It takes me a few attempts at forming words to get my mouth to coordinate with sounds. I can feel it moving, but nothing will come out. Like a fish stranded on dry land trying desperately to gulp air, my mouth opens and closes silently. It's Nathan who is the first to speak.

"I'm so sorry, Nicki. I didn't plan on this happening." He looks at me briefly and blinks hard before going back to staring into his water glass.

"But why?" I pause, searching my mind for the right question. My fingers tap my forehead as I search for the one that will produce the answer that will make this confusion go away.

"What? Why?" It's the best I can muster. I lick my lips and notice they've gone numb.

"Debbie and I feel awful about this. We really never expected it to happen, but it did."

My confusion gives way to disbelief. Is he saying what I think he's saying? Before I can ask him what he means he goes on. Now that he's started it seems he can't unburden himself fast enough.

"Debbie and I both felt the most important gift I could give you for your birthday was the truth. I felt awful keeping it from you these past few weeks. You have the right to know and to get on with your life."

Nathan has always had a crappy sense of timing and I find myself thinking how much nicer the little box with earrings would have been when he goes on.

"We really love each other."

Those words do it. I feel as though I've been whacked with a two-by-four straight across my stomach. I exhale sharply and then focus with everything I have on trying to get a single breath in. I start feeling light-headed as I grip both sides of the table as hard as I can. A buzzing sound fills my head and Nathan's face fades from my sight like a snowy television screen.

I hear strange faraway sounds, as if voices are thickly wrapped in cotton batting. The next thing I know I'm coming to in the ER of the local hospital. A ruddy-faced doctor with halitosis is repeatedly saying my name, three inches from my face, and asking if I can hear him. The bad breath works better than smelling salts.

"What happened?" I ask, bolting upright on the gurney, just as the sight of Nathan and Debbie enters my peripheral vision. I instantly feel very awake.

"What the hell is she doing here?" I hiss through my clenched teeth at Nathan, who moves behind Debbie using her as a potential shield.

"I thought you might need some help processing this."

She says it with such phony sweetness I imagine cavities forming in her even, overly white teeth.

"You want to help me process this? I've seen what your help gets me Debbie. Why don't YOU process THIS, I think you're a conniving, husband-stealing, BITCH!"

I say it loudly enough to turn almost all the heads in the ER. Dr. Halitosis observes the scene with a look of mixed confusion and fascination before he speaks up.

"I'm sorry folks, but you're going to have to go to the waiting room while we do some more tests. I want to keep her calm and your presence seems to be agitating her."

He herds them out of my curtained area. When they're gone he pulls a chair up beside me and studies my chart in his hand.

"Was it a heart attack?" I ask, clutching the front of my little black dress. "I couldn't breathe and I had this terrible pain in my chest."

"It definitely wasn't," he reassures me, "We're going to make certain but we think you had a panic attack. Has this ever happened to you before?"

I slowly shake my head, no.

"Could you tell me, did something happen just before the episode that could have triggered it?"

This time I nod mutely. He waits for me to elaborate and I reluctantly continue.

"I got some very upsetting news."

He mulls over my chart seemingly searching for more clues. "I see it's your birthday today."

"Yes," I answer, my voice trailing down my legs and disappearing into the new black patent leather stilettos I bought for the occasion.

A solitary tear rolls down my cheek followed by another, slowly at first, but quickly building to an impressive volume. I'm briefly aware of the doctor awkwardly placing his hand on my shoulder. As the ache in my heart becomes more intense, I realize in that moment, a heart is one thing that still works even when it's completely broken.

Chapter 2 ~ The Center of my Joy

I go through the next few months in a fog of too much sleep and massive quantities of Ben and Jerry's ice cream. At the end of three months, my steady regimen of sacking out on the sofa watching endless television, surrounded by sacks of cookies and various other junk foods has deposited twenty-five extra pounds on my small frame. Why is it that I feel as if I can't even gag down real food? At five foot five, I have gone for the first time in my life from lean to chunky. Not surprising, when you consider my diet is junk food twenty-four seven and my only exercise consists of either lifting the remote, or a box of tissues.

Nathan has moved out of the house and is renting an apartment ten minutes away, which is a plus when it comes to carting the kids back and forth and a negative when it comes to awkwardly running into him at the local grocery store.

The worst time was when I spotted him and Debbie canoodling their way down the frozen foods aisle, giggling as they filled the basket between them. They were so busy playing kissy-face and making eyes at each other that they didn't notice me with my ratty, unkempt hair, and overflowing cart. For a nano-second I imagined running as hard as I could straight into them with my cart, screaming at the top of my lungs and pinning them between me and the frozen food cases. Instead, I turned around and made a straight path for the checkout line even though I hadn't had a chance to grab my supply of Cherry Garcia.

I feel guilty about where I've let myself go every time I think about my kids. I can see the worry in their faces when they come home from school and find me still on the sofa in my bathrobe at three in the afternoon. Even though I know I'm only adding to their pain, I can't seem to stop myself. It doesn't seem possible that I can be alive and hurt this much. Each day I breathe in and out in disbelief.

Perhaps the most horrible part is my loss of a sense of self. I no longer know who I am. For the past fifteen years I have been Nathan Ferris's wife and partner. We had lived together for three years before we married. I have spent almost half of my entire life with this man and had had every intention of spending the rest of it with him. There was no plan B. I had never seen the need for one. Friends often told me that they envied us and that we seemed to have the perfect marriage. It wasn't perfect, but it was the center of my joy. I was never complacent about it. I never took it for granted. I had always felt blessed and fortunate. My single mistake was thinking it could only get better. Sucker punched. That's how I feel. Sucker punched.

There are moments when I want to slap him hard across the face and scream at him, "How could you do this to us? How could you?" and then there are the moments when I long to lay my cheek against his and have him stroke my hair the way he always did, while I tell him about the terrible thing

15

that's happened to me. But I can't. He's the terrible thing that's happened. My best friend, my go to person, is gone.

When I call my mom to tell her the news hoping for some emotional support, she pulls a Sicilian on me. She is one of the sweetest people on the planet as long as you don't screw things up for her.

Nathan had been the dream son-in-law from day one. He was always helping my dad with projects around the house. He ran errands for them on his way home from work and when it snowed, he'd be at their house with a shovel as soon as he was through with ours. When my dad passed away a few years back, my mom came to rely on Nathan even more. The way she saw it, I had just ruined that for her and she let me know in that uniquely vindictive way her sisters have informed me is a Sicilian thing.

"I can't say I'm surprised," she said, when I told her the news. "I can't believe it lasted this long. What kind of marriage is that when the wife doesn't take her husband's name?"

Keeping my maiden name had been a sore spot with my mother. In some ways she's very modern in her views, but that wasn't one of them. She always introduced me to people as Nicola Ferris instead of Botticelli and each year she would mail me birthday and Christmas cards addressed to Mrs. Nathan Ferris. It wasn't until she had heard the gory details involving our therapist that I could elicit any compassion from her and then it poured out in such a suffocating flood, I had to find a kind way to tell her to stop bringing by the endless pans of baked ziti and meatballs that were filling my freezer.

Chapter 3 ~ Potato Salad, Pastrami, and Paris

People talk about hitting rock bottom. For me it was the day I lost it in the deli department of the local supermarket. I was beginning to dread going grocery shopping for fear of running into anyone I might know, particularly my former therapist and my soon to be ex-husband. I would anxiously trek up and down the aisles craning my neck to peek around the corners, periodically remembering to glance at my list. I probably looked like an escaped convict on the run or some sort of paranoid schizophrenic. Inevitably, I would run into some well meaning, or not so well meaning soul. Today it's Betsy Farber who seems to be having an awfully good time telling me how terrible she feels for me. If she has a sincere bone in her body it's a small one, like her baby toe.

"Oh Nicola," she says, resting her hand briefly on my arm only to quickly remove it and place it on her own chest for dramatic effect, "I was so sad to hear about you and Nathan and I can't believe he left you for another woman."

She's smiling the whole time as she shakes her head in mock distress. She couldn't look more pleased. By the time I get to the deli counter I'm beginning to unravel.

It might be the way the man behind the counter asks, with just a little too much kindness in his face and voice, if he can help me. Whatever it is, it makes me want to climb over that glass case, grab him by the front of his clean, white apron, and beg him on my knees,

"Yes, please help me! I NEED help!"

I lose it. I start crying right there in front of the pastrami and potato salad. The poor man looks bewildered and quickly turns from his right to his left searching for a clue to my unexpected reaction.

Within my peripheral vision I can see people slinking away, pretending not to notice me creating a pool of tears that threatens to soon have us all floating. Standing by my elbow, a fearless little white-haired lady who has probably seen it all and then some, fishes in her purse, pulls out a tissue, and presses it into my hand with a comforting squeeze. I leave my half-filled cart right there, making my escape to the parking lot and the safe asylum of my car.

This is the day I stop returning phone calls from my concerned friends and I cancel any plans I had made to get together with them. For the next several weeks, on nights when I don't have the kids, I shut off all the lights, pull the curtains tightly closed, and hope it looks like no one is home. I swim in a river of self-pity. I let it carry me wherever it's dark murkiness flows.

It's on one of these 'lights out' nights that a knock comes on the front door. I ignore it the first few times I hear it, but whoever it is isn't easily deterred. The knocking becomes more insistent and it's eventually accompanied by some crazy-ass doorbell ringing that demands my attention. It suddenly occurs to me that there might be some

19

kind of emergency and since I had unplugged the phone earlier, I run to the door with fears of something awful having happened to the kids. Breathlessly, I open it to find my friend Paris standing there with her fist in the air poised to continue her relentless pounding. She takes me in with one sweeping look from head to toe and her mouth drops open.

"Jesus, you look like shit!" She's never been one to mince words.

"Don't hold back." I reply. "Tell me what you really think."

"I'm sorry honey, but I've never seen you look so bad and by bad, I don't mean good."

She says this as she moves past me in the doorway and begins surveying the living room, which hasn't been cleaned in weeks. It's liberally littered with empty pizza boxes and bags from eaten cookies and chips.

"Wow," she stands there with her hands planted on her hips and her head shaking in disbelief.

"It looks like you had a frat party in here. The only thing missing is an empty keg and a few unconscious, half-dressed bodies."

I hustle her into the kitchen, which is barely more presentable and put a pot of water on for tea. I take the scrunchy out of my hair and pull it all back into a ponytail in a lame attempt to look less disheveled even though I haven't changed the sweats I'm wearing in three days. Paris hasn't said a thing since we got to the kitchen. It seems like she's still trying to wrap her mind around what she's just seen

"Well, you certainly look great." I say, attempting a lighthearted tone.

Paris is a hardcore fashionista and so impeccable in her appearance, she has often joked that if her house were on fire, she would stop to put on lipstick before she would leave the premises. She's the daughter of a Russian-Jewish father and an African-American mother. The combined gene pool resulted in an attractive mix of high cheekbones, full lips, wildly curly warm brown hair, almond-shaped hazel eyes, a voluptuous body, and café-au-lait skin.

"Thanks sweetie," she smiles limply and shakes her head, "I kept calling you and leaving messages. You didn't call me back."

She says this as she looks everywhere, but at me. It's less of a statement and more obviously a question. I choose to treat it as a statement and stand there in guilty silence staring down at the salsa stain on the front of my shirt from two days ago.

"I should have come over sooner. I knew you were putting me off. I just figured you needed some time alone." She pauses. "I didn't realize you'd taken it so hard." Her voice fades to a whimper. "I'm so sorry I haven't been here for you."

She puts her face in her hands and starts crying, which sends me instantly over the edge. I put my arms around her and it's impossible to tell who is crying harder.

She sits me down in a chair and finds a clean wet cloth. She uses it to wipe my face and the simple kindness of that nurturing gesture brings another wave of tears from a place so deep inside of me I can barely breathe.

"It's okay", she murmurs, resting her cheek against mine and as she gently rocks me, my breathing slows. She wipes my face again and grabs a paper towel for my nose.

"Blow," she orders, as if I'm four-years-old.

She moves to the stove, turns off the teapot, and makes a pot of chai, which she knows is my favorite. As we sit sipping and talking, I realize the thing I had needed most I had pushed away, and that was the kind of support I get from my closest friends.

"I'm going to call Terry and tell him that I'm staying here tonight." She announces when she see me yawning.

"You don't need to do that. Really, I'm feeling so much better."

She picks up the phone and starts dialing. "Don't argue with me girl. Besides when was the last time we had a sleep-over?"

Chapter 4 ~ Interventions and Makeovers

I wake in the morning to the sound of Paris busily tidying up as she drags a large trash bag through the living room quickly filling it. As if she could read my mortified mind, she orders me into the shower with the same tone of voice she uses on her two kids when she wants to let them know that any kind of negotiating is out of the question.

When I reemerge from the bathroom, Paris is dancing around the living room as she vacuums. The sound of Al Green is cranking out of the living room speakers. This is the most upbeat energy this room has seen in awhile. I feel an oppressive weight being lifted off of my life along with the dust and debris and I breathe deeply for the first time in many weeks.

"Hey, you!" she hollers over the whine of the vacuum. "We're doing an intervention today. I called the girls and we've decided it's time for you to re-enter the land of the living."

"What?"

She shuts off the vacuum and turns down the music. "I've booked us all for a spa day at Eliza's." she says, with a matter of fact tone. "Lily, Kate, and Sophia are coming too. I called Nathan and told him he's going to keep the kids until three."

She TOLD him. Oh, lord. I start to open my mouth and she puts up her hand before I get a chance to protest. I've watched her use this same gesture on her kids and I'm amazed at how effective it is. Again, I feel like I've been reduced to four-years-old.

"It's our treat and you should never refuse a great gift. Now go get dressed and no sweats." She turns back to vacuuming.

She's shut me down. I mutter curses under my breath as I go through the pile of laundry half burying my bed trying to find something that still fits me, is clean, and doesn't fall under the category of sweats. I can't believe I'm being treated like a misbehaving child who's about to get a time out if I don't watch it.

Before I know what's hit me we're in the car making a quick stop to pick up coffee and muffins. Paris chatters away on her cell phone with her oh-so-patient husband giving him very specific instructions for running the household in her absence.

When we walk through the door of Eliza's the girls are all there. As soon as they spot us I find myself surrounded by a comforting cloud of nurturing femininity. Kate, who is as warm as her cinnamon spice coloring, crushes me in her version of a bear hug.

"Why did you make us all worry? I'm glad Paris came and knocked your door down, or we were all coming to get you and it wouldn't have been pretty." She teases.

Sweet, soft-spoken Lily with her wide open face wells up as she plants a kiss on my cheek, and dramatic Sophia almost scowls at me with her intense dark eyes.

"Yeah, you pull a stunt like that again and I will personally kick your ass," she half whispers in my ear, as she gives me a squeeze.

There are more hugs and kisses followed by head shaking and slightly scolding tongue clucking over my present state of disrepair. Eliza, the owner, comes out and like the grand mama hen she is, she gathers us all up and distributes us into various chairs in the room. Accompanied by three of her best girls she dramatically announces with a sweeping wave of her French manicured hand in their direction,

"Today we're going to give you complete makeovers; facials, manicures, pedicures, hand and foot massages, and we're going to do your hair and make-up." She claps her hands together delightedly. Eliza is a woman on a mission who is passionate about her work.

Paris passes around coffee and muffins and Kate puts some Ottmar Liebert on the IPod as we all settle in for some serious pampering. Eliza decides to take me on as her pet project. As I sit in a chair facing a large, unforgiving mirror, she recites the litany of horrors she's about to tackle. From my straw-like hair, to my untidy eyebrows and overgrown cuticles, she lets me know I'm a hot mess. I give myself over to her capable hands and as she conditions, waxes, and moisturizes, she dishes.

Eliza is not unlike a bartender in that people confide in her. She gets all the juiciest gossip in town. In no time we're all caught up on what's been going on in our neighborhoods. I even get to hear the latest on what's being said about me and I find it strangely comforting to know that most folks think Nathan is a bum and that Debbie should lose her license.

Of course there are those few women who are certain I must be the villain. Not surprisingly, they're the same ones who relentlessly flirted with Nathan as we all cheered for our kids at their soccer games on Saturday mornings. They're the same women who would say good morning to me without taking their eyes off of him.

The most unexpected bit of news though, and the one that seems to touch me the most, is how much my aerobics classes miss me. I had taught several classes at the local Y as a good way to make a little extra money while keeping myself in shape. The job came with the added perk of giving Nathan and the kids free memberships. I quit when I felt like I couldn't face people anymore.

By the time we leave with lots of kisses and gushing all around, I don't just look like a new woman with silky, shiny hair, and perfect make-up and nails, I'm beginning to feel like maybe I could be one.

Chapter 5 ~ Renoir and Max

I have spent the past few months cocooned in sorrow. I couldn't see out and I let no one see in. I was completely shrouded in all that pain. By the time I arrive home it's as if I have shed that opaque layer and I'm clearly seeing things for the first time since Nathan left.

I feel excited about having the kids for the weekend and I stop off at the grocery store to pick up everything we need to make pizza together. When Nathan drops them off I nervously watch from the hallway as they come through the door. They both stop short and look around checking out how clean the living room is, slowly taking it in before they turn their attention to me. Max, my twelve year old responds immediately in his usual open, unguarded way, throwing his arms around me in a big hug.

"Mom, you look so pretty!" he says.

"Thanks sweetie." I kiss his forehead. With the way he's been growing lately, it's right at the level of my nose. I look over at my daughter Renoir who, at fifteen has the usual issues with her mother that all teenage girls seem to have. But lately I have this sense that she blames me for the break-up. On some level I think she believes if I had made her father happier, he wouldn't have found someone else and left. I can't blame her. I have days myself when I entertain that notion and I should know better.

She moves toward me from where she has set her bags down. Close, but not too close. She tilts her head and narrows her eyes slightly as she scrutinizes my new look. I'm half expecting her usual sarcasm, but she surprises me.

"I like your hair," she says, sweetly. " It looks really good." I'm so touched by her moment of generosity I have to blink back tears.

"Thank-you," I say, reaching out and lightly touching the dark curls she inherited from her father, "that's a really nice compliment."

She shrugs it off, grabs her bags and as she starts to head to her room, I stop her.

"Can you wait a minute Ren?" I take a deep breath, looking at the two of them. "I need to say something to you both."

I look at their questioning faces and push past my guilt. "I know I've been a mess lately and I want you to know I'm really sorry. I promise, I'm going to make it up to you."

Renoir's expression doesn't change as her eyes blankly move from my face to the floor. She silently turns and heads off to her room. At this point in time I guess I can't expect more than that from her. It's Max, my little protector, who puts his arms around me one more time.

"It's okay mom."

Even though his kindness feels good, I know the truth is, it's not okay. We all go out to run a couple of errands for school supplies and while we're driving Max tells me about his friend Tommy's new dog.

"He's so cute and funny. He follows Tommy everywhere he goes. The only thing Tommy doesn't like is he has to walk the dog every day. If the dog doesn't get enough exercise he chews things up, like the furniture and Tommy's shoes."

My mind attaches to the word exercise. A dog. Exercise. I'm picturing myself racing up and down the beach with my four-legged friend.

"We should get a dog," I announce as if someone else has control of my mouth.

I might as well be speaking a foreign language. Max turns toward me with a confused look on his face as Ren moans from the back seat.

"I'm not walking any dog," she whines.

"You don't have to. Max and I will walk the dog. Right, Max?"

He looks utterly perplexed. "Do you mean it?" he asks pitifully, as if I was his sister messing with his head just for the fun of tormenting him.

"I mean it. We could go right now to the shelter in Beverly and see what they have. I look into the rearview mirror at Renoir. "What do you say? Are you up for a ride to Beverly?"

She casually murmurs her consent being very careful not to appear too interested, while Max goes berserk with delirious joy in his seat next to me. On our way there I lay down some ground rules. It can't be too big a dog and I would prefer it to be at least four months old and pretty much housebroken.

We get to the shelter and begin inspecting the crates. I feel like Goldilocks looking for the perfect chair and I keep finding ones that are too big, or too small, too hard, or too soft. Of course Ren and Max are completely smitten by the nine-week-old little balls of fluff that will someday, in the not too distant future, end up being the size of a riding mower. Some of the crates are empty even though they have information about a dog on the front.

I see one such crate that says its inhabitant is a six-month-old female mix breed from Mexico and I ask one of the women if they still have it. She tells me that the puppy just arrived there yesterday and is in the exercise pen while her crate is being cleaned. She points me in the dog's general direction. I'm not seeing a dog that would fit that age category until I move closer and then I see her sitting quietly while chaos reigns around her. She looks about eighteen inches high. Her short coat is a warm gold color and her large brown eyes look as if she's wearing dark eyeliner.

All around her dogs are jumping at each other and barking and there she sits, still and serene, as if she's waiting for someone. I walk over to the gate and ask the attendant if I can hold her and she brings her out and puts her in my arms. It's then that I feel she's shaking. I murmur and cradle her like a baby holding her on her back, and she immediately relaxes. Max and Renoir spot me and rush over.

"What do you think guys?" I ask.

Max scratches her behind the ears and rubs her belly. "What kind of dog is it?" He asks.

"She's some kind of Mexican wild puppy." I offer.

"She's really cute. She's got eyes like a person. Can I hold her?"

I hand her over to him and she cuddles with her head on his shoulder.

"Mom, look she's hugging me."

Max is all smiles and even my apathetic daughter seems enthralled as she coaxes Max to hand over the little bundle.

I look around for someone who can answer our questions and I'm directed to the office where I find a woman who would be equally at home running a penitentiary. Her nametag says, 'Esther Poor'. Esther takes her job very seriously. For every question I have of her, she has two for me. It's such an intense interrogation, I half expect her to hook us all up to a polygraph machine. She squints her beady little eyes at me with every answer I give her as if she's determined to find the hidden lie. It's a little intimidating and as a result my nervousness ends up looking an awful lot like guilt.

Desperately hoping to redeem myself, I give her half a dozen names and phone numbers of friends who can vouch for my character and ability to be a good adoptive parent to a puppy. Still squinting suspiciously, she asks us to wait in the reception area while she makes some calls and I pray that somebody will be home. After an interminable wait she reemerges with the first smile I've seen on her face.

"Ms. Botticelli, everything checked out fine. We can finish the paper work and then you can take the dog home. Do you have a crate with you?"

"Crate?" I ask.

We borrow a crate from the shelter, fill out all the necessary paperwork and as we head to the pet store to pick up supplies for the new addition to our family, we take care of the important task of naming her.

"Can we call her Aztec?" Max asks. I look over at Ren.

"What do you think?"

She sounds her most indifferent. "I don't care."

I turn back to Max. "I like it sweetie. It suits her." He has his fingers poking in through the grating and she's licking them as if human boy is her favorite flavor.

By the time Ren is in bed that evening, it's almost eleven o'clock and exhaustion hits me like a sledgehammer. I peek in on Max who's fast asleep with the dog, dry nose to wet nose on the pillow, each of them softly snoring. I give them both a pat and strangely they make the same creaky little sound of comfort.

This has been a day of transformations. For the first time in months I let myself feel hopeful and excited about the possibilities and grateful that I opened my door.

As I stand there looking at them sleeping it's hard to believe where I was only yesterday. So much has changed in just twenty-four hours mainly because a friend refused to stop knocking.

Chapter 6 ~ Serendipity, Sea Glass, and Sergio

As I begin the week I realize how much I need a solid game plan in place if I'm going to keep myself from sliding back into the abyss of the past few months. I'm not sure what will keep me moving forward and away from that dark place. I just know I can't go back there. I can also feel how fragile my new footing is. An answer presents itself the next day in the form of a serendipitous meeting.

I have found that sometimes the best way to solve a problem is to leave it alone so, I decide to take Aztec for a run. We climb into the car and take a quick drive down to Half Moon Beach, a small, perfect crescent punctuated by a few boulders. I love the way Main Street stretches beyond the beach with the curve of this little harbor. Because the beach sits below the street, it's the perfect place for me to let Aztec off her leash without worrying about her running into the road.

As soon as her leash is off she begins sniffing each and every inch of sand like a nearsighted little detective searching the ground for clues. We're alone on this mild spring morning except for a woman who appears to be picking up shells and stones. I rummage through my backpack and pull out the soft Frisbee I purchased in hopes of teaching Aztec to retrieve it. I soon discover that she has the attention span of a highly caffeinated ten-year-old boy with severe ADD. I've thrown it five times and I'm running down the beach about to pick it up for the fifth time when I see that Aztec has chased it. As I go to pick it up, she grabs at it creating an impromptu game of tug-of-war. A curious seagull lands a few feet away breaking her concentration and she abruptly lets go, sending me flying backward into a not so graceful landing on my butt. I sit there laughing just as the beachcomber walks up inquiring if I'm okay. I brush myself off and assure her that I'm fine. Aztec comes up to greet the newcomer, an attractive, elderly woman with a basket that contains sea glass, smooth stones, and some shells.

"What a darling puppy." She says, not seeming to mind at all that Aztec is covering her in sandy paw prints. She sets down her basket and reaches into her pocket.

"Do you mind if I give her a treat?"

She introduces herself as Jocelyn and I introduce Aztec and myself. We fall into an easy conversation and quickly discover we have a few mutual friends in town.

It turns out her brother owns Sadie's, one of my favorite gift shops, and he's trying to find a buyer for one of the two roomy condos above it that overlook the harbor. He lives in one of them and would like to hand pick his neighbor. He isn't using a realtor, or advertising because, like so many of the old-time locals, he prefers to find someone by word of mouth. It's so cheap, she tells me, that advertising would bring all the weirdoes out of the woodwork. I'm trying to think if there's anyone I know that's in the market for a three-bedroom condo, but no one comes to mind. She fishes in her jacket pocket and pulls out an old fashioned calling card with her name and number on it and asks me if I would phone her if I hear of anyone. With that, she picks up her basket and shakes my hand thanking me and giving Aztec a last pat before continuing her walk down the beach. It isn't until after I'm back in my house and I've tacked her card onto my bulletin board, that it occurs to me that she may have just offered me the answer I'm looking for.

One of the things I'm noticing, as I make my way through the house is how often something reminds me of all my years here with Nathan and all those reminders feel like an anchor mooring me to the past. Everywhere I look there's evidence of the life we lived together. The walls and shelves are full of photos and mementos of the life we created here. If it wasn't for worrying about upsetting the kids, I'd pack them all into boxes, put them into the closet in the attic with a big padlock on the door, and position a large breed guard dog in front of it in case I get a sudden attack of sentimentality. Since that isn't an option, this may be the solution.

I call her phone number and leave a message.

"Hi Jocelyn, this is Nicola Botticelli. We met at the beach this morning. I think I might know someone who would be interested in your brother's condo. I'd like to take a look at it this afternoon if that's possible."

After a quick shower I write a to do list. On it I put some easily accomplished things like:

35

Do the laundry.

I also include some more intimidating tasks such as:

Call the Y about teaching a class.

The thought of teaching a class in my out-of-shape, overweight state scares the bejesus out of me. I gather my courage and make the call to my old boss.

"Hi Nicki, it's so good to hear from you," she says, instantly putting me at ease.

"We all miss you and I wish I had something for you right now, but we're fully staffed. If you'd be interested in filling in for people here and there, we could do that."

"Thanks Sharon," I say, "I might take you up on that offer just to have something to get me going, but I really need to find something regular."

"You should try the gym over by the mall," she offers. "They've opened up a whole women's section and I know the guy who runs the place. He's a sweetheart named Sergio. Tell him I sent you."

I thank her for the helpful tip and decide to go over and check out the place. When I pull into the parking lot it's a little after eleven AM and the place is relatively empty. There's a young twenty-something guy behind the counter who's in incredible shape and suddenly I'm feeling like a flabby old lady. I casually peruse the brochures on the counter glancing around at the facilities as nonchalantly as possibly.

"Can I help you?" He asks in a friendly, low-key way.

"Are you Sergio?"

"No, I'm David, one of the trainers here. Sergio will be here in about an hour. Is there anything I can help you with?"

I decide to try to get over the fact that he's young and perfect by picturing him in his underwear. It doesn't help me feel less intimidated, but it does make me blush five shades of red. I try picturing him bald and with a beer gut. That works.

"I'm thinking of joining a gym and I heard you have a weight room for women." I lie.

"We do. I'll get someone to cover the desk and I'll take you for the tour. Okay?"

Over the next twenty minutes I get shown around the place and David answers all my questions. I learn that they have aerobics classes of all sorts and even yoga. There's a track, two free-weight rooms, a Pilates room, saunas, and a large open area with treadmills, Stairmasters, stationary bicycles, and other machines. When David tells me about the introductory special they're running, I'm so fired up I pull out my checkbook to sign up for a three-month membership.

Just as I'm finishing up the paperwork, a sturdy looking man in his mid-thirties shows up and David introduces me to Sergio. He has just a hint of a nebulous European accent, slightly receding curly dark hair and intensely green eyes. He doesn't really look like a sweetheart and I'm finding myself feeling more than a little scared. I introduce myself and before I lose my nerve I immediately mention that I'm a friend of Sharon Post's. I tell him I'm interested in teaching an aerobics class and she sent me since she heard he's looking for someone.

"Have you taught a class before?" he asks, and perhaps it's my paranoia, but I could swear that he looks down at my less than svelte body with look of mocking skepticism. I hold my head high, looking him straight in the eyes and with the most confident tone I can muster, I answer him.

"I was one of Sharon's most popular teachers at the Y."

"Why aren't you still there?" He fires back, his penetrating, unblinking eyes don't flinch from mine.

"I had a family crises."

I can see him mulling it all over in his head as he taps his pencil on the counter. " I could use someone for Friday night's seven o'clock class and Saturday morning's eight o'clock class. I'll be honest with you; those are hard slots to fill. The money isn't great, but if you can pull people in for those times I'll improve it and give you two additional classes with better time slots."

He doesn't have to wait for my answer. I give him an immediate yes. It's not ideal, but it's a start and it gets my foot in the door.

"Can you start this Friday?"

"I'll be here." I smile, answering calmly, but inside I'm quaking.

He shakes my hand. "Welcome aboard Nicola Botticelli. We'll see you Friday then."

He walks away and David takes the completed membership form from my hand tearing it in half.

"You won't be needing this anymore." He reaches under the counter and pulls out a packet of paperwork. "We will need all of these filled out. You can bring it with you on Friday."

When I get home I see the light on my phone is flashing and I check my messages while Aztec welcomes me by wrestling enthusiastically with the laces on my sneakers. The first message is from Lily asking me if I'd like to come by for coffee. The next one is from Jocelyn saying I could look at the condo either tonight after seven, or in the morning. She recommends seeing it during daylight for the full effect of the light and the view. I call her back, make a quick plan to meet her at the condo after my morning walk, then I call Lily to tell her I'll be right over. She's just the person I need to talk to.

Chapter 7 ~ Lily

Lily Summer has the perfect name. She's sweet and lovely with a sunny disposition. She's a natural beauty who is unaware of how pretty she is, shy and somewhat soft-spoken. I met her through wise-ass Kate a few years ago, shortly after she had moved here from the Midwest, and we hit it off immediately. She was one of those people I felt I had known forever, even before I discovered we had so much in common. We're both avid readers who love many of the same authors and we've turned each other on to some new ones. We're also both into fitness and particularly yoga. Lastly, we're huge movie buffs with a passion for film noir. Lily's a quietly spiritual student of life with an open heart and an open mind and because of those qualities she's one of the best people I can talk to when I need a sounding board.

She answers her apartment door in a cropped hooded sweatshirt and a pair of bicycle shorts. She has the most gorgeous legs I've ever seen in person. Each time I see them I half expect her to start high kicking like one of the Rockettes. I know if they were mine, I would. Her long sandy blonde hair is pulled back into a ponytail and her face has a just scrubbed glow that makes her look much younger than her thirty-two years.

"Nicki!" she says, as she clamps me in an enthusiastic hug. " I'm so glad you're here."

"I'm glad I'm here too. I need some objective feedback."

"Well, I'll try. Do you want coffee or tea, or perhaps a glass of wine?" She winks as if we're a couple of bad girls.

"After the day I've had, I'll go with the wine."

She takes out two glasses and pours while I tell her about my chance meeting with Jocelyn and about the condo her brother is selling. I tell her how being in my house is a constant reminder of Nathan and my life with him there.

"I just don't feel like I can really move on with the past constantly in my face and I think it would be too weird for the kids if I put all the reminders away. It'll seem like I'm dissing their dad. I've been sleeping in the guestroom for the past month because I can't bear being in my old bedroom any more."

"Yeah that would be hard," she sympathizes. "Maybe Nathan will want to buy you out," she says, off-handedly.

"I hadn't thought of that possibility. He does love that house."

"So call him and tell him the house is too much for you on your own and that a condo will be more manageable."

"You're right, that house is too much for me,"

I'm feeling more relieved by the moment. "But what if he doesn't want it?" I ask.

"Then you both agree to sell it and since it's a joint decision, the kids won't see you as the bad guy."

"This is great, even if this condo isn't the right place, it's really clear to me I need to move."

As she watches my face light up, she takes a big, self-satisfied gulp of her wine and sets her empty glass down almost too hard. I roll the idea over in my head and let out a huge sigh, which gets me giggling with relief. Lily grins at me across the table, obviously pleased with herself. I clink her empty glass with mine in a toast.

"To my most brilliant friend."

She tosses her head back in mock vanity.

"I'm just doing what I do best. So, can I go with you to look at the condo?"

That evening I give Nathan a call and run the whole idea by him. Boy, did Lily call it. He's thrilled at the possibility of having the house and offers to get started on all the financial arrangements that need to be made. Now that I'm realizing all the aspects of this change, I'm more than a little creeped out at the thought of that woman spending time in my house, but if I'm going to get myself where I need to be I have to let go of that. I decide to try to take every possible physical trace of my life here with me and I find that somehow comforting, as if all I'm allowing her access to is the shell, but none of the living, breathing heart of it. I make a plan with Nathan to sit down with the kids to discuss our decision with them on Wednesday.

Later that night, when I'm about to settle into the guestroom for the evening, I decide to sleep in my own bed in our old room. I need to say goodbye. As I settle back into the pillows I look around at the photos and mementos and all days and nights I've spent in this place wash over me in a tumbling wave of remembering. All the nights being in this bed with the kids when they were newborns and nursing them back to sleep, all the Sunday morning pig-piles on Nathan and me when they were toddlers, stories read beneath the down comforter till eyelids gave in to sleep, and Mother's Day breakfasts in bed with trays full of carefully carried plates of muffins, balanced pots of tea, and crayon colored cards. I smile behind my tears. A feeling of peace passes through me as I turn out the light knowing I'm only saying goodbye to a place and all the rest I carry with me wherever I go.

Chapter 8 ~ Kate

When I get to the beach with Aztec, Lily is not alone. She has Kate in tow. I met Kate Winslow seven years ago when Max and Kate's son, Homer, became friends in preschool. Yes, that's right. His name is Homer Winslow and that pretty much sums up Kate's goofball sense of humor and how willing she is to go the distance with it.

We were introduced after being summoned into the Way to Grow Preschool. Ms. Prine, the Director, ushered us both into her office and informed us that our darling little four-year-olds had demonstrated a terrible lack of constraint at the water table. Simply put, they had gotten into an out of control water fight drenching themselves and everyone else within a radius of twenty feet before someone was able to stop them. This included the teachers and their beloved leader, the aforementioned Ms. Prine. We listened to the story as solemnly as we could, considering the crime. Ms. Prine humorlessly related all the details to us.

There was a knock on her door and she excused herself saying she would return in a moment. No sooner had she left, Kate leaned toward me and with a lowered voice she said,

"I'd pay good money to see that woman dripping wet."

She gestured and made a face simulating a drenched Ms. Prine followed by several more faces and with that we began laughing. The more we laughed, the more out of control our laughing became. When Ms. Prine came back in we were hanging onto each other and practically falling out of our chairs. Tears streamed down our cheeks and with each attempt Ms. Prine made to restore some order, the poor woman sent us into another hysterical round of laughing. No doubt, by the time we left it was clear to Ms. Prine why we had such badly behaved children.

Since that fateful meeting Kate has claimed me as one of her mostly unwilling partners in crime. You wouldn't know she was a wild woman looking at her classy, understated, exterior. She drives a cream colored Mercedes with vanity plates that say simply, "IWIN". As one of the most successful Real Estate Brokers in the area, she's what I'd call rich. Her wardrobe is all understated J. Jill and Chico's. One of the only clues to her inherent spiciness is her coloring; shoulder length, wavy cinnamon colored hair, deep amber eyes and skin that becomes a light copper in the summer.

When it comes to consequences, she's fearless. And it's that kamikaze attitude that lures normally well-behaved people into behaving badly with her. It's also why she has done so well in business and why she has a hard time getting angry with Homer when he gets into trouble at school.

Lily and Kate are both excited about going to see the condo and I tell them not to get their hopes up. At the price he's asking, it very well could be a dump.

"If it's the place I think it is, I went to a party there a few years ago and it was fabulous!"

Kate says. She's picked up coffee for the three of us and hands me one.

We meet Jocelyn in front of the store and I make all the introductions as she shows us through a tall, sky blue gate to the porch on the side of the building. I'm already getting excited just seeing the view of the water from this vantage point at street level. Jocelyn unlocks the door and ushers us into a small foyer with a black and white marble floor tiled in a large diamond pattern on the diagonal. The walls are mustard gold with an ochre wash that compliments the molding and the character of this turn of the century building. As soon as she spots it Kate excitedly says,

"This is the place."

We climb the stairs to an open landing, which has plenty of room for the kid's bikes, skates and skateboards. There's a large window that lets in plenty of light. As we're all looking around Jocelyn unlocks the door and the light from inside streams out as if she had gone to the wrong door and accidentally opened the gates of heaven. We're temporarily blinded by the brilliance as we enter into a large open living area with a bank of huge floor to ceiling windows overlooking the harbor. The view is breathtaking.

"Wow," I say, with my mouth hanging wide open.

"Wow," Lily echoes.

"I told you," Kate mocks us with smug nonchalance.

Jocelyn begins showing us around. There's a sunny good-sized kitchen off to the left with a cozy built-in breakfast area with the view. Off of the kitchen there's a half bath and laundry room. Next is the dining room, which is open to the living room and all are overlooking the harbor through the bank of windows. Just beyond the living room a hall leads to two bedrooms with a full bath between them.

At the end of the hall past a large linen closet, is a wrought iron spiral staircase. Jocelyn gestures toward it.

"The master bedroom and bathroom are up there."

We all look at each other making big, soup-bowl sized eyes before we start to climb. I'm right behind Jocelyn with Lily and Kate close on my heels. I get to the top and find myself in a room of about fifteen by twenty feet with the same amazing windows and an incredible view of the sea. From this level I can see the lighthouse on Dog Island.

"No way," I say, in amazed disbelief.

"Way," Kate deadpans.

The master bathroom off of the bedroom is tucked under the roofline with a dormered window, which gives it interesting and romantic contours. It has an old claw-foot tub and a large built-in leaded glass cabinet for linens and things. On the other side of the bedroom there's a small room that could be used as an office, which has access to additional storage that runs under the eaves. Jocelyn asks me if I'd like some time to wander through again with my friends and offers to wait for us downstairs in her brother's shop. After she leaves, I turn to Kate and

Lily barely able to control my excitement and ask them,

"So what do you think?"

"Oh my gosh! I love it," Lily gushes with her hands on either side of her face like she's sixteen.

"If you don't buy it I will," threatens Kate. "This is the ultimate love shack, honey. Hell, if you buy this place I might even do you. This is definitely the kind of place where a girl could get her groove back."

"That's tempting sweetie, but I think I might pass on your generous offer and buy it in spite of the potential nookie with you, or anyone else."

We poke around checking out closet space and visualizing where to place my furniture. By the time we make our way back down to the shop, I'm so excited it's hard to steady my hand enough to write the deposit check.

Jocelyn introduces me to her brother Teddy, a distinguished elderly gentleman. I ask them if they mind if I post date the check while I run the idea by the kids and they suggest that I bring them by tomorrow to have a look. They're both so incredibly pleased that they take turns hugging me and we all get so caught up in the happy moment that soon Kate and Lily are in on the hugging too. By the time we're out the door I have cramps in my cheeks from so much smiling. Before we go our separate ways we make plans to celebrate with Sophia and Paris with drinks at Finz tomorrow evening.

I immediately call Nathan on my cell phone to let him know about the condo and my pressing need to get things expedited. I ask him if we can move the family meeting with the kids up to tonight and he says he can be here right after they have dinner and do their homework, probably around eight. He's being so nice and accommodating, I decide to pretend to forget, for the time being, what a spineless douche he is.

Chapter 9 ~ Sophia

I love slogans and mottoes. I know it's cheesy, but I do. If all of life were played like a game of pro football, or basketball, we'd each have our own squad of cheerleaders keeping us pumped as we made our way through the challenges of our lives. But we don't. Therefore, I believe we need slogans and mottoes. We need to be our own cheerleaders. One of my favorites is "Fortune Favors The Brave". I forget about it from time to time and it seems as if whenever I do, my life turns to shit. In this past week I have resurrected it in a major way. I made a big banner for the front of my refrigerator with the inspirational words printed on it boldly. I repeat it over and over like a mantra whenever I feel fear creeping in along the edges.

In only two days I am going to have to get myself in front of a group of strangers who will be looking to me for guidance, and lead them through a workout routine. Whenever I think about this, a powerful wave of nausea passes though me. I decide I need a lot of dazzling accessories to shift the focus from what I'm anticipating will be my less than stellar performance. First I hit the mall and buy myself an adorable, slimming, black workout suit with so much Lycra in it holding my extra stuff in and also lifting it up that I don't understand why my head doesn't look a whole lot bigger, and my eyes don't bulge. Next, I go through all the music on my IPod and find some compilations my former students loved, that had workouts to go with them that aren't too challenging. I do this not because I'm worried about my students, but because I need something that won't do me in on the first night. "Fake it till you make it," is another of my favorite mottoes. It seems for the time being to go hand in hand with the one on my refrigerator door.

Sophia calls to see if she can get a ride with me to Finz tonight. Her car is in the shop again. It's a twelve-year-old Saab she's planning to drive until the wheels fall off. For the past couple of years, it's been nickel and diming her with frequent trips to the auto shop. She completely ignores the drain on her wallet. Not only that, but each time we suggest maybe she should buy something newer, she acts like it's a personal challenge she has to see through. Plus, I think she doesn't half mind because her mechanic is so damn cute.

Sophia likes skating the perimeter when it comes to men. She's been divorced since right around the time her twin boys turned five. After seven years with a cheating husband who constantly told her she was fat and unattractive, it took a good three years away from him, with the rest of us building her up, for her to even consider dating. Although she has dipped her toes in that unpredictable sea, I can't say that she's felt compelled to dive in. Not yet. She still doesn't comprehend that many men find her dark, exotic, voluptuous looks beautiful and sexy.

I pull into her driveway and beep. Her head appears in the window briefly and she waves to let me know she'll be right out. I flip down the visor, put on some lipstick and check my makeup while

I'm waiting. I take a big breath and exhale out some of the anxiety I've been feeling. A night out with the girls will be better than therapy, and a lot less likely to have therapy's potentially unpleasant side effects. I'm singing along with the Alana Davis CD when Sophia gets in, turns down the music and breathlessly begins filling me in on her day in a torrent of words. It's so Sophia.

"God, I'm glad we're going out even though I don't usually like to go out on a weeknight. I really need to vent. School has been an absolute cluster fuck, pardon my French, the kids are off the wall, Mike is being such a prick about taking them on weekends and can you tell I have PMS? It's been a hell of a week and it's only halfway through. Don't let me drink too much okay? Am I talking like a maniac? I'm talking like a maniac aren't I?" She says it all without taking an apparent breath and dramatically digging her fingers into her thick mane of long dark hair. We both start laughing as I back out of her driveway. Apparently I'm not the only one in need of a night of girl therapy.

When we get to the restaurant I spot Kate's car just as she's getting out of it and park in an open spot a couple of cars over. As we walk in the door, Lily spots us from the end of the bar and waves us over. We get ourselves situated around the end corner with a spot saved for Paris and order drinks just as she arrives.

"Don't start without me," she says, as she rushes in and begins doling out kisses on everybody's cheeks. "What are we drinking?"

"I'm not fooling around," says Sophia. "I ordered a Martini."

Paris tells the bartender, "I'll have the same, extra dirty."

When we all have our drinks, Kate proposes a toast.

"Here's to not letting the bastards grind you down."

Paris looks horrified. "Well that's not very upbeat."

Sophia laughs. "Well I don't know about the rest of you, but for the week I'm having it totally works for me."

Lily sides with Paris. "I thought we were here to celebrate Nicki's new beginning and her wonderful condo."

"Okay, you're right," concedes Kate. "Here's to the promise of new beginnings in sexy love shacks and whatever you do, don't let the bastards grind you down. How's that?"

"Very diplomatic. It has something for everyone." I say, leaning over to give Kate the smart-ass, a kiss on the cheek.

We order several appetizers and soon we're sipping and tasting delicious bits of things from all the plates spread out before us like a mini-buffet. Between mouthfuls, we manage to discuss everything from what seems to be the rash of reported child abductions recently on the news to the homely woman Sophia's ex is dating. "He used to give me shit about being fat. What a joke. Have you seen this woman? She looks like Shrek!" Lily agrees with Sophia, but in her kinder, more tactful style. "Personally, I think Mike really prefers big girls, but he just can't admit it to himself."

"Speaking of big girls," I begin, seeing my opportunity for a seamless segue "This big girl is freaking out about starting my class on Friday. I look like I should be in the class not teaching it."

"First of all," begins Sophia with a tone that goes with her present mood and a finger wagging in the air. "You're not exactly what anyone would call big. You've got a little extra cush in your tush, but I understand. That's how I felt when the Y asked me if I'd like to teach that spinning class last year. Mike had me so convinced me I was a fat slob that I signed up for the class in the first place. When I first started I thought I was going to die, it was so freaking hard, but by the end of the first month, I loved it. I'd only been in the class for a few months when they lost their teacher and they asked me if I would be interested in the job before they ran an ad. They said I was one of the best students and I realized you don't have to be a skinny little thing to be in shape. The best part was that other people in the class told me how much more comfortable they felt having someone who didn't look anorexic teaching them. I wouldn't worry about it honey. You'll be back in shape before you know it. Besides, what is it you like say, "Fake it till you make it".

"Yeah," Kate says, a little too loudly and raises her glass in another toast, "Fake it till you make it."

We all clink our glasses. I don't know if it's the company, or the drink, but I'm feeling my confidence returning.

Chapter 10 ~ You Ain't Heavy, You're My Bother

I realize by Friday afternoon that the temporary boost in my confidence was without a doubt, fueled by the consumption of that Cosmopolitan. My anxiety hits such a peak that I'm having a flashback of the night I wound up in the ER. Panic attack. That's what the doctor had called it and I'm glad he gave me a prescription for it. After an hour of breathing into a paper bag off and on, I'm not feeling any better.

Since that first attack I've been reluctant to take anything for my anxiety and I opt for a glass of wine in the evening on those days when the panic creeps in and with that technique I've been pretty good at keeping it at bay. I'm so afraid to end up like one of those celebrities in rehab you hear about on the *E! True Hollywood Story*, another victim of prescription drug addiction. I don't know why opting for alcohol seems like less of a concern, maybe it has something to do with the fact that I never drink early in the day. It's definitely a fractured form of logic.

By three o'clock I'm fishing in my purse for my prescription. Since I'm not sure how it's going to affect me, I just take half of one of the little yellow pills. Knowing relief is on its way has the immediate effect of soothing me a little, at least psychologically. Paris, who has suffered from anxiety since she was a kid, has also advised that taking a bath can help so I run a tub and add some aromatherapy chamomile bath salts, which claim to be calming. I put in a quick call to my more experienced medication user and Paris tells me to wait an hour and if I'm not feeling a whole lot better, take another half. Another pill and an additional hour later, and I'm feeling completely smoothed out as if all those jagged nervous edges were magically sanded off leaving me as smooth as glass. I give Paris a call back and report how wonderful I'm feeling.

"You sound like you might be feeling too wonderful to be driving," she says, with concern.

"What time do you have to be at the gym? I think I'll drive you." She doesn't wait for an answer and I'm feeling so laid back, I don't even attempt to protest, which makes me think she's probably right.

"I should be there by six-thirty. The class is at seven and that will give me enough time to get myself situated. So I don't have to leave for a half hour. I should be okay by then. Don't you think?"

"Maybe, but why risk it sweetie. It's really not a problem for me to take you. I have no plans for tonight. Terrence is leaving to go play at the club around eight so I'll leave the kids with him and I'll have my mom come watch them when I come back to get you."

"You sure? I hate to be a bother."

"Don't worry about it baby. How does that old song go? *He ain't heavy, he's my bother.*"

"I think its brother."

"Close enough. You know what I mean." She says.

Since I now know that I won't be driving, I take one half more of the little yellow pills.

Paris drops me off at the gym at six-thirty on the dot and I unload my stuff from her back seat. I couldn't remember if there was an mp3 dock in the room, or not and I was too nervous to call and ask, so I've borrowed Ren's. I've got my IPod, a big bottle of water, a bag with shower items and a change of clothes. I'm prepared.

David, who I have dubbed, Boy Scout, greets me when I come in. He gives me a staff locker for my things and shows me to the aerobics room. It's actually smaller than the gargantuan cavern I was remembering in my panicked mind. There's an mp3 player there, but I'm more familiar with Ren's. David plugs it in for me. Boy Scout is an all around genuinely nice guy.

"I don't know if Sergio told you, but there are only six people signed up for this class and not everybody shows up every time." He says it apologetically.

"So he really wasn't kidding about Friday night being a hard one to fill." I'm relaxing more by the second as the image I had had of a room packed with hard-bodies suddenly gives way to a handful and I'm suddenly feeling very foolish for the day of panic I needlessly put myself through.

"Well, I think the big problem's been he hasn't had any consistency with teachers for that time slot. He can't seem to keep anybody for more than a month and then people drop out if they don't like the new teacher or they get tired of having to learn new routines just when the got the hang of the old one. You know?"

As I'm taking in everything he's saying, I'm getting new ideas of how to possibly turn this around and hoping to use this information to my advantage in a way that will benefit Sergio, the clients and me. As I brainstorm, I'm feeling more excited and less and less nervous.

By the time my students wander in and begin warily checking me out, I've formulated a strategy. There are two twenty-something women who are obviously there together, two slightly overweight thirty something women, a tall guy who's probably in his late twenties and a geek I would guess is hoping to meet girls. I put the music on low just to get their attention and move to front and center. I check my watch and see that it's just a few minutes past seven.

"I guess we'll get started." I begin, "I'm Nicola Botticelli, but most people call me Nicki." They stop chatting with each other and line up facing me.

"I'm your new teacher for this class and I understand I come from a long line of predecessors. I'd like to change that and actually stick around for a long while. I'd also like to make this class a place where we can specifically address your fitness needs. What I'd like to do is take a couple of minutes before we begin and have everyone introduce themselves and briefly tell me what your goal is in being here and how long you've been coming to this class."

I point to the tall thin guy to my left and ask, "Could we start with you and just go down the line?"

"I'm Paul Vincent and I prefer moving to music over lifting weights. I've been in this class for three months and you're my third teacher," he sighs with a dramatic heave of his shoulders. As he says it I realize he's probably more interested in meeting guys like Boy Scout.

The introductions continue along with their reasons for being here. Ed had a skiing injury he's recovering from. Diana is trying to lose all the weight she gained over the course of having three kids. Tina has a family history of heart disease and diabetes she's trying to sidestep. The twenty-something friends, Evie and Shaina reward themselves each Friday night after this much disliked, but necessary exercise with an evening out club-hopping in Boston where they get to flaunt their taut bodies in miniscule outfits. Well, they don't actually come out and state that, but after a workout in which I get everyone sweating, myself included, they emerge freshly showered and scantily clad with belly-button jewels sparkling and such a long expanse of bare legs that had it been one of the rest of us we would have been arrested for too much unwanted exposure.

I'm so tired after the class I don't even have enough energy to stand up in the shower and I decide to wait until I get home where I can lie down in my tub. I barely manage to lift my bag as I limp up the stairs and out to the parking lot where Paris is waiting in her car right in front of the door.

"Hey, teach. You're still upright. Way to go." Paris high fives my limply offered hand, as I drag myself into the front seat.

"Lycra is amazing stuff," I moan. "I think this outfit is the only thing holding me up. I swear if I take it off I'll instantly go horizontal."

"So how did it go? Did you stay calm?"

"I was so calm I was on the verge of a coma. Except for the part where I had to move it was a piece of cake."

I proceed to fill Paris in on all the evening's details including the petite size of my class. "So I pretty much got myself worried sick over nothing and I'll be surprised if the morning class isn't more of the same."

"Well at least you'll be able to get a good night's sleep."

As soon as I get through the door I drop my bags for easy access in the morning and shuffle off to the bathroom with my eyelids at half-mast. As I run the tub I throw in a couple of handfuls of Epsom Salt for my sore muscles. Within moments of crawling into bed, I'm deeply asleep and dreaming of hard and soft bodies moving to everything from show tunes to Polkas. It ends with a bizarre class led by Madonna in a wedding dress and Nikes, as I wake to the radio alarm playing, *Like a Virgin*. And then it's time to get up and do it all over again.

Chapter 11 ~ Keep, or Toss?

By the end of my second month at the gym, I'm feeling and looking a whole lot lighter and healthier. I've lost fifteen of the extra pounds I gained and my energy is back, along with a better outlook on my life. Not only that, but I've been told I've become something of an inspiration around the place. I let my class know from the get go that I was in the same place they were and it struck a chord that passed by word of mouth. There are now twenty-five people in my Friday night class and my Saturday morning class went from nine people to thirty-five. Being true to his word, Sergio gave me a great raise and another three classes. On this morning he comes by to check me out and after the class he walks up and congratulates me on a job well done.

"You know, you have a natural gift for motivating people. You'd make a good personal trainer, or Pilates instructor."

"You think so?"

"I do. If you'd like any information about getting certified let me know and I can hook you up. The money's a lot better and I could always use a woman trainer. What do you think?"

I hesitate to answer him, since I hadn't considered it before and he picks up on my trepidation.

"Think about it and let me know." He says, and begins to head out.

"I will, and thanks, Sergio." I call after his retreating, "I really appreciate it."

He waves at me over his shoulder and as I pack up my things I start to mull it over and the more I think about it, the more it makes sense to at least find out more. When I'm heading out the door I spot David and decide to take advantage of the opportunity to ask him a few questions. David works at the gym as a trainer and he has several private clients he works out as well.

His response to my questions is nothing but positive.

"Yeah, Nicki, I think you'd be great at it and there's definitely a need for more women in the field. Some women are much more comfortable working with a female trainer and if you're good, guys don't care either way. In fact some of them might prefer working out with a pretty lady such as yourself."

He winks at me, and smiles broadly. Boy Scout is a charmer and he knows it.

"It doesn't take long to get certified," he continues, " and if you love this kind of work it's a great gig." He casually slides his bag off his shoulder and onto the floor, his biceps flexing in their usual impressive way. He notices me noticing and smiles.

"It's just that you look like a personal trainer." I say, blushing.

"So will you. You've only been here for a little while and you look great already. If you keep at it, by the time you're through with the certification you'll be amazed at the difference. Go for it." He gives me a playful nudge. "Hey look, I've got to run for my nine-thirty. Let's talk more about it later. Maybe you'll let me take you for a drink, or dinner one of these nights." He flashes a row of perfect teeth at me, gives me a look that's something other than friendly, throws his bag back onto his shoulder and heads to the stairs. "Let me know, Nicki." He waves and smiles from the door as he heads into the gym.

"Thanks." I yell as he disappears into the club.

It's been a while, and even though I'm pretty out of touch with this whole realm, it seems pretty clear, that sweet young man was flirting with me. Not only that, but he also asked if he could take me for a drink, or dinner sometime. I feel a little weird. On the one hand I'm flattered and on the other hand, I'm more than a little uncomfortable. I could practically be his mother, his very young, and apparently attractive mother.

Everything is going so smoothly in my purchase of the condo it's as if the angels of perfect housing are guiding it to be so. Only a few days after I made my deposit, I just happened to run into an old friend. She just happens to be a mortgage broker. She got me a great rate and if all goes according to plan, I should be in my new home in just a few weeks.

I've been busily packing up and purging as much as possible. After ten years in one home with two kids, I can't believe all the stuff we've accumulated. Since the condo has less square footage and not as much storage, I really want to pare down. The only truly hard part is trying to decide what to keep of the gazillion things I've saved from the kids' childhood. I purchase two large plastic boxes with lids for each of their treasures. Report cards, artwork, cards and their school papers, are gone through carefully. It's a slow process. I make three piles, the must keep pile, the must toss pile and the not so sure pile, which turns out to be the largest. In the end, the whittling turns out to be a little too painful and I go to the store and purchase two more of the boxes. I easily fill them almost to the top.

Having Max and Renoir in school all day affords me the opportunity to go through their old toys and reduce that sizable collection down without having to contend with their constant objections. I do my best to remember which ones are considered valued old friends and which are still hanging around only because of their impressive pack rat tendencies. At moments, it's an enjoyable, sentimental history of their young lives.

Renoir, for all her present toughness, still has all the baby dolls she mothered when she was little. I remember the Christmas mornings and birthdays when these gifts were opened. Some are missing hair, or an eye and have evidence of magic marker vandalism inflicted by her little brother. Max has an extensive collection of dinosaurs. It begins with his first little stuffed Stegosaurus that he cuddled until he wore it threadbare in several spots, and it ends in the present with several incredibly realistic high tech models.

I fill my car with bags for my mother's church fair and drop them off at her house. She thanks me and then lets me know that fixing my hair and putting on a little lipstick couldn't hurt.

"Mom, I'm in the middle of packing."

"You're not packing right now." She says, bluntly. "Is there a law that says you can't look nice just because you're packing. You're such a pretty girl why not take advantage of it?"

I know this tone of voice. There's no arguing with her so, I quietly agree as I fish in my purse for a lipstick and give my mouth a quick coat of pink gloss."

"See," she gives me a pleased smile, "that brightens up your whole face." She kisses me on the cheek as she brushes the errant strands of hair back off my face. I reluctantly agree to go to lunch with her later in the week and head out to do more errands before the kids get home from school.

I'm so glad to feel more like my old self. I'm also grateful for how busy I am since it keeps me from noticing the part of my life I'm missing, but at times it does hit me and it hits me hard. It's usually at night. On this evening, it's after the kids have gone to bed and I'm alone in my bare room, the walls now empty of most of the photos. Aztec comes pattering in with a sleepy face and I pat the bed for her to jump up. She hesitates at first since this is something she usually gets scolded for but with a little encouragement from me she clumsily hops up and settles in. There's something comforting about the weight of her next to me and feeling her even, peaceful, breathing.

It's been more than five months since Nathan left and part of me still misses him and the life we used to have. Another part of me would like to see him publicly humiliated and put into shackles in the center of town with Debbie shackled next to him where they would be routinely pelted with rotten produce, by any local who felt so inspired. If it weren't for the kids being upset by this, I'd try to arrange it. Hometown sentiment being in my favor it probably wouldn't be that hard to manage. For the time being, I make do with the fantasy.

Chapter 12 ~ Moving

It didn't take much for Sergio and David to convince me to sign up for the personal trainer certification program. Only two weeks into the course, I'm surprising myself everyday. Between taking classes, studying, and packing, my life is a blur. The movers are coming in two days and I've gotten all my girlies in on the fun. They've been great. It seems like no one shows up at my door without at least a couple of empty boxes and an old newspaper. There have been days when I've come home to find Paris, Kate, or Lily in my kitchen, having used my hidden house key, filling boxes with my glasses, china, pots, and pans. They are the best.

The kids seem to be thriving on the chaos. In particular they love living on take- out pizza and Chinese food. The only thing they don't seem to enjoy is the part where they actually help with the packing. I tried to threaten them with leaving their things behind if they didn't pack them, but as soon as they reminded me they would still be living here part of the time with their dad, that strategy fell on it's face. It did help me realize just how much my thinking deteriorates when I'm exhausted. I also realized it isn't critical to have everything make it out the door on Saturday and then I relaxed a lot more.

On the morning of the move I get up very early in order to have some quiet time and collect myself before the day. I make a big pot of strong coffee, which I plan to use to fuel the movers. I pour myself a cup. Aztec curls up at my feet, warming my toes as I sit at the kitchen table looking out the window at the crab-apple tree, which has recently bloomed. May has always been one of my favorite months in this house. The newly leafed trees are that wonderful shade of green that almost looks unnatural and at this hour the birds are singing as if they're in a contest to out do one another. From my seat I can see my tulips and daffodils swaying in the breeze, creating a riot of color along the fence and for a moment I feel wistful about leaving them.

I shuffle over to the refrigerator in my fuzzy slippers and pull out what I need to whip up a batch of pancakes for the kids. Then I begin making my way through the house putting red stickers on all the pieces that I'll be taking to the condo. There are a few pieces I'm leaving behind for Nathan and it's not a matter of being an uncommonly kind, saintly, soon-to-be ex-wife. I just don't have room for cast offs.

After a quick shower I remember my mother's words and put on a little mascara, lipstick and blush. I give my hair a blast with the blow dryer and twist it up with a big chunky clip. Since I've lost all the weight I had gained, I'm back into my old clothes and I easily slip into a pair of my favorite, perfectly broken in jeans. I top it with a white, V-neck T-shirt and check myself in the mirror. I think even mom would approve. I look at my watch. It's seven-thirty and the movers will be here at eight. It's time to get the kids up and moving. Max's room is empty and when I go back down to the kitchen, I find him sitting with his eyes barely open at the table with a stack of pancakes in front of him.

"Good morning sweetie." I kiss the top of his head as he mumbles back.

"Mmmmmmm."

"The movers will be here in thirty minutes. You should get yourself showered soon."

"Mmmmmmm." He pours a puddle of maple syrup into his plate.

I go tap on Ren's door. When she doesn't answer, I open the door a crack and find her fast asleep with one arm draped dramatically over her eyes.

"Renoir Theresa Ferris," I say, in a soft singsong, gently nudging her awake, "It's moving day."

She grabs the covers and pulls them over her face, muttering beneath them.

"I just thought you might want to be showered and dressed before a bunch of strange guys show up and start taking things out of your room. They'll be here in less than a half hour." I slap several red stickers on her furniture.

She sits up so quickly she looks spring loaded. As I head out her door, she lets a curse fly. "Shit!"

"Language!" I say, closing her door behind me. I can hear her scrambling and complaining under her breath. Ren's never been a morning person and we've all learned to try and steer clear of her for the first hour of the day. Since she was two we joked about how much better mornings would be when she got old enough to drink coffee.

At eight on the dot the movers arrive, a noisy bunch of good-natured Brazilians who were recommended by Lily after she used them to move into her apartment last year.

It's clear within the first two minutes of meeting them that Louis is the only one of them who actually speaks English. The rest of them are speaking Portuguese. There are four of them and they seem to range in age from early twenties to late forties. I communicate with them using their leader as a translator and occasionally resort to a form of charades that gets them all laughing and talking amongst themselves. They seem to find me entertaining which is fine with me. Max is able to communicate with them in spite of the language barrier with the same effortless ease he has with most people and Renoir continues giving them cranky sideways glances all the while maintaining her usual morning grumbling.

As I'm about to pick up a box it's quickly scooped up by one of the young guys. "No, no, no pretty lady." He admonishes me. "I do it."

The second time he does it he winks at me. Ren notices and reacts predictably.

"Oh gross, what is he doing?" She asks with disgust.

"I think he's just being friendly."

"He better not be friendly to me."

I look at the nasty scowl on her face and reassure her, "I don't think you have to worry about that happening, sweetheart."

71

I pile the kids and Aztec into the car and we drive to the condo to meet the movers. When we get there, Renoir is only too happy to be given the job of taking Aztec down to the beach to keep the puppy from being underfoot. Max and I are just taking the first boxes out of the trunk of my car when the guys pull up.

Everything goes in with relative ease until we get to moving furniture up the spiral staircase to my bedroom and the office. Since I don't speak Portuguese I can't say for certain, but I'm pretty sure there are some serious expletives flying. My mattress only makes it up there after being forced into a pretzel-like shape. I hope it will recover from that. However, the box spring isn't even a possibility. Aside from those two challenges it all goes fairly smoothly and quickly. By noon they've finished up and as they're waiting in the truck for me to pay Louis, my young admirer leans out the window and blows me a kiss. Louis looks a little embarrassed. "He thinks you're a very nice, pretty lady." He says, apologetically.

"Well, you tell him I said thank you for such a nice compliment." I say this thinking that a good-looking twenty-something, with a strong back, and no ability to converse in English, may be the perfect man for me.

Chapter 13 ~ Mimosas, Courtrooms, and Boutiques

The next few days I experience an exhaustion of Olympic proportions. The circles under my eyes are so dark and deep, that I look like a Goth in training. All I need is a bunch of tattoos and a few facial piercings.

Sunday morning begins auspiciously when Kate, Lily, and Sophia show up at my door and I answer it still in my bathrobe.

"Hi! We're here for the housewarming party. Need to do some unpacking?" Kate asks, mischievously holding up a bottle of Champagne and a half-gallon of orange juice. "It's Mimosa time."

I turn around scanning the maze of boxes. "I have no idea where the glasses are."

"No worries." she says, smiling impishly and nudging Lily, who lifts up a bag with plastic cups, bagels, lox and cream cheese.

As Kate pours, Sophia asks, "Do you think we drink too much?"

Kate looks at her solemnly, with the bottle of Champagne poised mid air. "No Soph, I think we drink just enough."

To that, we make an unsuccessful attempt at clinking our plastic cups together.

Within a couple of hours we've got most of the kitchen and the downstairs bathroom squared away before the early morning cocktails make us all too sleepy to do any more and we all end up falling asleep curled up on various pieces of furniture with the warm sun streaming through the windows and across our bodies.

I spend the next day putting the kids' beds together and taking care of other top priority comfort issues. Each day I whittle away at the mountains of boxes and little by little more floor space gets clear until by the end of the first two weeks it looks as if we've been here all along.

The kids flipped a coin over the bedrooms. The one facing Main Street is larger than the one overlooking the water. At this point in their lives, a larger room wins over one with a view. The plan is that after six months they'll switch off if Renoir still wants the larger room since she lost the coin toss to Max. Repeatedly.

In so many ways things are going well and in spite of my exhaustion, the new space gives me a feeling of renewed energy, which I haven't felt since before Nathan left. It's as if I've been suddenly cut free from the heavy weight of the past I was dragging along behind me like an old rusted ship's anchor. At night, when I climb up the spiral staircase to my room, I'm retreating to a much-anticipated sanctuary. On the warmer evenings I've been opening the windows and letting the sound of the waves lull me into an incredibly deep sleep. Each morning I wake feeling more refreshed then I have in years, but by the time the day is through, I'm once again so exhausted I can barely speak English well enough to form coherent sentences. By dinnertime I've been resorting to monosyllabic grunting and gesturing. Interestingly, the kids seem to understand and respond to me better in this simplified state.

The divorce proceedings are not as horrible as I had anticipated. Nathan has been agreeing to everything I'm asking for, not that I'm taking advantage by asking for much of anything. Sophia told me it's because he feels guilty. Whatever the reason, I feel grateful that something this hard isn't a lot worse. I don't know what I would have done if he had decided to be a shit about it. I just don't have the stomach for that kind of battling.

According to Sophia, Mike was the same way during her divorce after she repeatedly reminded him of all the times he'd cheated on her during their marriage. The worst time was when she was pregnant with the twins. That was his biggest guilt button and she had no qualms about pushing it in order to get what she needed for her and the kids to survive.

So when my day in court arrives, I'm surprised to find how mixed my emotions are. I'm glad it's finally going to be settled and sad that it's officially over. That morning as I'm getting ready to go, Kate, Lily, and Sophia all call to offer support and encouragement. I've always been able to feel as though I'm okay in the midst of something painful until someone who really knows and loves me, offers consolation. It's only then that I really emotionally connect with how I'm feeling. When I hang up the phone after talking with Sophia I have a cry that comes from a place so deep inside of me I feel like I'm two years old again and I'm wishing my mother could pick me up, rock me on her lap, and tell me everything will be all better.

I'm glad I have Paris with me when I walk into that courtroom and see Nathan sitting next to his lawyer with Debbie sitting right beside him. Paris gives my hand a reassuring squeeze when we sit down next to my lawyer, a somber, no nonsense kind of woman who I've never seen smile in all the times I've met with her.

I sit there waiting my turn, as other couples file before the judge. I find myself wondering if my lawyer was like this before she became a divorce lawyer and if it was her temperament that led her to this profession, or if the work has hardened her. I watch as three couples end their contract with each other, the same agreement they entered into with such joy and happiness when they married this person that they couldn't imagine living their life without. I find myself searching their faces, studying them for clues and wondering in what way are we similar. Did it cause us all to find ourselves here? I want to ask them,

"What happened? What happened to all that love? Where did it go?"

A stream of sorrow flows through the room swirling around the judge's robes and running off into the corners where it seeps into the walls leaving a dark stain. I don't hear what's being said as Nathan and I stand there before the judge with our respective lawyers. I'm too busy shifting from one foot to the other trying to keep that sorrow from having a chance to soak in through my shoes. When I finally have the official pile of papers in my hands

I can't get out of there fast enough. Paris has a tough time keeping up with me as I make my way down the front stairs and out the door. When she catches up to me, she breathlessly asks,

"Are you okay?"

"Yeah, that sucked." I feel the furrow between my eyebrows starting to relax.

"What do you say, we do a little retail therapy and go shopping?" Paris suggests brightly.

I nod my head. "Yeah, we deserve a little reward."

It's a strange day of courtrooms and boutiques, a kind of jigsaw puzzle that doesn't fit. I push the pieces close together and pretend they do.

Chapter 14 ~ Boy Scout

I don't usually work on Saturday nights any more, but Sergio let me know he was in a bind. He's been so good to me throughout this past year, I couldn't say no. I had been hoping to go out with the gang to celebrate finally getting my certification as a personal trainer. The girls had been planning a dinner party at the Love Noodle and that had to be changed to drinks when I get out around nine so it won't be a total loss. From the look of the full parking lot when I pull in, this Saturday night is a busy one, but strangely, as I head down the stairs, it looks as if the place is empty. When I get to the door I see that there are no lights on. With confusion, I slowly push it open into complete darkness and silence. Someone flips the light switch and I'm so stunned by the sudden bright lights and a room full of excited people jumping up down and screaming SURPRISE, that I drop my bag on my foot prompting me to hop around holding onto the injured part and cursing. The mischievous group of friends instantly surrounds me laughing and picking up my spilled things.

"Were you surprised?"

They're all asking me at once, as if it wasn't obvious by my spastic reaction and the look on my face. I can't believe all the people who are here. Almost everyone from my classes seems to have shown up, along with most of my private clients. And there at the back of the room I spot Sophia, Kate, Lily, and Paris and I wave them over to me.

Sergio's looks very pleased with himself for pulling off such a great surprise, as he hands me a glass of champagne. Most of the other trainers are here too. I give Sergio a hard time for being such a good liar and find out he got a lot of help not only from my friends, but also from the other trainers at the gym.

The space has been transformed. The juice bar has a buffet of appetizers from the Love Noodle spread across it and David is manning a make shift bar at the front desk. There's a long paper banner across the front of it that says, "Congratulations Nicki!" The couch from Sergio's office has been pulled out and someone brought in a bunch of beanbag chairs and huge pillows that are randomly scattered about. David lowers the lights with the dimmer and puts some dance music on over the sound system as Paris goes around lighting dozens of candles, creating a surprisingly sexy atmosphere. I keep grabbing people and hugging them as I go through the room and when I get to Sergio he picks me up in a big bear hug and says,

"I'm very proud of you."

My eyes fill up as I whisper in his ear with my cheek pressed against his, "Thank you, Sergio. Thank you for everything."

After everyone's been eating and has had a drink or two, Sergio begins loudly clinking on the bottles at the bar and he signals to David to turn down the music. When he gets our attention he proposes a toast.

"I would like to make a toast to our guest of honor this evening." He lifts his glass toward me. "Nicki, look how far you've come in the time that you've been here. When you asked me for a job that first day you were a chubby lady in a tight spot."

Everybody laughs, myself included.

"But you worked hard and look at you now. You're a lean, mean, certified machine! To our Nicki."

I raise my glass to Sergio. Several of my friends clink glasses with me. I look around the room at all these warm faces smiling at me and I feel blessed.

David cranks up the music and people start using the space to dance. I'm standing there watching them when David comes up behind me and pulls me out into an open area. I'm feeling so happy and comfortable that it doesn't feel at all awkward to be dancing with this man who's so many years my junior. Sophia has even managed to get the usually reticent Sergio to shake his booty with her. Kate, Lily, and Paris are shaking it in a group with a bunch of the other young trainers. When they spot us they dance up and drape themselves over David and me in a noisy group hug.

As the evening slowly comes to an end, Sergio calls cabs and confiscates keys from several of us. David, who hasn't been drinking offers to drop off me, Kate and Lily since it's on his way home. He drops off Lily and Kate first, since my house is closer to his. When we pull up in front of my condo I effusively thank him for the ride home and for all he did to help Sergio with the party. He grins at me.

"You're welcome. Boy you're lit. You're really cute like this."

I laugh and thank him for the ride. As I lean over to give him a quick kiss on his cheek, he turns his face and meets my lips with his. I pull away quickly.

"You did that on purpose." I say, and instantly regret how stupid I sound.

"Yeah," he says, grinning and rumpling his hair with both hands, "I did. I couldn't help it. If you haven't noticed, I'm really attracted to you Nicki and I've been thinking about doing that for a while." He pauses, "Sorry."

He doesn't look, or sound the least bit remorseful as he sits there still grinning at me and I'm so wordless by his confession and the kiss I just sit there blinking stupidly until I find my voice.

"But David, I'm so much older than you." I say it with all the confusion I'm feeling.

"So what," he shrugs, "you're interesting and you're hot." He leans in to kiss me again and I put both of my hands up to block him.

"This is very flattering, but I'm really not comfortable with this." I realize my heart is pounding and I'm feeling something strongly resembling a panic attack. All the adrenaline seems to be sobering me up a little.

"So I guess you don't want to invite me up then?"

"Invite you up? Oh. God. No." I keep a hand placed on his very strong chest mindful that his face is only about six inches away from mine and as I look into his handsome young face it takes a certain

81

kind of willpower to prevent the alcohol that's circulating through my body from taking over the logical, but presently impaired part of my brain.

"You're a great guy and I don't have to tell you, a very attractive one. If I were fifteen years younger I'd probably be all over you, but I'm not."

"I don't care about our age difference Nicki." He lowers his voice, "You're interesting and you're sexy."

He puts his hand over my hand on his chest and looks soulfully into my eyes. He ain't making it easy. I squeeze my eyes shut and gather my resolve.

"Even if our age difference wasn't an issue for me, which it is, I'm just not in a place in my life to be with someone right now in any capacity. It's only been a year since my divorce and I'm just not ready for anything."

He makes a sad face, pouting his beautiful lips, and then manages to lean in just an inch or two with his face close to mine and says in a slow and sensual way,

"I just want to make love to you." He rests his forehead against mine and I playfully push him off.

"Give me a break will you? You're killing me."

He laughs, "Well if I can't make love to you, will you at least let me have one kiss, one real kiss?"

I contemplate it a moment, let out a huge sigh and ask, "If I do, will you leave it alone from here on out?"

He grins and holds out his little finger. "I pinky swear."

"Okay." I say, reluctantly.

He takes my face in his hands and looks into my eyes for a brief moment. Then he kisses me with such sweetness and urgency that it runs through me like a live circuit. No one has kissed me this intensely for a very long time and it's more intoxicating than the alcohol I drank. It makes me glad I made that speech not just for his sake, but also for my own. My body feels like it's being shaken awake from a very deep sleep.

"Thanks for the ride," I mutter, trying to collect my keys, my purse and myself.

"Thanks for the kiss," He grins mischievously, trailing his fingers along the side of my face. I shiver involuntarily.

When I finally climb into my bed, I lie there staring up at the ceiling slowly breathing in and out trying to calm the energy that's circulating wildly through my veins. This thing that's been asleep in me stirs rebelliously trying to rise to the surface of the place that it's been confined beneath. It's not going to allow me to keep it locked away anymore. Boy Scout fed it something it's been starved for. Now that it's gotten a taste, I wonder what will happen when it finally breaks loose.

Chapter 15 ~ Pain, Pleasure, Pain

My hangover the next morning is accompanied by some equally painful regret. Now in a sober state, I alternate between kicking myself for kissing David and playing the delicious moment over and over in my head. It's pain followed by pleasure followed by pain. Paris calls to see if I made it home all right.

"Boy, were you drunk." She gloats.

"Yes, I was." I see no sense in arguing an obvious point with her. "Drunk and stupid." I fill her in on the details of my goodnight kiss.

"Oh my God! Do you mean that gorgeous hunky young guy you were dancing with? I knew it! I told the girls he had a crush on you. Did you sleep with him?"

"Sleep with him! No, I didn't sleep with him. Seriously, would you sleep with some guy who was sixteen years younger than you?"

"I would if I looked like you and I didn't have a great husband. There's nothing wrong with having a little fun if you're both consenting adults."

"Barely." I mumble under my breath.

"I saw him honey and that was no child. I'm just saying there's nothing wrong with it in my opinion."

"I just can't do that and besides, I'm not ready for anything yet. Do you think I'm crazy?"

"No sweetie, I think you have to be true to who you are and if something doesn't feel right it probably isn't. But at some point it's going to be time to take a chance and open your heart and your other parts to another person and I just hope when that time comes you won't let your fear stop you."

"How will I be able to tell if I'm still not ready, or if I'm just being afraid?"

"Don't worry about it. I think you'll know."

I hang up the phone with my doubts trailing behind me as I move from room to room picking up around the house and doing dishes and laundry. Is Paris right? Will I know and how will I know? The only thing I know for sure is I don't want to ever go through the kind of painful loss I went through with Nathan. I'm so preoccupied I accidentally toss a red sweater in with my whites leaving me with a load of baby pink towels and sheets.

By the end of the day, I've heard from Kate, Lily, and Sophia who all call with their questions about my sexy interlude with Boy Scout. They're like raunchy guys in a locker room wanting to know if I got any. Even Lily, who's usually the perfect lady, seems to have a salacious interest. I'm hoping nothing like this is spreading on David's side of it since that could make for a really awkward situation at work with the other trainers. As evening comes around, I find myself dreading having to go in to work out a client in the morning.

Nathan drops the kids off, which is a welcome diversion since they instantly require all my attention as we figure out what to have for dinner and attend to any last minute Sunday night homework. By the time they're getting ready for bed, I'm so exhausted I can barely keep my eyes open long enough to make it upstairs and I'm glad to have sleep drop over me like a thick, comforting blanket.

As we're get ready the next morning to get out of the house for the day, I'm dragging my feet more than the kids are and for the first time they're giving me a hard time about how slowly I'm moving. I realize I'm trying to delay the inevitable and after I drop them off at school, I give myself a serious talking to. It isn't a big deal unless I make it one. Right? I resolve to enter the gym with no regrets about kissing David and no guilt whatsoever. I'm a grown woman and what I do is nobody's business, or something like that. I'm doing pretty well with my plan and as I work out my client there seems to be no evidence that anyone knows, other than David and me. When he comes in for his first client he passes close behind me as they walk over to the treadmills.

"Hey beautiful," he walks backward, grinning at me.

"Good morning." I reply as professionally as possible turning immediately back to my client. Within my peripheral vision I can see he's still looking at me and I purposely ignore him hoping he'll get the message.

When my client heads off to the shower I go to the desk to check my appointments. Sergio is finishing signing up someone new and asks me if I have a few minutes to show her around. I give her the tour and a schedule of all the classes and then I grab a smoothie before I head back to the desk to make a few phone calls.

"Can I have some?" Sergio asks, I hand him my glass and he takes a big gulp.

"Thanks," he says, handing it back to me. "That was some party huh?"

"Yeah, thank you again, it was a lot of fun. I was completely surprised."

He gives me a wide smile. "So you had a good time?"

"I had a great time." I smile back.

He nods his head, still grinning at me. "I'm glad to hear that. You deserve to have some fun you know."

He seems to be getting at something, but I'm not sure what, so I just say,

"Thanks." and turn to make my phone calls.

As I'm dialing the first call, Sergio begins humming next to me. It takes me a few moments to recognize the familiar melody. He's humming 'Mrs. Robinson'.

I hang up the phone before the call goes through and give him the death stare. He takes his time and pretends not to notice. He stops humming and looks up at me.

"What?" he asks, innocently.

"That's not funny." I punch him in the shoulder.

"Owww. I think it's funny and kind of surprising. I had no idea you were such a naughty girl, Ms. Botticelli, or should I call you Mrs. Robinson."

My mouth drops open and he starts to laugh.

"Lighten up little girl. I'm just messing with you. I really meant it when I said you deserve to have some fun. There's nothing like a younger lover to make you feel alive," he purrs and winks at me. My mouth continues to hang open.

"Sergio, first of all I have no lover. I was drunk. We kissed. That's all. Nothing else is going to happen."

He frowns, "That's a shame. If David was making me that kind of offer I'd take him up on it in a second." He looks wistfully out across the floor at David as he works out his client.

"He's very beautiful." He sighs, "I'm jealous."

I'm having a moment of realization and Sergio watches it creep across my face. He looks annoyed before he confirms what I'm thinking.

"You're not going to say you didn't know I was gay are you? Everybody knows and don't say I don't seem gay. I hate that."

Before I can come up with a tactful response, he looks around to see if anyone is listening.

"So, tell me." He leans toward me and lowers his voice. "Is he a good kisser?"

Chapter 16 ~ Lots of Jellybeans With Very Few Chocolate Truffles

About a month later, as I'm heading in to work, I spot David getting dropped off at the gym by a very pretty young woman in a blue Jeep. He sees me and calls me over.

"Nicki, I want you to meet Charlotte."

I extend my hand. "Nice to meet you, Charlotte."

"It's nice to meet you too. I've heard a lot about you."

"Thanks." I say, feeling a little uncomfortable at the thought of what David might have said to her.

"I think it's so cool that a woman your age is a personal trainer and you look so awesome. My mom is only a few years older than you and she doesn't look anything like you do." Charlotte says, with genuine enthusiasm.

I smile limply and try my best to be gracious, "That's really sweet of you. Well it was nice meeting you." I slunk off feeling like some kind of freaky example of geriatrics. Over my shoulder I can hear David giving her one of the kisses I've been fantasizing about on a pretty regular basis. He catches up with me as I'm heading in the door.

"Hey Nicki, how's it going?"

"Good. Charlotte seems really nice."

"Yeah, she's great. She's almost as sexy as you are." He gives me a playful nudge.

I roll my eyes. "Give it a rest handsome."

He laughs, "Hey, I knew I wasn't going to get a chance with you so when Charlotte came along." He trails off shrugging his shoulders.

"You don't have to explain anything. This was the right thing to do. She's perfect for you." I give him a motherly pat on his face.

"Thanks Nicki, you're such a cool person." He gives me a kiss on the cheek and as we're standing there smiling at each other, Sergio walks by and mutters just loud enough to be heard, "Does anybody work here?"

The rest of the day I find myself thinking about the thing that's been on my mind and circulating through me ever since David kissed me and woke those dormant feelings I've been stuffing deep down inside of me. Will I ever find my perfect someone and if I do, how will I know for sure? It seems lately, everywhere I go I see happy couples engaging in public displays of affection, something I was never completely comfortable with in the past. Now I found myself looking at them with a mixture of longing and envy. Where is my perfect someone and how will I find him? I make John Mayer's *Love Song For No One,* my new ring tone. I'm officially sappy.

When Nathan calls a few days later and tells me that he and Debbie have split up because she's realized, after many months of working with her therapist, that Nathan had only been a revisited adolescent fantasy, I know where he's was going with it. For a brief moment I entertain the idea of going back to that relationship, but I can't. I'm not the same person I had been the night he handed me those divorce papers. If anyone had told me that night that all that pain would lead me to being happy in ways I could not imagine, I would have ripped them a new one. But, here I am. It's not perfect, but it's good in ways that surprise me everyday. I now know something I never knew before. I am strong. I'm a survivor. So I tell him I'm sorry to hear that and gently move him on to the topic of the kids. It's strange to think that even eight months ago I probably would have jumped at the chance to reconcile. When I later tell the girls about it, even they find themselves throwing the devil on the wall.

"Maybe now he knows how right you two are for each other," says Lily with a face full of childlike hope.

"You two always had such a good marriage," says Paris.

"I knew those two would never last. I think he was the one having an adolescent fantasy," says Kate.

"Maybe you should take him back and make him spend the rest of his life making it up to you," adds Sophia with a defiant toss of her black curls. I just smile at their fierce support of me as they look back at me, expectantly awaiting my response.

"Once you're a pickle, you can't go back to being a cucumber." I say it simply.

"You're a pickle?" Lily asks, softly.

"Yeah, Lil, I'm a pickle. I don't really want to be a cucumber anymore."

I debated telling my mother and I immediately regretted it when I did. Her reaction was the most easily predicted, "That's great honey!"

I had to tell her, "No Ma, that's not great because I don't love him that way anymore. I'll always care about him and love him as a person, but I don't want him."

She looked like she was going to cry, or maybe just hit me with a heavy object.

So, now I find myself looking around expectantly whenever I go out with the girls and wondering. Will tonight be the night I meet *him*? Part of me is glad to be even feeling this way and part of me still feels like this is an area to be avoided at all cost. I read recently in some women's magazine that the supermarket is becoming one of the best places for single people to meet. Grocery shopping now becomes a hunting excursion. I go out wearing make-up and I think about what clothes to put on. Six pm seems to be one of the best times for spotting single men picking up something for dinner. Weeks pass by and I see no one who inspires me to even take a second glance. I let the girls know I'm now feeling ready and looking. Ironically, we're all in the same boat, except Sophia, who is in one of her periodic phases when she's swearing off men, and Paris who manages to be blissfully married.

On one of our girl's nights out Kate brings an article with her about online dating. Kate has had a few dates using the personal ads, but nothing to get excited about. She reads the article to us as we eat sushi and sip sake.

"I don't like the idea of putting my picture on the Internet," Sophia says, "you never know who's going to see it. The school would give me so much grief."

"People can do awful things with Photoshop," Lily adds, "like putting your head on somebody else's naked body and then putting in out all over the web."

"Now that sounds like it could only help," deadpans Kate.

We all agree that it seems like a pretty scary proposition. Who knows if the person you contact is who they say they are? Plus the potential volume of rejection could be pretty painful. Still, it piques our curiosity and when we get back to my place we decide to check out a site, or two. Without signing up you can browse the photos. So we do a search of men within thirty miles of us between the ages of thirty-five and forty-five. There are hundreds of them. They come in all shapes, sizes, and colors. It's like a candy shop with lots of jellybeans and only a few chocolate truffles. The bulk of the profiles are pretty inane with a few interesting ones sprinkled in. After about an hour of browsing we agree that this is definitely something we can't see ourselves doing.

After the girls have said goodnight and I go to shut down the computer, I have this strange sense

I'm closing up a world full of men who are looking for the same thing I am. What if he's in there? What if my perfect someone is searching for me in cyber space just waiting for us to find each other? "Maybe," I think to myself, "maybe.

Chapter 17 ~ Dodging the Mrs. Dowds

It's the third time in as many weeks that I find myself face to face with Mrs. Dowd. We're in line at the grocery checkout and since I'm ahead of her I have no hope of escape. She does her usual polite inquiries as to my mom and the kid's health before she launches into her standard plugging of Donald, her middle-aged, adenoidal, paunchy son who, not surprisingly, happens to still live with her.

"You should come have dinner with us sometime." She says. "I just know you two young people would have a lovely time together."

"Thank you, Mrs. Dowd that's really kind of you." I smile limply. "I'm just so darn busy these days with work and the kids."

She leans toward me and pats my hand. "I understand dear, but you're not getting any younger and you should take the time to find yourself a nice young man. A lovely girl like you shouldn't be alone."

I imagine hauling the loaf of French bread out of my cart and bludgeoning her with it right there. Instead I politely say, "You're probably right, Mrs. Dowd."

Thankfully it's my turn in line. I pay for my groceries and make my get away. That was a close call. I don't know how much longer I'm going to be able to dodge the Mrs. Dowds that seem to be coming out of the woodwork. I'm amazed that so many of my mother's friends have varyingly dysfunctional single sons and not a remotely attractive, interesting one in sight. Even my mother is breathing down my back inviting me over for lunch and when I arrive, her friend Grace is there with her icky son Dick who smiles at me hungrily from behind glasses that make his eyes look like two eggs over easy.

As I'm putting away my groceries, I take serious stock of the situation. It's time to get realistic. Being a single mom with two adolescent kids, I'm not exactly burning up the clubs doing the whole singles scene. This is a small, dominantly geriatric retirement community, where the average age is around sixty-two. Since I've never really had a thing for older men, the chances of me meeting Mr. Right in line at the Post Office is about as likely as me showing up on the beach next summer in a thong. I mean it could happen, but we're talking only in the event of some minor miracle like, they really do find a cure for cellulite.

As soon as I finish putting away the groceries, I go to my computer. The recent image of Mrs. Dowd and her son is so fresh in my mind I wince. I look up a couple of online dating sites, browse some of the ads and based on the format I think will work best for me, I pull out my credit card and join one.

I spend more than an hour writing and rewriting my winning little profile. I try to make it funny, interesting and smart. I include what I'm looking for in a partner and hopefully it's not too intimidating. After agonizing over it for several minutes I decide that the right guy won't find my laundry list of desired qualities at all overwhelming. He should be:

>Kind
>
>Spiritual, but not religious
>
>Good sense of humor
>
>Into health and fitness

Now, I have to post my photo because, as the literature on the site says, "Photo ads get twice as many results". It takes me a while to settle on one. I find a nice black and white shot that's a few years old, but if you squint when you look at me, I haven't changed a bit. Besides, according to the article that Kate read to us the other night, everybody does it and you just have to expect the squint rule applies across the board. The whole process takes me over two hours. I'm hoping it will be two hours well spent. I submit my ad and a window pops up to tell me that after my ad is reviewed, if there are no problems with it's content, it will be posted on the site within the next twenty-four hours. I feel excited and terrified.

During this past week, as I was toying with the idea of doing this, people suddenly began sharing countless stories with me about online dating. Some are encouraging and some a bit frightening. I hear everything from people who met in cyber space who are now happily married with kids, to women being harassed by some very disturbed men. None of those stories has prepared me for the onslaught that comes next.

The next morning I receive an email from the service informing me that my ad is up and that I can now send and receive email from other members. I go to my account with no expectations. I'm shocked.

In cyber space, I am a babe. It's a little overwhelming. Where did all these men come from? By the end of the first day I've received over one hundred emails. I get a slightly nasty one from the provider telling me I've exceeded my limit and that if I don't start emptying my mailbox, they will. I'm going to have to check my email several times a day to keep up. It's potentially a part time job and I feel like a celebrity opening fan mail. The letters run the gamut from thoughtful and sweet to borderline raunchy and moronic with the common denominator being, they want ME. They come from all over the planet. One from a guy in Jerusalem reads, "If you want a REAL man, you go and find him!" I laugh and hit delete. Another arrives from Paris in French. I forward it to Kate who translates it and sends it back. It's tre' hot. My previously deflated ego is feeling pumped!

I'm virtually wading through this stuff. I've already stated in my ad that I won't respond to emails without an accompanying photo and I've also set a limit on the distance I will travel. Right away that eliminates quite a few of the responses. It's a process of whittling things down.

Some guys look better than the all you can eat chocolate buffet at the Copley Plaza, but sound like they're sharing their brain with someone who got the superior half, while others write these wonderful mini odes but when I scroll down to check the photos they've attached, I find myself wondering if my Aunt Josephine might like them. I tell myself it's a numbers game. Eventually, with enough perseverance, I'm hoping the two elements of beauty and brains will come together.

Chapter 18 ~ A Tightrope Lubed With Grease

I'm a soldier in the trenches of cyber dating. I'm quickly discovering this is no place for thin-skinned sissies, or weak stomachs. I've just opened an attachment of a nude man who is very proud of what nature saw fit to bestow upon him. It was such a large file it took me more than a few moments to realize what I was looking at. Unfortunately, it was more information than I needed at seven-thirty in the morning. This also makes me realize that I have to be careful about opening attachments with Max and Renoir around. They already think I've turned the corner when it comes to my sanity. I can't hand them the proof.

Some of the responses to my ad are so heartfelt I feel I must say more than just a polite "*No thank you*," when the author is not what I'm looking for. Letting someone down graciously is a little like farting in a crowded movie theatre. Even though you wouldn't have done it if you could help it, it still stinks and bums people out. So I mention some of their positive attributes and tell them that somehow I know the right person for them is waiting just around the corner. I know it's cheesy, but it makes me feel better and I hope it makes them feel a little better too.

I get an email from a guy who sounds pretty incredible in spite of the fact that he's a lawyer. I decide not to hold that against him because he's intelligent in a deep way. Surprising, he's spiritual and he's funny. He writes that he doesn't have a photo he can send, but promises to send one soon. His writing is so engaging I decide to make an exception on my rule about missing photos.

By the fifth email, I'm feeling like I really like this guy, but I'm also feeling some kind of reservation I can't put my finger on. Maybe it's just my fear of disappointment due to the still missing photo. I don't want to get my hopes up about him, even though he's painted an impressive verbal portrait of himself. I get the feeling he's hiding something from me. I've always had what I would call an accurate gut. I just didn't realize it would work in this strange new realm. His sixth email arrives with the confession. Mr. Spiritual is married. He tells me his sad tale of marital woe complete with the heartbreaking details of the difficulties involved in extricating himself from his emotional prison. Poor baby. Yeah. Right. Even though I consciously realize he has no way of knowing what a hot button this is for me, I lambaste him cyber style and in his whimpering response back, I can practically see him slinking off to his corner, tail between his virtual legs. I'm definitely disappointed and I'm very aware I let myself get a little to into the idea of this guy. From here on in, I am practicing the Buddhist act of non-attachment. If any situation calls for it, this one does.

I let go and move on. I find in the midst of a lot of uninteresting responses, an email from a cute guy named Eddie. Adorable. Pretty green eyes with thick lashes, dark curly hair and a jaw Jack Palance would be proud to call his own. He seems a little reserved on the written page, but it could be he's just not comfortable with this format. He's articulate enough and nothing jumps out at me to scream serial killer. After several emails back and forth we do some fairly meaningful sharing. I decide to give Eddie a chance. I ask him for his phone number to go to the next step in this strange process, communicating in real time. I call him from my landline, being sure to block my number in case he has caller ID and he does turn out to be a psycho. He has a nice quality to his voice, but a heavy Boston accent. I pretend he's a young Pacino and it starts to work for me.

After we have a couple of conversations on the phone we decide to take step three and set up a date for drinks. Now, I've been thinking this over carefully because, after all, the idea is to actually meet people for what I would call, *the sniff test* because no matter how great the thing is on the written page, if the physical, in the flesh chemistry isn't there, it isn't going to happen. So, I'm thinking you meet for drinks, that way if it's bombing you aren't trapped for an interminable amount of time. Because as we all know, when you aren't having fun, time moves at the speed of a glacier.

The evening of our meeting arrives and even though I'm solidly in non-attached mode, or so I tell myself, I change my clothes four times. I want to walk the line that says, 'I can be wild, but also someone you can respect and consider taking home to your mother.' Like a tightrope lubed with grease, it's one, hard balancing act. I go with jeans, a black top with a ballet neck that shows skin, but not too much skin and easy on the makeup, jewelry and perfume. I'm as neutral as Switzerland. I give myself a good pep talk in the rear view mirror as I chew a couple of Tums and head into the restaurant.

I've been learning in a very tangible way that truth is indeed, a relative thing. Example; the other day I get an email from Harry. It reads:

"Hi, I'm Harry. I really liked your ad and your photo. I'm thirty-nine, I've never been married. I own my own very successful auto body business. I'm very attractive and I work out four times a week. I love candle light dinners and long walks on the beach. I've included a recent photo and I hope you write me back. I think we have a lot in common. Thanks, Harry."

I open the attached file. Harry is a pleasant, nondescript looking fellow in a bright yellow and blue striped polo shirt I'm sure my Uncle Frank would lust for. Judging from his physique, Harry's into cross training, with his favorite workout being a rigorous night of lifting the remote combined with some serious aerobic snacking and he definitely does this workout more than only four times a week. He's posing in front of a calendar featuring a photo of a woman in a bikini that, judging from its size, she probably borrowed it from her seven-year-old daughter. She's sporting two quite impressive non-biodegradable breasts. Oh yeah, Harry is my kind of man. I am as tactful as I can possibly be with my response.

"Dear Harry, Thanks for writing, but I don't think it's what I'm looking for. I wish you the best of luck!"

Silly me, I thought that would be the end of it. I'm about to learn that some of us are suckers for punishment. Harry writes back.

"Maybe I'm a masochist, but I'd really like to know, what about me isn't for you?"

I respond hopefully one last time.

"Hi Harry, I just didn't get the feeling from what you wrote that we're really suited to each other. Take care."

He just can't seem to stop himself and writes,

"I hardly wrote anything. How can you get that kind of impression from a few measly lines? Did you find me attractive?"

Now, I'm getting pissed. "Harry," I write, "you're a nice looking man, but you're just not my type."

Harry has the last succinct word. "BITCH!"

I'm tempted to write him back and give him grief about his horribly generic use of the candlelight dinner/beach walks cliché, but decide to quit before it gets really ugly. At least I have the satisfaction of knowing I'm a bigger man than Harry.

I pull into the parking lot and take a deep breath. I tip the rearview mirror, put on some lipstick and give my mouth a spray of breath freshener. It's five o'clock and already dark. It's warmer than it's been recently. Still I shiver in spite of the mild October air as I head into the restaurant to meet Eddie. I step inside and I'm welcomed by the smell of garlic. We're meeting at a wonderful Italian restaurant, that way if things go well, we can segue into dinner. I glance around, my eyes skimming the faces at the bar. No Eddie in sight. I check my watch. He could be late, or lost, or he could have decided to forget about it altogether. As I'm mentally preparing for all the possibilities, I pivot one more time and feel a hand on the back of my shoulder.

"Nicki?" I turn and there he is. He gives me, what he must know is a killer grin, complete with amazing dimples. "Eddie?" I ask, instantly feeling stupid. Who else would it be? But, he continues smiling beneficently. "Yeah, shall we get a drink?" He does this cute little leading thing with his hand on my lower back and helps me off with my coat. Before we sit, we subtly give each other the once over. It might be my imagination, but it seems like he's turned up his smile a notch.

We order a couple of glasses of wine and beginning sipping and talking.

"So," he sighs, "this is nice."

He seems as relieved as I am. We start with basic, harmless stuff and talk about our day. He works for an investment company and loves his job. He then tells me some stories that are now viewed as humorous, about some past cyber dates from hell.

"One," he tells me, "was with a woman who sent me a photo that must have been at least ten years old. I'm telling you I didn't even recognize her. She had to be seventy-five lbs. heavier than she was in the picture and she was only about your height."

He gestures with his hands held way out from his body to demonstrate her girth.

"We're talking big!"

I'm immediately thinking about the squint rule. As I understand it, it allows reasonably intelligent men and women to misrepresent their physical attributes only slightly, for the purpose of increasing their ability to lure people in. I'm wondering why someone would risk pushing it that far when he says,

"People lie. It's almost impossible to find honest people anymore." he leans in toward me and gives me a steely stare. I find myself feeling this strong urge to confess to something. Instead I ask,

"So, you never lie?"

He looks appalled and leans back in his chair. "Never! I used to lie when I was a kid and even in my early twenties, but not anymore. I hate lying. Liars disgust me!"

I believe him. He *looks* disgusted. I decide to have some fun with it and see if my new friend can laugh at himself.

"I lie," I say, "Not all the time, but sometimes I lie. I might do it to avoid an uncomfortable situation, or to save my ass. You know, I'll tell the kids I have an appointment in an hour so I can't drive them to the mall and it's really that I just don't feel like it, but I know if I tell them the truth it will be a huge hassle. It's just easier to lie." I smile at him demurely and casually take a sip of my wine checking to see how my confession is

106

registering. He looks like he's not sure what to make of my impromptu confession.

"So," I ask him, "when you met the 'big girl' and you let her down afterwards, did you tell her that you don't go for overweight women, or did you lie?"

For a moment, he looks like I hit him hard in the head before he regains his composure and lights up that grin for me complete with laughter. Apparently, I'm funny even when I'm not trying to be. He gives me a playful little shove across the table and changes the subject.

The subject turns to fitness - a passion we both share. He teaches Karate a couple of nights a week and he's also into rock climbing. He has the body to prove it. He leans over while I'm talking and brushes a strand of hair out of my eyes and I get a little rush. We hold each other's gaze as we talk and he subtly touches my arm. It's all feeling pretty nice. I excuse myself to go to the Ladies Room. As I walk away, I can feel him checking out my butt. I'm feeling smug. In these jeans, it's one of my best features. I get back to where we're sitting and he's ordered another glass of wine and an appetizer. I'm glad to see a little food, because I'm feeling the first glass, probably from nervously drinking it too quickly.

I've noticed, as we've been talking that he has this nasty looking scar across the knuckles of his right hand. I ask him about it.

He looks sheepish and proud at the same time as he tells me the story. It's one from his early twenties. Apparently, before he gave up lying,

Eddie was also a bit of a hell-raiser. So the story went that one night, after too much drinking, he got into a fight with a guy and punched him in the mouth. The guy's teeth split his knuckles open, which wouldn't have been too big a deal if he had gotten proper medical treatment right away.

Unfortunately, the human mouth is one of the most bacteria ridden places on the planet and after he began to sober up a few hours later, his hand had swollen to cartoon-like, Pop-Eye proportions. He was rushed to the hospital where major surgery was done and he was treated for a systemic bacterial infection, which left him a very sick boy. He wound up being in the hospital for a couple of months. The experience was a wake up call and the beginning of the end to his wild days. He was certain in informing me that he was now a peaceful warrior only. Eddie was an interesting character.

"So, you mentioned in your ad that you read palms." he says, leaning forward and putting his hand out to me. I tease him, as I take it.

"You sure you want me to tell you the truth?"

"I think I can handle it." His dimples seem to wink at me. He's leaning very close and I can feel his eyes on my face as I scrutinize his hand. There is something really nice about the way he's looking at me and I can feel the color rising in my cheeks. I give him a very basic reading and when I'm through he reciprocates by taking my hand and giving me his version of a reading. He seems to be using the Braille method and is having fun running his fingers up, down, and across my palm. I can't believe that something so simple can feel so good. After so many months of touch deprivation, I'm like a walking nerve ending.

Three hours and two appetizers later, we decide to call it an evening and he walks me to my car. We chat a bit more and he says he'll call me and that he had a good time. I thank him for a fun evening and go to give him a quick hug. Somehow he manages to add a quick, awkward kiss to the mix. We both giggle in embarrassment. He apologizes and I say,

"It's ok."

"Really, could I have another one?"

In my mind, I'm waving a white flag. The word "Sure" flies out of my mouth. My common sense, which would tell me *no kissing on a first date*, seems to have temporarily shut down overridden by the desires of my body. The next kiss comes with intent of purpose. He's a good kisser and it sure feels nice, but something is missing. No tingles. We say good night and I get into my car. I give him a smile and a wave as I pull out of the parking lot. The missing tingles have me wondering, all the way home.

Chapter 19 ~ The Color of Love

My alarm goes off at eight. After two kids, this is my idea of sleeping in. I hit the snooze and as I lay there replaying the events of my date with Eddie in my head, I doze off only to be woken abruptly by the alarm's radio and Tracey Chapman singing about that fast car. I'm meeting Kate and Sophia for brunch at eleven so I get showered and give the dog a quick walk.

We're meeting at a great little breakfast place on the water. It's the kind of place we locals like having to ourselves in the late fall. In spite of the lack of tourists it's still so popular, there's a line out the door. Sophia's already they're, shifting from one foot to the other in the cold. We wait on the front steps doing our chilly little jig together. Kate comes running up, breathless and giggling her apologies just as a space opens up inside.

We order some hot cider and soon we're warming up, scanning the place to see who's here and saying hi to different tables in the room. The conversation starts with kids, which is the usual, with venting about pretty much the same things: homework, psychotic teachers, sibling rivalry, adolescent hormones, and all that goes with them. The conversation then moves on to the exes and more venting. One thing the three of us share is an ability to laugh at it all. The way I see it, when you stop finding the humor in these things it's time to get in the tub and open up a vein.

"So," Sophia starts, "are you going to volunteer information about the date, or are we going to have to beat it out of you?"

Kate stops, with her muffin in mid air. "Oh my God! That's right, the date with Enrique was last night wasn't it?"

Poor Eddie, he already has a sarcastic nickname given to him by Max after he saw Eddie's photo and said he thought he looked like a South American drug smuggler. I give them all the gory details right down to the kiss.

"Oh my God Nick, I can't believe you played tonsil hockey on a first date!" Kate pretends to feel scandalized.

Sophia smirks. "Yeah, I'm really surprised. That's so not like you."

I give her the finger.

"You both know that's not something I would ordinarily do. He was just so damn cute."

"Yeah, and you're just so damn horny." Sophia smiles at me from beneath her lashes and flips me the finger back.

Kate starts eating fruit off my plate. "So, how was the kiss?" she asks.

"It was a fundamentally good kiss. His technique was good. He was expressive, not too much tongue, no drooling, but the weird thing is it did nothing for me. No tingles. What do you think that means?"

"Oooh, that was a little clinical. I wouldn't worry about it though, honey," Kate, teases. "I mean, it's been a while. You're probably just a little shut down from being in nun mode for so long."

I run that statement through my internal data banks. My head thinks she may be right, but my gut just isn't buying it. Something just wasn't right. I'm not sure at this point whether it's him, or me. I decide to change the subject.

"Have either of you heard from Lily?"

"That girl is working like a dog," Kate mumbles through a mouthful of spinach and cheese omelet, "I half think she's doing it to piss her mother off. You know how she's constantly breathing down her neck about not having a man and not being married." "And not producing grandchildren!" Sophia adds.

Lily's the only one of us who has never been married. She lives in a habitually clean apartment with ridiculously white carpeting and no sticky surfaces. She inhabits a completely different planet. It's one devoid of car-pooling, or a freezer full of Bagel Bites, or mountains of clean and dirty laundry. It's a world I vaguely remember as B.C., or Before Children. Who can blame her for being a little reluctant about leaving her peaceful, orderly oasis?

As we step out of the restaurant we make a plan to all go out together for some quality girlie time.

I get home and there's a message on my phone from Eddie saying he had a great time and asking if I could give him a call that evening. He wants to make a date if I'm up for it. I'm definitely up for it. I want to get another look at those dimples and that gorgeous smile. Plus, the whole kissing issue certainly requires further exploration. I'm a girl with a mission. The last thing he says really puts him through the roof with an abundance of brownie points for team Eddie.

"I noticed when you pulled out of the parking lot that one of your headlights is out. If you pick up a headlamp, I can fix that for you." I'm melting. What a man! Okay, so the list of pluses looks like something like this:

1.Seriously cute!
2.Into health and fitness
3.Takes care of his woman

I pick up the phone and dial his number, it rings several times and I start composing in my head a message to leave on the machine, when Eddie answers sounding out of breath.

"Hi! Did I get you at a bad time?" I ask. " I can call back."

"Oh no, not at all. I was just getting in the door. I was wondering, I know it's short notice, but what are you doing tonight?"

"Tonight?" I ask and he immediately starts to backpedal. Part of me thinks, don't seem over eager girl, part of me completely overrides it and causes the words, "Sure, tonight would be great," to come out of my mouth.

The next thing I know, I'm walking toward a table at the same restaurant. Eddie sits there with that grin that seems to be pulling me in like one of those tractor beams on Star Trek. I'm helplessly pulled in. He stands, pulls out my chair and gives me a quick kiss on the cheek.

"Sorry I'm late." I apologize.

He leans forward across the table and takes my hands in both of his.

"It was worth waiting for." he says, and locks eyeballs with me.

Man, his eyes are green. I sigh a little too audibly and his dimples become bottomless pits.

We order drinks and the conversation gets more animated and seems to go all over the place. We start comparing some stories of people we've connected with online and we're having a good laugh at how similarly weird our experiences have been so far. Eddie's been at this for almost a year now. I'm thinking may have something to do with his enthusiastic response to me. From what he tells me, it's been pretty slim pickins'. He asks me if I get a lot of responses from younger men and I begin telling him about this twenty-five-year-old, six-foot-four inch body builder who looked like an African-American version of the incredible hulk.

He pauses with an odd look on his face. "You didn't go out with him did you?"

I laugh, "Of course not! He was way to young."

Judging by the look on Eddie's face that still isn't the answer he's looking for and he asks, "Would you go out with a black guy?"

I shrug and answer, "Sure, if we click, I don't care if a guy is striped, or polka-dotted. Why? Wouldn't you date a black woman?"

He shakes his head. "No, I wouldn't date one. I really don't have anything against those people. I have some of them for friends, but I couldn't go out with one."

An uncomfortable silence follows and seems to go on forever. I work at composing my features, hauling my chin back up from where it's dropped on the table. I try to figure out where I can go with this. Maybe he can redeem himself. I offer him an opportunity. "Don't you think attraction is really about connecting with another person's energy? If you met a woman who was intelligent and attractive and just your kind of person, I'll bet you wouldn't even notice what color she was."

Okay, so maybe I said it a little too enthusiastically and in my best Pollyanna voice, but did that really warrant the completely irritated look he was now giving me. He sat there blinking repeatedly with his mouth slightly open and his brow knitted. He looked like an annoyed, Wide-mouthed Bass. I hold my breath and wait for his reply with my eyebrows raised in an expectant and hopeful way as he searches for, I guess, what he feels will finally get me to understand the essence of Eddie.

"No. Nicola. I just wouldn't even go there."

Well there it is. Simple. Succinct. I'm picturing introducing him to Paris, and her husband Terrence and their two adorable mocha kids. I give Eddie's gorgeous green eyes and sexy dimples one more appreciative inspection. Ah well, close in some ways and miles away in others. Adios, Enrique! The search continues.

Chapter 20 ~ The Slate Gray Door

The girls are sad to hear about the early demise of Eddie, but in total agreement with my decision to kick him to the curb. It was more than just the issue of his being a screamin' bigot. He was also a little too rough around the edges for my taste. I want a man with a modicum of sophistication and if I'm out shopping as it were, why not look for a man with as many of the features I want as possible. I know it sounds like I'm talking about buying a major appliance, but think about it, is it really that far off? Is it all that different from putting together an order for a new car online? In essence, I'm building myself my ideal man.

More inane email arrives complete with lackluster photos. The volume is dying down a bit, which is a welcome respite. After only twenty-five days online I'm no longer considered fresh meat. I decide that tonight I'm going to take a pro-active approach and become the hunter rather than the hunted.

I get the kids off to bed, make myself a cup of tea, and settle in front of my computer. To do a search I have to type in some basic information as to what I'm looking for. It can get pretty detailed to the point of being specific about hair and eye color. Apparently, some women only date brown-eyed, brown-haired men, and right there you've narrowed the field from which to pick and choose. I go for a guy who's any myriad of visual possibilities my only needs are that he be a non-smoker, who is in reasonable shape. He needs to live within thirty miles of me and should fall between the ages of thirty-seven and forty-five.

I press the submit button and wait to see what will be regurgitated back at me. The first page of ten profiles out of three hundred appears, and I begin. This is more complicated than I thought it would be. I start with the photo, which isn't even the size of a postage stamp. I need a magnifying glass. In some photos their heads are smaller than baby peas. Some are wearing sunglasses, or posed so mysteriously that even their own mother's couldn't pick them out of a police line-up. Fortunately, with others, it's an obvious no go. If the physical appeal isn't somewhat there, I just don't see the sense in torturing myself by then reading a really wonderful bio. Instead, I just move on. Is that superficial of me? You bet it is and I embrace that part of myself without guilt. Heck, the men have no qualms about it. If physical attractiveness is not the first thing they say they're looking for, it's certainly the second. Besides, I'm visual. Eye-candy is not for men only. We women need to demand equal time and start expecting a little more pizzazz.

Lily once told me she never really thought about whether a guy was good looking, or not and I almost fell off my shoes. Here she is, this very attractive, physically fit woman, dating schlubs. The way I see it, half the fun is gone right there. I have since educated her in the joys of dating cute men. Now don't get me wrong, I'm not saying G.Q. men only and I acknowledge that beauty is definitely a subjective thing, that changes from eye to eye, but that's just it, my eyes need to be pleased. So if the photo looks remotely interesting I continue.

I'm finding that the old cliché seems to hold true. Beauty and brains combined are a rare combination. This is frustrating and if I let myself go there, a little frightening. I'm contemplating joining the schlub club. After going through about one hundred and fifty of the three hundred profiles, it's either that, or quit, when I come across a cute photo. He has dark thick hair in a funky cropped style, nice strong features and a dazzling smile with teeth so white, they practically glow. He's definitely the most attractive guy I've seen so far, so I'm figuring the profile is going to suck out loud. I'm pleasantly surprised. It's witty, insightful, and urbane. He's a writer. Oh my God! I reread it and it's even better the second time through. I go back and read his stats again. He's only thirty-four, which makes him five years younger than I am and puts him three years below the edge of my age curve and wondering why he turned up in my search. The hell with it, I've mostly dated men younger than myself, even Nathan is four years younger. I decide to go for it. I'm feeling energized and powerful. Hope looms at me from the monitor of my computer. I go to 'email this member' and compose a brief response, trying not to gush and asking him to check out my profile. I end with an optimistic, "I look forward to hearing from you." and hit send. With that, my work is done for the day. I glance over at the clock and see that I've been at this for more than two hours. Finding Mr. Right is labor intensive.

The next morning I find an email has arrived from Smiling Guy. His name is Slater Gray and as you may have guessed, his friends call him Slate. I'll admit it's a little Hollywoodish, but I've always had an affinity for men with unusual names and a guy named Slate Gray would definitely fall into that category. He seems really pleased that I wrote and isn't at all at a loss for words in his response back. It's an absolute novella complete with stories from his childhood, past relationships, and his extensive travels. He's presently writing an article for the New Yorker on politics in the city's theatre industry. Slate Gray is no slouch.

He talks a bit about making the transition from the emotionally open climate of southern California to the much more socially reserved atmosphere of New England. It's been a bit of a shock to his sensitive system and from what he's told me about himself so far, sensitive seems to be the operative word. Now don't get me wrong, I'm all for sensitive men, why some of my best friends are sensitive men. But he does mention one thing I find myself questioning, regarding his softer demeanor and that, is the perception some folks here in the conservative northeast have expressed regarding his sexual orientation. Hmmmmm. Could this be a red flag? He does have two pierced ears. Perhaps the Slate Gray door swings both ways. I'm a little concerned, but not overly since I'm blessed with incredibly accurate gay-dar. If we meet, I'll know.

I compose an email back and do my best to be similarly engaging, but I just can't compete at his level. I decide to compensate for my literary shortcomings by attaching a bunch of photos and ask him to send me some more in return.

The next few days are pleasantly spent opening these interesting emails from Slate. More photos arrive and they give me more of a sense of who he is. There is one of Slate with his Dad that's really quite sweet. They've just gone white water rafting and They're standing beside their raft; arms around each other's shoulders, soaking wet, and beaming for the camera. Slate is a big rugged man and even cuter in these more candid shots. After several days of emails we move to the telephone.

In real time he's surprisingly shy, even reticent. He's one of those unusual guys whose forte is the written page. There's something endearing about it. Here he is this great big capable man with all these accomplishments to his credit and he's at a loss for words on the phone. It takes a little doing on my part and eventually I'm able to draw him out. I notice that he has this affectation to the way he speaks that comes off as a bit effeminate. Perhaps that is what people have interpreted as his being gay. It's very obvious from speaking with him that he's not as confident as one might think he would be, given his accomplishments, but he also has a sweetness that's endearing.

We make a tentative date to meet on Friday for dinner at the same place I met Eddie. On Thursday night, Slater calls to confirm our date and to get the time and driving directions from Boston. While we're talking, I finally decipher what it is in his voice that makes him sound effeminate. It's just the slightest hint of a lisp. Perhaps this little speech impediment is the thing that moved him in the direction of favoring the written word. I'm sure it also contributed to his way of speaking so softly and tentatively. In realizing that this is a sensitive man who probably was teased mercilessly as a child and still wears the pain of that, my heart goes out to him.

I get to the restaurant a little early and he's already there at the bar waiting with a slightly frightened look on his face. As I walk toward him, the bartender gives me a smirk. In the past two weeks, he's seen me here with two different men. He probably thinks I'm a hooker. I meet his smirk with an, I could give a shit stare and turn my gaze to Slater. I smile warmly.

"Oh wow!" he says, a bit too loudly, "You look so nice! I hope you don't mind, I thought I'd come early so I could have a drink. I'm sooo nervous!"

Adding Slater's physical presence certainly completes the picture. He says this with broad, flapping hand gestures and the bartender doesn't even try to hide his smirk.

"Can I get you something?" he asks me, as he leans over the bar trying so hard to hold back laughter, he looks like he's suffering from gas pains. I glare back at him and order a glass of Chardonnay. Taking a couple of big gulps, I quickly assess the damage. I mean really, what's the big deal? So I'm on a date with an obviously gay man. Obvious, that is, to everyone but him. I can easily get though a simple dinner. Hell, I've treaded in this territory before. One of my first boyfriends in high school was in gay denial. When he finally sorted it out years later, he told me that part of the reason he dated me, was he wanted to be me. I had suspected it the whole time, but also thought he was, in some ways, the perfect boyfriend for that time in my life. He never pressured me to have sex and he always complimented me on what I was wearing right down to my earrings. Though, there was something a little unappealing about having my boyfriend say,

"Oooooh I LOVE your dress!" with so much longing in his voice, I was tempted to let him borrow it.

I ran into Danny in New York City five years later wearing more eye make-up than I was and cozying up to a guy who was prettier than I'll ever be. It was great to see that he had finally found his niche.

I've always prided myself on my ability to make the most out of whatever life puts in front of me and to find value in all kinds of circumstances. True, I know from the get go that there is no romantic relationship to be had in this situation, but Slater is an interesting and sweet man who shares my passion for a lot of things. This could be, as they say, the start of a beautiful friendship.

A table opens up for us and we head over. Slater had made the cute suggestion that we both dress in the typical N.Y.C. uniform of black on black and as I walk ahead of him he expresses his appreciation for my outfit of black leather pants and a black lace shirt. Under his chic black trench he's wearing black jeans and a black, Cashmere V-neck sweater with a gorgeous silver watch and two small silver hoops in his ears. His blue-black hair is cut in a trendy, cropped style. He's such a cute man I start trying to think of any single guys I know who I could fix him up with.

Over our drinks and I ask him how the article for the New Yorker went. He looks pleased that I've asked and tells me it will be in the December issue. I congratulate him and tell him I can't wait to read it. As he blushes up to his ears, he averts his face to the side. He's been turning his head this way since we sat down. There's a very noticeable scar on one side of his face that starts at his cheekbone and ends above his jaw near his earlobe. It's something he seems to feel self conscious about and I want to help put him at ease.

"You might think this is odd," I begin, "but I like scars. I find them interesting. Like that one on your cheek, it really gives your face character."

I toss it out there offhandedly and immediately his whole demeanor seems to melt. His hand absently moves to his face and he shrinks down in his seat. His shoulders roll forward and in a little bitty 10-year-old voice he asks,

"Do you mean it?" if it were possible for Slater to be in love with a woman, I think he would ask me to marry him on the spot. Gratitude gushes out of every pore in his body. Unfortunately, my plan backfires horribly. Instead of feeling at ease, he chooses to put himself in a one down position for the rest of the evening asking me such questions as, "If you're five years older than I am, how come you look younger?" and, "Why would someone like you email someone like me?"

Slater Grey is a man who is not comfortable in his own skin and it's becoming very apparent that even a friendship is out of the question. I have found in my travels that people so lacking in self-confidence, have a tendency to eventually despise those of us who have a good rapport with ourselves. They start out being attracted to us, but it soon deteriorates into petty, jealous, sniping. I've always done better with people who like themselves flaws and all.

We're almost to the end of our dinner and I'm feeling exhausted from two hours of fluffing his delicate ego. My imaginary pom-poms are ratty and frayed from all the Rah, Rah, Rah. I just want to go home, fill the tub, and call it a day. At this point it feels like it's been a day and a half. After what seems like an interminable wait, the check comes and I reach for it because somehow I feel guilty and responsible for Slater's shortcomings, even though the logical part of my brain knows that's just bullshit. He quickly puts his hand on top of mine and gives me a look, which I remember from when my kids were about three and on the verge of crying. It consists of big puppy dog eyes and a slight protruding of the bottom lip. I call it the boo-boo face. Oh My Gawd! I want to run from the place screaming, but instead I calmly ask,

"Why do you look so sad?"

As soon as I ask the question, I regret it. I must be suffering from temporary insanity brought on by the stress of the evening. He does the whole shrinking down in his chair routine again and answers me in his smallest voice yet.

"Because I know I'm not going to see you again."

"Oh Slater," I find myself struggling to rally, "Now that's not true. I think it would be fun to hang out with you sometime." I don't say it out loud, but I think to myself,

Yeah, sometime in the far distant future when I'm to senile to know what's actually going on around me.

This sucks. He reaches into his pocket and pulls out a little wrapped box.

"I had a feeling this would happen so I brought a little something for you to remember me by." He hands it to me and the whole thing is so saccharin sweet I swear I can hear violins playing something by Andrew Lloyd Webber.

Now I'm pissed. It hits me that Slater Gray is one of the most manipulative men I've ever met. I wonder if I look even remotely as angry as I feel. I open the box, which contains worry dolls. I thank him and give him a quick kiss on the cheek. We wrap things up and he offers to walk me to my car. I thank him for offering to do that and tell him I need to do some shopping in the mall for my kids, and tell him I'll email him later. Two minutes later I'm doing a joyful dance of liberation in the aisles of Target.

When I get home I write him immediately. I want to tidy this up as soon as I can and as kindly and tactfully as possible. I start by thanking him for a lovely evening. Then, I comment on the wonderfully interesting conversation and point out all his good qualities as a person. I finish by saying that I hope he'll understand that I don't think we're a good match. I wish him luck in his continued search and decide in the name of kindness not to elaborate any further. I crawl off to bed feeling so wiped out my energy barely clears my ankles.

The next morning I awake feeling renewed. It's amazing what a few Zs and eight hours away from an energy sucking, emotional vampire can do for you. I make a cup of tea and a batch of pancakes for the kids. My whole world looks rosy. My children seem positively angelic as they nag and antagonize one another at the table. It's like that first day of being well after you've had the flu for two weeks. It just feels so good to feel good. At about ten o'clock I check my email. There's one from Slater. I hold my breath as I open it, like someone trying to delicately diffuse a bomb. It starts out,

"You pseudo-intellectual, crunchy-granola, Bitch!!!" It deteriorates from there. It would seem that on the written page Slater Gray no longer feels the need to use his little ten-year-old's voice and beyond that he actually grows some sizeable balls.

It is quite possibly the nastiest, most unkind letter I've ever received and further proof of how much the man does not like himself. I reply, "Good luck with all of that." and then block him from sending any more cyber venom. It's done and I am

126

one relieved, pseudo-intellectual, crunchy granola bitch.

Chapter 21 ~ The Devil we Know

Sophia's car has to go in the shop for a brake job and I follow her over as she drops it off at the garage. She transfer's the mountain of bags she schleps to work every day as the art teacher of the local high school and climbs into my car. I grab one of the bags from her and awkwardly try slinging it over the back of the seat.

"Geez Soph, what have you got in there, your rock collection? I think I just tore my rotator cuff."

"Actually," she smiles, "it does contain part of my rock collection. I use them for collages and shit."

She gives me a kiss on the cheek and asks how my date with Slater went. I fill her in on all the grim details including the flashy hand gestures and his brief synopsis of me.

"Wow!" she says, "Pseudo-intellectual, crunchy granola, bitch, huh? What a perceptive young man. It's taken me years to figure that out. I wouldn't be too crushed, honey, that whole gay thing would have eventually become a problem if not in the near future, than definitely a few years down the road."

We both giggle. "So," she asks, "are you ready to give up and join me in the trenches of not so sexy celibacy or are you hungry for more torture?"

She peers at me out from underneath the thick fringe of her black lashes and I'm thinking what a waste of a great woman it is. Too many years of being put down by an emotionally abusive husband left her with a less than healthy ego and little appreciation for her many charms. She's all too comfortable hiding out in her work as a teacher and nurturing her students, as well as her ten-year-old twins.

In some ways Sophia is fearless and I admire her moxie. As a single mom, she went back to school to get her degree when the twins were seven and did it with very little help from anyone. Mike is far from a supportive ex and more often than not, he can't even manage to come through on the weekends when he has visitation. The three of us are always trying to get her to expect more for herself and I think she's slowly getting it. She just can't seem to stop picking guys who practically have the words, "I will fail you horribly." tattooed on their foreheads, all in caps, and it's as if nice guys give off some kind signal like radar that she detects and uses to continually steer away from them. Perhaps we all have a certain amount of that in us. My mother used to say to me,

"Better the devil you know, than the devil you don't know."

Perhaps we all keep picking the same familiar devil and we just don't realize it. All too many of my past relationships have seemed to have a recurring theme. Do we keep recycling them until we get it right or until the lesson is learned like Bill Murray's character in the film Ground-Hog Day?

Sometimes it seems the more I know, the less I'm sure of.

I drop Sophia off at school and we make plans for me to swing by later to go pick up her car. She gives me a hug and starts draping bags all over her body like a woman in need of her own personal Sherpa. Teetering, she makes a sad attempt to wave from the steps, as a cute kid with an obvious affection for his art teacher comes up and helps her with her bags. I wonder how many of those boys have a mad crush on Ms. D'Antonio. A crush her low self-esteem doesn't even allow her to see, or enjoy for the flattering and harmless ego boost that it is.

I remember when my friend Theo met Sophia one night when we were all out at a club. He pulled me aside and asked me if she were single.

"That," he said, widening his expressive brown eyes, "Is a whole lot of woman."

Theo is a fun, sexy, successful, black man. He was the CEO of his own computer start-up that he created five years ago. When the company went public about a year ago, Theo was suddenly a very wealthy guy with no one to share it with. I had tried many times to find someone among my various friends to fix him up with, but the chemistry was never quite there. He wasn't exclusive in terms of dating only black women, but he definitely wasn't attracted to what he calls, the skinny little pancake-assed girls. Sophia's curves were just what this man craved.

The two of them danced the whole night and seemed to be enjoying each other's company so on the way home, I put it out there.

"What do you think of Theo?"

"He's adorable, why?"

"Well, I was just wondering if you might be interested in going out with him?"

She groaned. "My father would roll over in his grave!"

I gave her a puzzled look. "I didn't know your dad was dead."

"He's not," she continued groaning, "but he will be from the massive coronary he'll have if he ever hears I'm dating a black man. I'm sorry Nic, but he would kill himself, or me. I swear. He's just so set in his ways."

I did one of my best, exaggerated world-weary sighs.

"I'm sorry to hear that sweetie cause, that man wanted you bad. He thought you were fine, fine, fine."

"Really?" She grinned from ear to ear.

"Oh well." I sighed.

"Oh well." She echoed.

And that's the way that went. Two people who could have been great for each other never got the chance to check it out because of someone else's foolish issues. It sucks eggs. Sometimes, it seems that trying to get this whole love thing to happen is a little like waiting for the planets to line up.

After I drop Sophia off after school, I head home. I check in with both of the kids on the phone. They're playing at friend's houses for the afternoon

131

and then heading over to their Dad's for the weekend. I set up a couple of appointments with clients for the coming week and I'm ready to begin my weekend. It's been a couple of days since I checked my mailbox on the dating site. The Slater fiasco has left me feeling less than enthusiastic about the whole process. I pour myself a glass of white wine and go to the site. There are several emails in my inbox. A few are from the same guy, but I don't read those yet. I open the first one and I can't believe what I'm reading. Slater has been one-upped in the nasty department. What follows is a detailed description of this guy's favorite organ and it's not his brain.

It seems his member is mutant-like in it's gargantuan proportions and he's not modest when it comes to informing me of it's exact width and length and he's anything but shy about letting me know what it is he'd like do to me with his bionic baton. Sick. I suddenly lose any semblance of the Buddha. I've had it. I'm not worried about bruising any delicate egos here. In fact, this guy's ego is perhaps the only thing that's larger than his penis. My reply is to the point, so to speak. I start by congratulating him on being the obviously pleased owner of such a substantial part and then make the helpful suggestion that due to its remarkable length, perhaps there's a really handy place he could shove it. I finish by telling him that I hope he and his huge appendage will be very, very happy.

As an added thought I let him know that my own personal preferences have always leaned toward a package of a more serviceable size, which

I also find far more esthetically pleasing. I hit send, then block him from writing me again, and immediately report him to the service. At this moment I don't even want to look at the other email. Maybe Sophia has it right. The trenches of not so sexy celibacy are looking more appealing by the moment.

Chapter 22 ~ Dancing, Dorks, Diamonds

Saturday night out with my girls. What's not to love? We're all going to see Paris' husband's Blues band play at one of our favorite clubs, for a night of dancing. It's one of those places where you'll see people from twenty-one to sixty-one out there on the dance floor shaking it. The crowd comes for the music, which is always great, and the funky-chic atmosphere. We pick Paris up in Kate's car and all drive in together. I tell the girls about Megadick and my not so demur response to his email. They can't stop laughing and seem to go back and forth between horror and hilarity.

"So you reported him," Paris asks, "then what happens? Wait a minute, he said it was how big?"

"Well, they wrote me back that he's basically banned from the site. That kind of email is completely against the rules and according to him it was about the size of a baseball bat."

"I'm glad you gave it back to that sick pervert, but it is a little scary. You never know who you're dealing with. It could be some maniac serial killer for all you know. I just hope you're being careful, honey."

"I am," I reassure her, "I always meet people at very public places. I get a lot of information beforehand. Granted, they could be telling me anything, but I'm finding as I go along that when I get a gut feeling that something isn't quite right in a certain area, it usually isn't and I find that out in the phone call. If it feels really off I don't bother to even get as far as a phone call. The ones that have potential are the only ones I talk to and from there I see if they seem worth meeting. I have their phone number and photos and I always let other people know where I am. I had to promise my kids I would do this in a very particular way and I don't want them to be worrying about me. Believe me, I'm very careful."

"Oy!" Paris slaps her forehead in her inimitable, drama queen way, "Maybe you'll meet someone nice tonight and you can forget about all this online-dating crap."

"Right," Kate rolls her eyes. "That's where all the great guys are, in clubs and bars. Seriously, have the past two years taught us nothing?"

"Wait a minute!" Sophia chimes in, "I met Jay the fire fighter in a club."

"Yeah," Kate says, "and we all know what a prize he turned out to be. Wasn't he the guy who sucked in bed, but wanted to do a three-way?"

She then adds, when Sophia feigns being hurt,

"He WAS pretty damn cute."

"DAMN cute." sighs Sophia.

"Girls," I interrupt, "Let's face it, the only one of us that has found love in a bar has been lucky-in-love Paris."

Paris beams at us. Her man is her pride and joy and who can blame her. He's intelligent, good-looking, and thick skinned enough to deal with how intensely outspoken she can be. Plus he has a damn sexy job as the highly talented front man of an in demand internationally known blues band. She loves it when women try to hit on him. Something about all those girls craving her man just makes her that much hotter for him. He loves that she not only doesn't get jealous, but she gets turned on to the point that later that night, he gets lucky in a big way. Ten years, and two kids have not diminished the fire those two have burning for each other. It's downright inspiring.

We get to the club and energetically make our way to the table Paris has reserved for us. As heads turn and stare I take account of the picture we're presenting. As five attractive, vivacious, fashionable women, it would seem from the reaction we're getting, we're an interesting sight.

Theo is already there and orders a round of drinks, all the while making eyes at Sophia. Kate starts scanning the club to see if Jeff is there yet. She's been sort of seeing this guy for the past few months. None of us has met him yet, which makes him a definite maybe. An impressive line of guys we never laid eyes on precedes Jeff. If a guy makes it to the stage of meeting us, he's not only a rarity; he's pretty much in.

Jeff is ten years her junior, which makes her nervous for several reasons. She's afraid that all the areas where she's had experience and he hasn't are going to do the relationship in. He's never been married, never had kids and he wants both. Kate's been married and isn't sure if she needs to do that again. She has two kids and at age forty would like to believe the having babies part of her life is behind her. From what she's told me, she and Jeff have amazing sexual chemistry together and she's not ready to give that up. I can't blame her. Great sexual chemistry is a powerful thing. It's like a force of nature, a tidal wave, or a hurricane. Sometimes you just can't get out of its path.

By nine-thirty the band is about to go on and we all have a pleasant buzz except Lilly who has volunteered to be our designated driver. I offered and was pleasantly pleased when she insisted. After the week I've just had, a little unwinding is in order. The band begins their set and Paris and I hit the dance floor. I've never been one to wait for the crowd to get out there and neither has she. I've always felt that if you get out there first, it breaks the ice for the shy folks.

It's not long before our whole crew is out there shaking it. By the third, or fourth song a couple of guys cut in on Paris and me. Neither of them are my type physically. They look like guys who spend too much time behind a computer screen and too little in a gym, kind of pasty and paunchy. As the song ends, we graciously say thanks, but no thanks and send Bob and Ted on their way. We use our tried and true formula. Paris simply flashes her wedding ring and points out her husband wailing away on stage and I use Theo as my imaginary boyfriend even though at the moment, he's flirting blatantly with Sophia. Hey, it works and hopefully no one gets his feelings hurt.

This is one of those nights when I just seem to be a dork magnet. I'm beginning to think it's me when, Lily comes dancing over, grabs me by the hand and drags me to the ladies room.

"GAWD!" she says, "I hate to be mean, but the weirdest guys keep asking me to dance."

Now, you would have to know Lily to realize how extreme this statement is. In all the time I've known her, I can count on one hand how many times she's said something even remotely unkind, or negative about anyone, and I still have fingers to spare.

"Me too!" We both crack up laughing, but I'm wondering if she feels as bummed as I do. Most of us single people have a hard time admitting it, but every time you go out the door there's that hopeful, little voice in the back of your mind telling you that maybe this trip to the cleaners, grocery store, or friend's party, will bring you face to face with the person who, like you, is out there in the universe just waiting for that eventful collision to occur.

"Is it unusually bad out there tonight, or is it just that I'm totally sober?" She asks me, fluffing up her hair in the mirror.

"No, sweetie it's bad. I've had a couple of drinks and it's still bad. There must be some kind of dweeb convention in town." I pull out a lipstick and put some on just from force of habit.

We make our way back to our table and find that with the exception of Sophia, who is having a great time with Theo, everybody else is ready to call it a night. For us, it's an unusually quiet ride home. Kate's upset because Jeff didn't show and I imagine Sophia's wishing her circumstances were different when it comes to Theo. Lily made a comment about being a spinster and I told her she had way to hot a body to fit into that category, but I can feel her discouragement and it's not so different from mine.

They drop me off at my condo and I'm greeted at the door by Aztec looking a little bleary eyed from being woken up at one A.M., but wagging her cheerful hello nonetheless. In spite of the hour, I'm feeling too restless and buzzed to go right to bed and after the slim pickins' of the evening my computer seems to beckon me. I give in to its siren call. There are three more emails from the guy who had had several in there the last time. I open the most recent one, which sounds like he's thinking perhaps he should give up on hoping to hear back from me. It has a playful, almost self-deprecating tone to it. I go back and open his first one. It reads:

"Bonjour from Javier in L.A.! I just read your ad and I think it very interesting. We have many commonalities (sp?). I too love music and film. I have a web site that you can check out to find out much more about me and see what I look like. I don't have an ad myself, but I think the web site will do. I hope to hear from you.... Merci!"

A man who uses French, has a Spanish name, and lives in Los Angeles, I'm intrigued. There's a link, which I click on and instantly there's a photo of a very sexy looking man with intense eyes and a muscular body wearing a tight white t-shirt, very worn jeans, playing a Fender Stratocaster guitar in a club. There are some moody black and white shots of him and lots and lots of information. The site is like an expose'. It's an interesting bio of a man who is the epitome of the renaissance guy.

He was born and raised in Paris, had visited L.A. fifteen years ago and loved it so much he came back three months later and stayed. He's a musician and an aspiring actor with a string of small parts on his resume' from soaps to sitcoms. When he first got to this country, he had financially kept himself afloat doing everything from stripping to selling Jaguars. He now owns and operates his own voice-over and dubbing company in L.A.

His mother is Spanish and his father a Parisian Jew. To say that my curiosity is piqued at this point is a huge understatement. I go back to my email and read all of his other letters. They're witty, adorable, and they're perplexed and obviously disappointed about not getting a reply. He speculates that, "a woman as beautiful and intelligent and interesting as you has probably found someone already."

"No Javier!" I yell across the ethers of cyber-space. "I'm still here, hang on."

While I had been out dancing in Dorkville this hunk of virtual burnin' love had been sizzling undetected in my computer. I feel a little like one of those people you read about who finds a lone, rough diamond of ridiculous size and perfection just sitting on the ground in their backyard right next to the barbecue grill. You just never know when a treasure is going to appear out of the ethers.

Chapter 23 ~ Skating on Wafer Thin Ice

The alarm goes off and my groggy state somehow incorporates the traffic report into my dream. In it, I'm struggling to fly a helicopter over the highway. Suddenly, Sheryl Crow materializes in the seat beside me and begins singing that I'm her favorite mistake. I wake up just as we're about to hit a billboard that reads, "If you lived here, you'd be home now."

Wow, we're talking serious Cosmopolitan damage. I'm a lightweight when it comes to ingesting alcohol, which is just as well. Knowing that about myself usually prevents me from being tempted to use it as a serious stress buster. One, or two glasses of wine are my usual wild night and the two Cosmos of the night before has left my head feeling like the inside of a rotten cantaloupe. I carefully slide into my slippers and shuffle to the bathroom since actual steps are far too jarring for my tender state. A long, hot shower and two cups of coffee eventually render me semi-conscious, as I sit down at the table to compose my Saturday 'to do' list. It reads as follows:

1. Bank
2. P.O.
3. Dump
4. Grocery Shop
5. Write Javier!!!

I decide to start with the things that will require the least brain power and save writing Javier for after a power nap even though I'm anxious to get back to him. It's been five days since he first wrote me and I'm hoping he hasn't given up and connected with someone more responsive in the meantime. I tell myself what will be will be. The hung over part of me wants to tell this sensible part of me to piss off. I make a mental note never to drink more than one Cosmo again.

When I get back from running errands, Aztec is waiting in the kitchen with her leash in her mouth. I raise one eyebrow in her direction.

"That's subtle, Az."

She stares back at me without blinking. Her tail sweeps back and forth on the floor.

"Okay sweetie, let's go."

I grab my keys and sunglasses and we head down to the beach. It's one of those rare spring days when you start letting yourself believe that warm weather will come again. The sun is out and if it weren't for the wind it would almost be warm. I've brought the Frisbee and I immediately get busy trying to wear this dog out as she chases it up and down the beach. The combination of the sun and the salt air begin to perk me up and I'm almost feeling human again. As I look out over the dazzlingly beautiful sea I think about that man out on the west coast looking out at the Pacific and it just feels amazing to think about this world we live in, this world in which people who live on opposite sides of the country find each other without leaving their homes.

By the time I'm back in my kitchen, I'm feeling completely inspired. I open my email and see that for the first time in five days there's nothing new from Javier. Oh Lord, he's really given up. I imagine him as a man in the middle of the ocean sinking below the surface for the third time and I scramble madly to toss him the proverbial life ring, which will keep him afloat. After reading through his web site again, I'm feeling oddly close to this person. There is something in his words and images that's emotionally more open than anyone I've connected with in this place and because of that I find myself feeling free to be the same with him. His candor in presenting himself creates this sense of a safety net that I believe I can softly land in, or maybe it's because there is something unreal about so many miles between us, making the possibility of us ever really meeting, unlikely. Whatever it is, I find myself pouring my soul out without reservation to a stranger who lives in a place far from my kitchen.

The sound of the phone startles me out of my nap, which judging from how dark the room is, has turned into at least a couple of hours. I fumble for the light and squint through bleary eyes at my watch. It's five fifteen. The kids should be here any minute and I'm glad I picked up something not only simple for supper, but also something they love. Whenever I make tacos I'm suddenly transformed into a great cook and one of the world's best moms. It's like freakin' magic.

I brush my teeth, which has the immediate effect of waking me up as if it's six AM. I'm as programmed as a lab rat. No sooner have I pulled myself together, I hear the kids coming through the door, kicking off their shoes and scattering their bags on the floor.

"Whoa guys, that stuff doesn't go there. Take it to your rooms please."

The groaning starts immediately. It always amazes me how quickly I get over that feeling of having missed them. Kids are a mixed blessing. Although I can't imagine my life without them, they are definitely the greatest source of stress in my life. People love to tell me that at fifteen, Renoir is a challenge because of her age, but the truth is, she's always been this way. When she was two we used to joke that for Christmas, we were going to get her a small country to rule. I guess I would rather have a headstrong daughter than one with a doormat personality. I tell myself that whenever I have one of those days that end with me creatively fantasizing about killing her, or myself. Max is as laid-back as Ren is intense and he's been that way since the day he came smiling out of the womb. Unfortunately, even Mr. Mellow has his breaking point and now that he outweighs her by ten pounds and is only one inch shorter than her five feet, four inches, she's learning, slowly and sometimes painfully, he's not someone she can easily push around anymore. Payback, as my mom used to say to me when the kids were little and driving me insane, is a bitch.

After they get themselves settled back in they find their way to the kitchen to share the events of the weekend with me, something I have always thoroughly enjoyed.

They are both engaging storytellers and sometimes I'm amazed at what interesting people they've become in their own right. Then again there are those moments when I can completely understand why my father used to threaten to bang my head and my sister's together like coconuts.

"Mom," Ren begins, with a tone of voice that doesn't bode well for a happy tale,

"Will you tell Max to get his own friends? He acts like a total dip shit around Zoë."

Max calmly shoots a goldfish cracker at his sister like a hockey puck and pings her off the forehead. I laser beam him with the look that says, '*You're skating on wafer thin ice'*.

"Zoë seems to like Max, sweetie." I give Max a conspiratorial wink without Ren seeing me.

My daughter loudly lets out a dramatic sigh. "She so totally doesn't. She's just trying to be nice that's all and he acts all stupid and gross around her."

"Well," I say, matter-of-factly, as I dice tomatoes. "He *is* a dip shit."

My attempt to get her to lighten up completely backfires.

"I knew you wouldn't take me seriously, you're always on his side. This SUCKS!" She turns on her heel, makes a dramatic exit to her room, and slams the door. The sound of the band of the month comes cranking out through the walls so loudly the fillings in my teeth are practically rattling. I tap on her door and ask her to turn it down a bit. When she complies with a barely tolerable decibel level I decide to let her cool down and talk with her later.

I return to the tacos and Max who is looking a little guilty.

"I didn't do anything Mom, she's freakin' got PMS."

"You know what Max, that may be true, but you're also not being sensitive to how she's feeling and you could be. I know that Zoe is a very interesting, cute girl, but she also happens to be your sister's best friend. I'm just asking you to try to put yourself in her shoes."

"She doesn't like it when I wear her clothes." He gives me a slow grin and I stare at him blankly.

"Lord Jesus, take me now." I say to the cutting board.

"I thought we're not supposed to swear."

"I'm not swearing, I'm praying."

I knock on Ren's door to see if she is calm enough to have a civil conversation. As soon as she looks up from the bed I can see that she's still crying.

"You seem pretty upset," I say, "is this just about Max and Zoe, or is there something else too?" I rub her back and wait.

"It's everything." She sobs, sucking in air in jagged, shuddering, breaths.

"Everything seems like crap lately. I really don't feel like talking about it."

I smooth her hair back off of her face and kiss her sweaty forehead, "Okay, but if you change your mind I'm here, and contrary to popular belief, I can be on your side too. I'm not so old that I don't remember what it feels like to be fifteen. Back in the day it really wasn't that different from now. We may have had bigger hair and guys had mullets, but we were dealing with pretty much the same stuff. You're going to have to trust me on this one, having a thirteen-year-old brother is a whole lot better than a thirteen-year-old sister. I'll have to tell you some heartwarming stories about all the boyfriends I had that your Aunt Michelle went after. Sometimes I think the only reason we get along as well as we do now, is because she lives in Florida. I don't know how Grandma kept her sanity. Oh, that's right, she didn't."

I get a smile out of her, "So what do you say we go eat? I've got some tacos out there with your name on them."

"Okay," she says, and leans against me, resting her forehead against my neck. She lets me hug her and for a few moments I feel like I'm holding my little girl again.

The rest of the evening is quiet as we go through our usual Sunday night ritual of getting organized for the school week and then watching a movie together. Max falls asleep half way through it curled up at the end of the sofa with Aztec. I finally get them off to bed and check my email. Various new ones have trickled in, but nothing from the man on the west coast.

Chapter 24 ~ Bumps, Hills, and Mountains

Why do Monday mornings always seem to be such a challenge? Eventually, we gain momentum as the week continues, but we start out at a complete standstill slowly moving forward like a herd of sedated turtles. Max has to go back in the house two times after we get in the car because he's forgotten something he needs for school and the phrase, "Hurry Up!" seems to reach his ears as undecipherable scrambled code.

"Max!" I yell out the car window as he saunters in for the second time, "Pretend you're being chased by a stampede of angry elephants will ya?" Judging from his continuing pace, my son has no fear of being brutally trampled to death.

When I get back home I take Aztec out for a run and do a quick email check before I head off to the gym and my first client of the day. There's nothing new from Javier. Shit. I open a new one in the hopes that it will distract me from the crummy feeling I have that I blew it. It's from a distinguished looking gentleman of sixty-four who sounds very sweet and very wealthy. The crux of his email is he would love to spoil me in the manner to which he thinks I should learn to become accustomed. Unfortunately, the gold digger gene is extremely recessive in me. There have been a number of times when I've envied other women who possess it.

Before I was married to Nathan, Paris introduced me to this man she knew from England. He was several years older than I am, had a PhD in philosophy and was a troubleshooter for several high tech companies all over the planet. He was a very interesting man to say the least and rich as Croesus. Paris was all excited about the idea of her best friend living the life of a fairytale princess on his twenty-acre estate. As much as I would have liked to been able to fulfill my friend's fantasies, I couldn't do it. The chemistry just wasn't there. Poop.

As time will allow, I decide to open one more email before I have to head out the door. This one's from a guy who asks me to check out his ad because he thinks we have a lot in common blah, blah, blah. I click on the link and there's a bunch of photos of this adorable guy who looks like he may be part Asian, or Native American. He has these dark almond shaped eyes, high cheekbones and a sexy mouth. I barely scan his bio because he's ten years younger and wants to have kids, so why bother. He has several photos on his profile all showing him in different activities and styles of dress, it's like a GQ layout. He's a hottie and with a twinge of longing, that has more to do with my hormones than my heart, I toss this fish back into the cyber-sea. I write him a polite email back thanking him for his response and cite our age difference and his desire for children as my reasons for passing. I hit send and wave bye-bye. Well, it was a nice momentary diversion even if it wasn't the right fit. I grab my bag of gear and a bottle of water and head off to the gym.

My ten o'clock client is a sweet woman who is a few years younger than I am, but looks at this point in time like she's got a good ten years on me.

I'm Barbara's birthday present from her husband Jerry. She recently thrilled him and their kids when, after close to twenty-five years of smoking, she quit. I've been telling her that working out is going to become her new addiction and her willing enthusiasm is inspiring. We're into our third week of working out together and not only has she hung in there with me, she's getting excited about the already evident changes in her body and energy. It's helping people like Barbara that make me feel like I have the best job in the world.

"Hi Nicki!" she waves, "come see what Jerry bought me. He calls it an incentive."

"Like you need one." I say, as I admire the diamond studs she's wearing.

"Well I'm not about to stop him." she winks, "He did promise me a life of wine and roses."

I'm thinking some of us get promised wine and roses only to end up with beer in a can and dandelions.

Barbara and I start out with a brisk walk around the track and as we walk, I talk with her about nutrition and we go over the things that are working for her and where she feels she's getting hung up. We do the Stairmaster and I point out how she's no longer getting winded. Some stretching follows that and then we head to the women's gym area where she uses the machines and free-weights. Forty-five minutes later we cool down and she heads off to the shower, but not before showing me the definition she's starting to see in her arms. When I go to high five her, she gives me a hug that practically knocks the wind out of me. "Thanks, Nicola." She says, as I catch my breath.

I head out of the club to my car to drive to my next client, who has a private session in her home. She's a wealthy woman with an impressive home gym that gets my salivary glands into overdrive every time I walk into it. I usually work out Ariella and her kids later in the day, but she's flying out to the west coast for her company this afternoon so we're squeezing a session in before she goes.

Ariella Pendleton is a pedigreed blue blood from the top of her highlighted blonde, chignon to her Prada clad feet. Her home is impeccably decorated with beautiful paintings and objects d'art, but somehow still manages to feel sterile, as if you've entered a very exclusive hotel lobby. Looking around you would never know this house is shared by Ariella, her husband Stewart, two teenage sons, and a Great Dane named Hamlet. There's no evidence of the prerequisite messiness of life within these walls.

"Can I get you anything?" she asks when I arrive and waves her perfectly manicured hand in the direction of Luisa her housekeeper, who looks at me expectantly.

"No, thank-you I'm fine." I hold up my bottle of water and Ariella smiles wanly.

"Great, I'll go change and meet you in the gym in a minute."

She returns in a new designer workout outfit. In the past few months I've been working with her, I've rarely seen the same outfit twice. As I put her through her paces, we make the usual friendly chitchat and try to connect with our common bond as women and mothers. When she first hired me as her personal trainer, she noticed the lack of a wedding ring on my finger and asked me about it. I told her I was recently separated and about to be divorced, and a month later she tried to fix me up with her landscaper. Due to her upbringing, Ariella has a strong sense of what could be called 'class distinction '. In that world a landscaper and a personal trainer are a perfect match. Unfortunately, Dave and I couldn't have been more different in terms of our interests, his being country music, football, and drinking beer with his buds. I'm more of a wine, PBS, and alternative music fan. I made sure to thank her for the thoughtful gesture and I let her know that I had a game plan for meeting men on my own. At that point I was beginning to toy with the idea of doing online dating, which I had mentioned to her. She crinkled up her nose as if I had just walked into her house with dog shit on my shoes.

"You mean you go on dates with total strangers?" She looked one degree shy of disgusted and began fiddling with the gargantuan diamond on her left hand, no doubt finding comfort in its presence, and the knowledge that she would never have to trek through such distasteful territory. I think I may have said something horribly cheesy like,

"A stranger is just a friend you haven't met yet."

She gave me what I think was meant to be an encouraging smile, but her eyes clearly said, "You poor, delusional, desperate creature." Something about her reaction and the negative reactions of a few more of my friends only served to strengthen my determination to not only do this thing, but to make it work.

Today, as she works out, the conversation turns to her trip out to Los Angeles. Ariella is the owner of an import export company that deals exclusively in antique furnishings from other countries. She has offices both here in Boston, and also in California. I stupidly mention that I've recently received some emails from a really cute guy in L.A. As soon as she starts asking questions, I realize what a mistake it was to bring it up at all.

Her questions sound like this:

"He does WHAT for a living?"

"He's HOW old?"

"He's been married HOW many times? He has How many kids?"

And I sound like this:

"He's an actor and musician."

"He's thirty-eight, and he's been married and divorced twice."

"He has two kids and he has custody of the kids."

At this point she's looking at me like a psychiatrist observing an unstable patient in a psych-ward. The look is both nervous and concerned. Hearing it all come out of my mouth at one time, I realize that Javier not only doesn't sound like something to get excited about, he sounds like something to run in the opposite direction from.

As I drive to my next client, I do a reality check. This guy could be a total flake; twice married, twice divorced. At almost forty, he's still chasing after something pretty elusive and what kind of single dad with little kids can crank it out with a band half the night in clubs and still be a responsible father the next day? Red flags are waving all over the place. Plus, the dealmaker and breaker; he's on the other side of the country with young kids and ex-wives. This is a man who is not going anywhere and I'm sure as hell not in any position to relocate in the near future.

What was I thinking? The divorce disrupted my kid's lives enough. I can't imagine disrupting their lives any further. Maybe his not writing back is a blessing and a sign. I realize in this moment that meeting people this way creates the illusion that the world is a smaller place than it actually is. It's easy to get caught up in the romantic notion that true love will transcend any bumps in the road, even a road, which stretches clear from one sea to another, but this is a road traveling over more than bumps and more than hills. This road is traveling over mountains.

Chapter 25 ~ Drifting on a Sea of Confusion

Years ago, I read this bizarre theory that God is the ultimate addict. The author went on to say that the reason so many of us struggle with addiction issues that run the gamut from food, shopping and sex, to drugs, alcohol and gambling, is because we are indeed created in His image. According to the theory, the source of the Almighty's *buzz* is a by-product created by our pain and suffering. The writer believed our pitfalls and the resulting angst created this by-product, which gets our Heavenly Father, for the lack of a better word, high. At the time I wondered what the author was smoking. It's been six days since I last heard from Javier. On days like these his crazy theory doesn't seem quite so whacked.

I'm bummed. I've let go of any hope of hearing from him. There's been a steady flow of email coming in and none, so far, have been remotely interesting. I'm still hanging on to the hope that it's simply a matter of numbers and time. I'm sending back another no thank you note and about to end this uneventful visit to my email, when suddenly there appears one from the missing man himself. My heart is pounding. I can't open it fast enough. It begins with profuse apologizing.

"Please, PLEASE you must forgive me Nicola...BTW, very pretty name for very pretty woman, but I digress. I'm so sorry for it taking me so long to write back to you. You MUST forgive me. If I were there I would let you beat me with your very beautiful hands. I couldn't help noticing in your photo what pretty hands you have, but I digress again. I am not a game playing man who wishes to make you wait. It is nothing like that. Oh GOD! I hope you are still there and wanting to write back to me especially after that beautiful email you sent me. Nicola, I feel you all the way to here in your words. You are a tender woman and I have long been looking for a woman who possesses that very quality.

My mother and father have a marriage I can only dream to someday have. I asked my father what he believed was the secret to their love and he told me he believed there were two keys to such a marriage. Those two things are deep friendship and great tenderness. So, I am searching for a woman with a tender heart who will be my best friend. You have such a heart and now it has taken me so long to write you, I am sure you are thinking I am a big fat jerk. Well not so fat, though I would like to lose a few pounds. Could you hear me screaming your name from here in L.A.? I was so frustrated that I couldn't reach you. I have not been able to get into my account for days. There was some kind of technical problem on the site and I am thinking my whole account has disappeared. So, I went back to the site where I first saw you, but I could no longer find you. Does that mean you are gone? WHERE DID YOU GO? Have you given up pretty little Nicola with the tender heart? I await more of your words with, how you Americans say, 'baited *breath'*, which to me does not sound so very appealing. Kisses, Javi."

A huge smile takes over my face only to quickly disappear. He sounds so sweet and cute. Torn. People use that word. I too have used that word, but in this moment, I'm physically feeling it in a way I've rarely felt it before and it stops me short. I have to get some perspective before I reply. After I pace back and forth for a few minutes, I pick up the phone and call Lily, my compass when I am drifting on a sea of confusion. She has this amazing ability to make judgments about situations without somehow, being judgmental. I feel like luck is with me when she answers on the second ring.

"Summer Designs. This is Lily Summer."

"Hi Lily, it's me. I'm so glad you're home, but did I get you at a bad time?"

"No Nicki, I'm not busy. Are you okay? You sound really stressed. What's going on?"

"I got an email from this guy, actually I got several emails and I don't know what to do about them. Can I read some to you?"

I fill her in and then I read her several of the emails he had sent before and the one I just received and she comments on how adorable they are and then asks me, "So what would you like to do about them?"

"What I'd like to do and what I should do feel like two different things. I don't know. Part of me feels like this is a useless pursuit and part of me wants to check it out anyway."

"Maybe it won't develop into the kind of relationship you're looking for, but what's the worst thing that could happen if you check it out?"

"I could get very attached to something I can't have and that could be really painful."

"So, don't get attached, " she s, as if that's the easiest thing in the world to do,

"Do the whole Buddhist non-attachment thing you talk about and try not to worry about what's going to happen way down the road. Life doesn't come with any guarantees. Right?"

"You're right," I say, "and I definitely find this man really compelling. I owe it to myself to at least check it out. Who knows why he crossed my path. I'm going to stay open and this will be good practice in learning to not get attached to the outcome. So... I'm writing him back?" I ask.

Lily giggles, "Yeah, you're writing him back."

When I hang up the phone, I find myself thinking about all I've experienced since I started this whole adventure several months ago; the hundreds of emails that ran the gamut from good, to bad, to ugly. I think of the awkward phone conversations, the sometimes nerve wracking, but mostly interesting 'dates' over drinks, or dinner, and I would have to say all in all, it has been enlightening. I've learned a lot about men and certainly about myself, and I have no doubt there's more to learn. I have the feeling, as I sit to write my reply to Javier that some of the most interesting lessons await me.

Chapter 26 ~ Wildflowers

I drop the kids off at their dad's, which still feels strange and then head home to start cooking. I've invited the girls over this evening to have dinner and watch a movie. Kate is bringing a salad, Lily's bringing garlic bread, and Sophia's bringing the wine. Paris has baked a pan of brownies since we're all a bunch of choc-aholics. I put spinach lasagna in the oven and run the vacuum around the place doing what I like to call "cosmetic cleaning." I'm a master at it. With only minutes of strategically sprayed glass cleaner and furniture polish, I am creating the illusion of a clean apartment. Add to that my signature low watt lighting, lots of candles, and the place looks great. Sort of.

Sophia shows up first with the wine, which she immediately opens and pours. I put on some music and we start munching on cheese and crackers while we wait for the others to arrive.

"I want to tell you something," Sophia begins, "but, you have to promise to keep it just between us."

I pause, as I'm about to stuff a cracker in my mouth. "Really? Something you don't want Paris, Kate and Lily to know?"

She shakes her head and takes a sip of her wine. "Not yet."

I'm curious as hell, so I agree. Sophia has a mischievous grin.

"I had a date last Friday." She pauses and looks at me with seemingly nothing more to add.

I finally ask, "Okay, so you had a date and?"

She blurts it out as if I've painfully done the Heimlich maneuver on her. "I went out with Theo!"

It takes a moment for her words to sink in and then I can't stop smiling.

"Oh, my God Soph, that's great! What made you change your mind?"

"Remember the night we went to see Terrence play?" I nod and mutely stuff another cracker and cheese in my mouth without taking my eyes off her face. She goes on, "We just had such a great time together. He's so much fun and a genuinely nice guy. Well, the next day I got a delivery of this gorgeous bouquet of flowers and not the typical roses either. It had peonies and delphiniums and lilacs. It looked amazing and smelled incredible and he wrote a poem on the card that started out 'to a wildflower.' I was blown away, but it didn't stop there. He has sent me flowers every day since."

I roll my eyes and feign fainting. I love this stuff. I can only manage to muster one word. I utter it like a woman opening her eyes for the first time since waking from a forty-year coma, "Wow." I make the one syllable go on forever.

"Yeah," she says, "I caved, Nicki. He wore me down."

Somehow she doesn't look too upset about succumbing to Theo's charms. She looks pleased and dreamy-eyed. I can't stop grinning at her.

"So, you had a good time?" I ask, with my entire face a smile.

She nods and smiles back. Over the top of her wine glass, her dark chocolate eyes are melting. I'm about to ask her for all the juicy details when I hear Lily, Kate, and Paris noisily coming in the door. Sophia grabs my arm as I get up to head into the kitchen.

"Promise me Nick, not a word."

"Cross my heart sweetie, and if it seems like I'm about to have an accidental slip up, you have my permission to give me a preemptive kick in the shins."

"Oh believe me I'll be kicking you and don't forget how easily you bruise."

We're both giggling as we head into the kitchen, where we greet the rest of the crew. Kate scrutinizes us. "Okay, what's up with you two? You look thick as thieves."

Sophia doesn't miss a beat. "Nicki was just telling me about her most recent email from Frenchie-boy. It's pretty hot stuff."

Paris jumps in, "Doesn't he have a website, or a blog, or something? I don't know about you girls, but I want to get a look at this man."

"Oooooh, yeah," Lily says, "can we see?"

I pour them all wine and we all head over to my desk in the corner of the living room. I bring up Javier's website and there's a collective murmur of appreciation at the first few photos. As I read aloud the accompanying text, which tells about his life as a little boy in Paris and continues to two more pages and the rest of the story of Javier in L.A., which

161

include photos of him performing, the appreciation level elevates. The site is by turns funny, interesting, and touching especially when he talks about his kids and how much they mean to him.

Paris comments, "He's not your usual physical type honey, you seem to always go for the pretty boys."

"That's true, but there's something just so interesting about him. Plus I like ruggedly handsome too, not to mention that body."

"Mmmmmmm." purrs Kate, "that body. Could you print me out a copy of the photo of him in the white t-shirt and jeans?"

"I love his funky salt and pepper hair, but he looks a little dangerous to me," Lily says, and we all laugh.

"Not tame enough for you, huh?" I ask, "You know me though, I like a little sinner mixed in with a saint and this man seems to be a nice combination of both."

"I don't know," Lily, continues, "I don't think I could date someone who'd been a stripper." She makes a face like she's five and he's an icky boy with a frog in his pocket.

"Oh, come on Lily," says Sophia, "we're talking stripper past tense. You've got to give the guy a break, plus consider how that might translate to the bedroom." She arches one of her eyebrows and does a little hip roll. We all give a collective "oooooh," including Lily.

The oven timer rings and we're all back in the kitchen. I pull the lasagna out of the oven and Kate dresses the salad. In a few minutes we're all sitting around the table sharing stories of our week and enjoying a meal together. Looking around at my friends as they're laughing and eating, I feel blessed and fortunate to have these wonderful women in my life.

Chapter 27 ~ Is It In The Cards?

There's a psychic fair going on in Salem this weekend and Paris calls me early Saturday morning to see if I'll go with her. One of her friends is going to be doing readings and Paris says it's eerie how accurate she is. I'm not so sure I'm in the mood for eerie.

"You can find out if Javier is the one," she says, using the same kind of tempting tone I've heard her daughter use when she tries to coerce Paris into buying her a new dress or shoes.

I'm the very skeptical believer.

"Well," I say, "isn't that sort of the standard thing psychics tell you, that they see you going on a trip, or finding love? I don't think my circumstances present much of a challenge. I think the kid who bags my groceries could probably give me a pretty good reading."

"No honey, I'm telling you, Rachel gives you details, facts, and figures for chrissakes. She makes believers out of the most hardcore cynics. Don't you remember when she predicted I would meet Terrence and all the things she said would happen?"

She proceeds to remind me of those long forgotten details. Rachel had told Paris she would meet a black man who was a singer and she would be completely impressed with his talent. That in itself didn't seem so unusual to me since, Paris practically lived in clubs at the time, but the thing

164

that did end up impressing me, was Rachel told her she wouldn't be attracted to him at first and they would start out as friends who would be instantly inseparable and within a month this man would win her heart by being one of the kindest men she had ever met. Her feelings of not being attracted would completely turn around to the most intense level of attraction she had ever felt for a man. Rachel had gone on to tell her that she would be married within a year of meeting him and that they would have two children, a boy and a girl. There had been more details as to all the things that they would have in common right down to their love of antiquing. All of it had come true.

"Okay," I relent, "Let's go."

We get to downtown Salem and it's swarming with people. Salem is one of the few cities in the country where witches can move about in theatrical black garb, complete with floor length capes, without getting a second look from the locals. Of course the tourists, of which there are many, are snapping photos and taking videos. It's a wonderfully eclectic place where, within a few blocks, you can have a delicious meal at The Love Noodle, find a prosperity potion, get your tea leaves read, and go dancing to a local band. The place is steeped in some pretty dark history and somehow manages, in spite of that, to project an atmosphere of playfulness.

We quickly find a parking space, which is an auspicious beginning, and walk over to the New Moon Boutique where a line of people are waiting to sign up for a reading with Rachel. She has an assistant who is scheduling people in for available time slots and we can see Rachel further back in the shop doing a reading with a young woman who is leaned forward in her chair listening to her intently. A couple of months ago, the Boston Globe ran an article about Rachel in their Sunday paper. It talked about her impressive talent as a psychic and since then, she's been in big demand. As if her psychic radar is working, she looks up just as we walk in, waves to us, and motions for us to come back. Excusing herself for a moment, she walks over to greet us. She gives Paris a big hug and then turns to her assistant.

"Alyssa, what times do we have available for these lovely ladies?"

Alyssa checks the list. "The next two available slots are twelve-thirty and one."

"Will that work for you?" Rachel asks.

We both nod at each other and Paris says, "That will be perfect. We'll go grab a bite to eat, do a little shopping and then come back. Do you want us to bring you back anything?"

"No thanks, Alyssa is getting me some lunch. I should get back to my reading. So I'll see you two at twelve-thirty." She gives Paris a peck on the cheek and we head out.

I spot an adorable little cafe that has a menu of yummy sounding vegetarian entrées posted on the front window and we grab a great table by the front window where, we can enjoy the local color as it saunters by. We tell our waitress we're a little pressed for time due to our scheduled readings at the New Moon and she knowingly nods and suggests one of their wrap sandwiches as a quick choice. We order those with a couple of fruit smoothies and enjoy a quick lunch.

We still have a little bit of time left and we decide to stop at one of our favorite shops on our way back to the New Moon. It's a traditional looking bookstore with anything but a traditional selection of reading material. It has an eclectic selection of books, jewelry, tapes and other more unusual items. You can find everything from a book on the history of Gnosticism to one on dream interpretation. If that doesn't thrill you, there's even a primer on do-it-yourself levitation, complete with some mighty peculiar looking photos.

We pass on the books, and head straight to the jewelry counter. It contains pieces made by local artisans, and like the books, they run the gamut. Some of the items are meant to be purely decorative and others can be used as tools in the esoteric arts. Some are simple and others are elaborately ornate. As much as I know that a magic wand can only be a help to me, I decide to go for something a little less practical and opt for a pair of smoky topaz earrings. I find out that they're not a completely frivolous choice. The helpful sales person informs me, that smoky topaz is a good stone for attracting romantic love. She offers up this interesting tidbit, as she clears the stones for me of any negative energy they might have, by smudging them with sage smoke. This is all done in a very matter-of-fact fashion. I love this city. Paris buys a beautiful art nouveau ring with a huge Citrine. We do a little more window-shopping and get to The New Moon with only a few minutes to spare.

"Can I sit in on your reading?" Paris asks when we get there.

"Sure," I say. "Actually that's a good idea. I have a hard time remembering everything that's said, especially the parts I don't want to remember." I smirk at her and she quietly chooses to ignore me.

"Cool," she says, "You can sit in on mine too. I wish I had brought my little recorder."

Alyssa, Rachel's assistant, hears us and interrupts.

"Rachel can record it for you and I have cassettes available for just three dollars each."

"Excellent!" I say. "We'll take two, Alyssa."

And with that Rachel comes over and ushers us to her table. Alyssa pulls up an extra chair so we can sit in on each other's readings. Rachel definitely doesn't look like your typical psychic. She looks like the winner of the Paula Dean look-alike contest; a striking woman with startlingly blue eyes and a big warm smile. She closes her eyes and does a blessing over her Tarot deck. She hands me the cards and asks me to shuffle them until it feels like I should stop and to think of the question that I want answered while I'm shuffling. I focus with everything I've got, my question repeating over and over in my head.

"Is Javier the man I'm meant to be with and how will we make that work?"

Focusing. Shuffling. Focusing. When I finally set the deck on the table and begin cutting the cards in the way that Rachel instructs me, I begin a process that creates more questions for me than answers. In the end it doesn't surprise me. I'm in Salem after all, a city steeped in mystery.

Chapter 28 ~ Four Letters

Rachel places the cards on the table, scrutinizes them, and makes odd noises under her breath that I can't quite interpret. She takes off her reading glasses, rubs the bridge of her nose intensely for several seconds, and then looks back at the cards as if all that rubbing cleared her vision allowing her to now see everything. She nods her head slowly and begins,

"This is very interesting Nicola. I want to tell you what I see without hearing your question, because sometimes knowing the question can taint the reading."

I look over at Paris who looks at me with an excited smile on her face, like this is a good thing. I'm suddenly feeling a little freaked out. Is knowing always such a great idea? I feel like someone in a canoe that's about to go over a waterfall and no matter how hard I paddle backward, there's no stopping. It's just a matter of holding on and praying I'll survive the five hundred-yard drop down.

Rachel tips her head from side to side and a few vertebrae in her neck pop loudly. She picks up a card from the table and scrutinizes it.

"This card is the Empress and she represents you." She swirls her hand in a circle.

"I see a lot of men around you. You have this appeal that makes a lot of men want you."

I involuntarily let out a loud, "HAH!" Paris gives me the kind of look you give your kids when they're about to embarrass you in public and you want them to believe that you will, without hesitation, kill them where they stand.

Rachel continues, "You can laugh Nicola, but it's true. I see old men, young men, white men, black men, tall men, short men and the common denominator is they all want you, but what I'm also seeing is a kind of atmosphere around you that insulates you from them. Somehow their desire doesn't really touch your life in a physical, concrete way. They see you and they want you, but they can't actually connect with you."

I'm stunned. What she has just said is a pretty accurate description of the online dating I've been doing. I have been getting email from lots of men of all ages, colors, and shapes and it hasn't been concrete. I take a deep breath as she goes on.

"Does this make sense to you?" She asks. I nod, and try to compose my face into a neutral expression as she continues.

"I see two men who stand out from the others, two men, you eventually make an intimate connection with and not necessarily in the sexual sense, but in an emotional sense. They're both younger than you, but one is close to your age. The other one is much younger. The younger of the two has dark hair and eyes and the older one has blue eyes. I'm not sure what color his hair is, I think it's light." She picks up a card, scowls at it, closes her eyes again for a moment, and then continues.

"The lesson in all of this is that things are not always what they seem and sometimes what you think is the least likely answer, is the right one. I see that you will feel a lot of intensity of emotion for both of these men. I also see you trying to make something fit because you love the idea of it and it will take you a while to figure out that you are on the wrong path. You will have these romantic ideas about one of these men, but they emanate from your head and from a place of illusion not unlike the desire all these other men feel for you. It's based on a fantasy. You won't accept the truth of what is best for you, until you start choosing with your heart only."

This is not what I was expecting to hear at all. Two men? Javier sounds like he could possibly be the blue eyed man, but who is this other guy and where will he come from? I risk a scary question.

"Do you see me ending up with one of these two men? This isn't going to happen at the same time is it?"

She contemplates the cards, closes her eyes for a moment and when she opens them she replies,

"I see that love will find you, but it won't be easy for you to accept the form it comes in. You will fight it, thinking it should look like something else and yes, they will be in your life during the same time period. You will at some point feel your trust betrayed by both of them, but only one will truly betray you."

For some reason I feel sweaty, and after that last comment about being involved with two guys at the same time, I'm not feeling remotely convinced. That's not something I would ever do. I've never been involved with two people at the same time except for once in high school when I was sixteen, which really shouldn't count. I can't see myself in this kind of scenario at all. Besides, Javier is the only man I'm even considering right now and there's no one else.

"So, when do you see this happening?" I ask.

"Time is one of the hardest things for me to predict but, I do see warm weather and flowers blooming and you at the beach. My guess would be, in a few months, going into this summer. I'm also being told that the name of your true love will be four letters long and it's not a nickname like Mike, or Nick. You will feel an immediate sense of comfort with this man, and a strong physical attraction. Do you feel like this answers your question?"

I say yes, only because I just don't want to hear anymore, but it doesn't answer my question at all. It only raises new troubling ones. Paris and I switch seats as she has her reading and I'm glad it's being recorded because I'm having trouble paying attention. My mind is ricocheting off the walls like it been taken over by a kid with a sugar high.

I drop Paris off at her house and head home. The cassette is sitting on the seat next to me and I toss it in the glove compartment with an enthusiastic slam.

"Out of sight, out of mind," I proclaim to the air around me. I find The Stones, Exile on Main Street on my IPod, crank it up and sing along at the top of my lungs. By the time I get home the fear demons have been exorcised from my system. With the help of Mick and Keith, I have been set free and

I laugh to think that I let myself get so rattled. It's just a freakin' Tarot reading!

I drop my bags on the couch when I get in the house, kick off my shoes, and pour myself a glass of wine. I put on an Adele CD and sit down to my computer with Aztec curled up against my feet. There's a new email from Javier, which I open like a gift. As he tells me about his day, he includes all the sweet details, which make me feel like I'm there with him. He tells me about a funny thing his little boy said to him while he was giving him a bath and I imagine those strong hands being gentle and nurturing. The email ends with him saying that he needs to hear my voice. He gives me his phone number and some good times when I can reach him since we have to calculate the time difference between the West and East coasts. He says he will gladly call me if I feel comfortable giving him my number and he ends by saying he can't wait to hear me breathing in his space. He wants to have my voice in his head. I get a rush as I send him my number and ask him to call in the next two hours if he can. I take a big gulp of wine, exhale, and wait for his call with the kind of anticipation I haven't felt since sitting by the phone in high school.

Chapter 29 ~ A Fox in The Hen House

At four-thirty the phone rings and I see his name on the Caller ID. My heart is racing and my chest feels like a flock of birds are beating their wings against the cage of my ribs. Breathing deeply, I collect myself and pick up the phone.

"Hello?" I say, and that single word feels delicious in my mouth. I can feel him smiling there at the other end as he replies,

"Hi, you." There's a slight pause and we both laugh together. Then he says,

"This is really good."

I answer, "yeah."

His voice is rich, deep, and sensuous and the French accent puts me over the edge.

"There are so many things I want to ask you," he says.

"What do you want to know?" I ask, "I'm an open book, so feel free to ask me anything." I'm grinning and I'm sure he can hear it in my voice.

"Anything? Really? Okay, do you like oral sex?" He asks.

It's a ridiculous first question. It's the kind of question, which normally would have offended me so much that I would have hung up instantly. Strangely, it doesn't feel at all inappropriate and I laugh as I answer without hesitation, surprising myself.

"I love it!"

He laughs at my enthusiastic response and asks,

"Giving it, or receiving it?" he asks.

"Both!" I say, and he moans and then laughs.

"That's a wonderful thing." He goes on, "I feel that making love can be like a beautiful piece of classical music with many different aspects, some pianissimo, some adagio, some allegro. When you are free in it you can create something very rich with lots of variations and you can express all aspects of your heart with each other and the many aspects of your soul."

I'm melting. His beautiful voice and his words fill my head and travel through me. Every nerve in my body feels awake.

He continues. "I'm impressed that you were willing to be so open to my question. I must admit it was a little test. I find most Americans are kind of schizo when it comes to sex, or so it seems to us."

"What do you mean?" I ask.

"Well in some ways Americans seem obsessed with sex, if you look at your media, your pop stars, and your fashion, and when it comes to lovemaking, you can't comfortably talk about it in the context of intimacy. You seem to be hung up about expressing yourselves in bed. At least that has been my experience of American women. For the French, it's just a part of life like eating and sleeping. It's one of the things, which are important to give to your body to be healthy and happy and also one of the things we savor and truly enjoy."

"It sounds like you've been with the wrong American women," I tease, and he laughs.

"Well, I've been told," I begin tentatively, "that French men perhaps do a little too much savoring and enjoying when it comes to lovemaking, and it's kind of a given that married men also have mistresses. Is this true?"

I've wanted to run this question by him ever since I heard he was twice married and twice divorced. I've been wondering if this tradition had caused of the demise of those relationships.

"Ah, not true, a false portrait of the Frenchman painted by jealous and threatened Americans who feel inferior because they have heard of our prowess as lovers. They know that the French invented romance." We both laugh, but I still need to be convinced. He goes on.

"Look at it the way we see it. Americans have one of the highest divorce rates in the world and what usually causes that breakup? It's infidelity, right? So, what you Americans call 'having a mistress' when you refer to us, is called 'committing adultery' for you. Am I right? So then, who is guiltier in this area? The French, or the Americans? We are all sometimes weak when it comes to temptation, but I get the feeling what you want to know is, did I have a mistress?"

Okay, so now the guy is reading my mind and since we're being so straightforward, I decide not to deny it.

"Well, did you?"

"I will tell you the truth, Nicola. I never had a mistress but I also was not faithful to my first

177

wife. We married very young. I was only twenty-one and I don't say this to excuse what I did, but to explain where I was in my life as a man. At that time we were living in a small apartment and barely, how you say, making ends meet. It's kind of a funny thing to say because we were also barely making our ends meet, as in our bodies. I was dancing with the Paris Corp de Ballet while she worked all day and I would come home very late to find her fast asleep in our bed. So here I am, a young man with all these hormones, working all night with these beautiful dancers, and coming home to a wife who is not available to me sexually. I was completely frustrated and eventually I gave in to the temptation that was all around me. I was one of the few male dancers who wasn't gay. So, it was a feast spread before a man who was starving. I was like a fox in the hen house. It was not enough that I loved my wife deeply and that she was the one I wanted, because I could almost never have her. When I would climb into bed at night, just the smell of that woman would make me hard. But I was unfaithful to her and it got worse after our daughter was born. I ended up losing my family because of it and I've never been unfaithful to a woman since. Does that answer your question?"

"It does, and I appreciate you being honest with me."

"I think life is to short to spend it bullshitting ourselves and each other. Besides, I want to get to know you and you to know me. How can that happen if I hide the truth from you? You would get to know someone, but who would he be?"

I want to know more so I go for another question.

"So. What was the cause of the end of your second marriage?"

"Ah," he says, "you are really wondering about my bad track record and I don't blame you. I'm glad you ask me these questions. So, my second wife I met shortly after I got to this country to pursue becoming an actor. She was a big help to me in that area and she is a good person with a big heart. Unfortunately, she was addicted to prescription drugs and also alcohol, which I didn't know when we first got together. I realize now that I was pretty naive about all of it. The L.A. scene involves a lot of partying and someone with such a problem can kind of hide out in the whole scene. It took having a kid with her for me to see how far gone she was."

"That must have been a hard thing to face."

"It was. She was the mother of my child and a good person, but she was an addict and she became a danger to him and abusive to me."

"Did you two try rehab? If this is all to personal, you don't have to tell me."

"No, it's ok, and yes, we tried several times. She just kept relapsing and she seemed to get worse, or maybe my ability to tolerate her addiction, with a little kid, just went down. I filed for a divorce and fought for custody of my son and got it. It's been hard, but I'm glad I did it. I make sure she gets time with him, but this way I know he's safe. She's getting better. At this point she's been sober for almost a year now."

"That must be a relief for you and I'm glad for the sake of your son too. So, do you see any chance of you two reconciling now that she's on the road to recovery?"

He laughs, "I like your questions, you are a woman who gives things a lot of thought."

I laugh back, "Especially when it's something that concerns me. I've got to watch my back here."

"Don't you mean your heart?"

I consider his words and I answer, "Yes, you're right, my heart."

So when Javier asks me, "Is it my turn to ask about your ex?" I try to be as forthcoming as he has been and in the course of the next hour we share some pretty intimate aspects of our past and it all feels strangely and wonderfully comfortable, which reminds me of the psychic's reading. I hear the sound of a wristwatch alarm over the phone and he says,

"Shit! My time's up. I've got to go pick up my son from day care. Boy, that hour went by fast. Are you going to be around later? Maybe we could talk again if you are a night bird."

"A night bird? Oh, do you mean a night owl?"

"Yes! That's it." He chuckles, "A night owl. Would that be, ok?"

I'm thinking to myself, how could I say no and answer. "Sure I'll be here!"

"Great! Ciao Bella."

"Ciao Javier!"

Several hours later, just as I'm getting into a deep sleep, the phone rings. I groggily answer.

"Hello?"

"Oh, I woke you sleeping beauty. I'm sorry."

"Javier? That's okay."

"No," he says, "you should sleep. I'll meet you in your dreams. We can talk tomorrow. There will be an email waiting for you in the morning. Goodnight Nicola, and kisses on your heart."

I clumsily slide the phone into the stand, close my eyes, and smile my way back to sleep.

Chapter 30 ~ Dreaming in French

Perma-grin. That's what Kate calls it when she sees me the next day after work and it's true. I can't seem to stop smiling, as I tell her about my phone conversation of the day before and also about the delicious email from this morning.

"You know what I'm looking forward to doing?" I ask her, without waiting for her to respond, "Getting rid of my profile on that website."

"Whoa girlie!" Both of her hands fly up like a cop stopping traffic. "Just one minute, lady. What do you mean get rid of it? Please don't tell me you're putting all your eggs in Frenchie's basket. You've had one phone conversation with this guy and your ready to retire your screen name?" She scowls in total exasperation.

"You think I should keep my ad going?"

"Oh Puh-leeeze, why wouldn't you?"

"I don't think I need it and what if Javier sees my ad still up, isn't he going to think I'm some kind of player?"

"First, why would he still be looking to see if it's there? Second, if he does, he'll think he hasn't got this one in the bag, which is exactly what you want him to think."

"I do?" I ask.

She rolls her eyes. "You do. Trust me on this one, honey. Have the past few months taught you nothing?"

Kate silently shakes her head and gives me a motherly smile. I mull it over. I'm a strong believer in treating others the way you want to be treated, but is Kate right? Is this a kind of no man's land with different rules than the ones that apply in the real world? In this one, you seem to owe no one anything other than politeness and respect. I'm guess I'm only used to being a married woman. This dating world is alien territory. I think Kate is right. Loyalty isn't part of the picture yet. That comes later, much, much later.

"You're right," I finally acknowledge, "the ad stays."

Over the course of the week, I continue writing lengthy emails to Javier and brief ones saying *no, thank you* to the few guys who trickle into my mailbox every day offering something I'm not interested in. I know that it's partly due to the fact that Javier is an impossible act for mere mortals to follow and I feel more than a little sorry for these guys who are unwittingly trying to jockey for a position that is being, at this time, so deliciously filled. Javier and I talk on the phone every day and I look forward to the evening ritual of having him talk me to sleep.

His voice, being the last thing I hear before I drift off to sleep, has the lovely side effect of landing him in some pretty steamy dreams. Lately, I find myself often waking in the middle of the night in a serious sweat. When I tell Javier about the result of our bedtime chats, he's delighted and asks for details, which of course I give him.

"Ah, yes that definitely sounds like something I would do," he says, when I describe the head to toe exploration of my body he performed in a dream with his hands and mouth.

"This is good, because it tells me what you like and all the things I will be able to do when I finally get to touch you. It sounds like we are sexually, very compatible. You're an earthy and sensuous girl, Ms. Botticelli. Are you all Italian?" He asks.

"I'm mostly Italian, from the north though and Sicilian. That's why I'm blue-eyed and blonde."

"That explains it! I love Italian women. They are very fiery lovers. Oui? The Italians are almost as skilled lovers as the French," he teases.

"Almost?" I respond, matching his attitude, "we'll see."

"Yes, we'll see."

There's a pause and we both remain silent and listening to the other breathing. There is nothing awkward about the silence and for a moment I can imagine laying my face against his chest, listening to his heart and feeling the rise and fall of his breathing beneath my cheek. Javier breaks the quiet.

"I was just imagining holding you next to me and smelling your hair."

I sigh deeply and answer, "I was imagining something very similar. Are we crazy for even doing this? And what, exactly are we doing?"

There's another pause between us before he goes on, "I hear the frustration and confusion you're feeling and I feel it too. I don't know what to tell you Nicola. I have no answers for you yet, but I have this feeling we will find a way if it's meant to be. We can either give this thing a chance, or we can go our separate ways before we get in too deep. So, what do you say, continue or stop?"

The thought of stopping at this point seems far less appealing than continuing to tease and torture each other, so I answer with only the slightest hesitation. "Continue."

"It's agreed then, we will continue with our exploration of each other in this somewhat limited way and we will see where it leads us. I have a little surprise I think you will enjoy. Next Sunday night, I have a small part on a TV show. You will get to see me walking and talking in your house. What do you think? Pretty cool, huh?"

"Are you serious?" I say, excitedly, "That's wild and it gives me a good idea too. I'm going to have one of my friends follow me around with a video camera for an afternoon and I'll send it to you. How does that sound?"

"I love it! I was going to suggest that we Skype. Have you ever done that?" I hear his doorbell ring in the background and it's one of those normal sounds that create the illusion that he's just down the street.

"Can you hold on a minute? I'll see who it is and be right back."

He puts the phone down and I can hear muffled voices in the background. Even though I can't make out what's being said I can hear a woman's voice and a strained tone to their voices. Javier comes back to the phone and his whole mood has changed. "I've got go, something's come up. Gabriella is here and she's very upset."

I know this name from our conversations, as belonging to his recent, now ex-girlfriend of the past two years. They split up about four months ago and according to Javier, she's having a hard time accepting that things have changed.

"Do you want me to call later?" I ask.

"No," he says, "I'll call in a while and talk you to sleep. Okay?"

He hangs up abruptly and a feeling of thick weight presses down on me. I'm uneasy at the thought of him and Gabriella struggling to come to terms with where their relationship now stands and as much as I try not to, I can't help imagining them there in his living room together at this very moment miles away from where I sit alone in mine. I slowly set the phone in its receiver.

Eleven o'clock comes and goes and there's still no call, or email from Javier. I look in on the kids who are fast asleep. Max and Aztec are unknowingly in a snoring contest with each other. I do my evening bedtime routine and shuffle off to bed. As I lay there, I think about what Javier said earlier today. If this is meant to be, a way will be found. Perhaps Gabriella showed up today to show us both the way we are meant to go. For now I will have to wait to see what her visit reveals. I stare at the phone willing it to ring until my eyes will no longer stay open.

Chapter 31 ~ Nobody's Doggy Doo

I'm meeting a new client today. Sergio called me early this morning to tell me he'd gotten a call from a guy who made a special request for my services. It's kind of an ego boost that this has been happening more and more lately. The guy's name doesn't ring any bells and I wonder who might have referred him since Sergio neglected to get that useful bit of information.

The club is usually a twenty-minute drive from my house, but I immediately hit bumper-to-bumper traffic. After about ten minutes of crawling down the highway, it becomes apparent that I'm going to be late. I call Sergio and ask him to give the client the heads up, with the option of rescheduling if the delay presents a problem. I ask him to call me back if the guy decides to cancel for today. There's no sense making the trip for nothing. I'm only minutes away from the club and I haven't heard anything from Sergio, even though I'm twenty minutes late. I have to assume the guy is still waiting and I'm hoping he's not too pissed off. I'm prepared for that possibility with the offer of a free session. I rush into the locker room, stash my stuff, and head out to the floor, practically colliding with Sergio as I come flying out.

"Whoa! Speed racer," he says, laughing, and grabbing me by both arms. "It's okay. He said he's in no rush. Seems like a really cool guy. Not bad looking either."

"He isn't pissed?" I ask, expecting the worst.

Sergio shrugs "No, he seems fine." He points to the main floor,

"He's right there, with his back to us in the navy pants and the white T shirt. I made him a smoothie and had Joey show him some of the machines." I give him a hug. "Thanks, sweetie, I owe you one."

"Yeah," he replies to my rapidly departing backside, "take a number."

I come up behind this mystery man and realize I've forgotten his name. I decide to simply lead with as charming an apology as possible.

"Excuse me," I begin, as he turns to face me. "I'm so sorry for being late, I hope I haven't inconvenienced you too much." I extend my hand. "I'm Nicola Botticelli."

He takes my hand and shakes it slowly, all the while looking intently at me, and scanning my face as if he's trying to place me.

"C.J. McCarthy," he replies, "nice to meet you and no, it's no inconvenience at all. "Botticelli?" He asks. "Like the Venus on the Half Shell artist?" There's just the slightest hint of a smile at the corners of his mouth and in his eyes. I'm looking at his very handsome face and wondering if he's looking at me this way because I've met him before.

"Yeah, Sandro Botticelli is supposedly a distant ancestor. I'm sorry, have we met?"

He runs a hand through his hair and shakes his head, "No, I don't think so. I'm pretty sure that's something I would remember." He continues smiling at me.

I can't help staring at him, trying to figure it out. Much like almost remembering a dream, it's right at the edge of my memory, just barely eluding me. He looks for just a moment the slightest bit uncomfortable with the scrutiny and turns his attention toward the machines.

"So," he says, "I was told you could give me a really good workout, I'm ready to find out if that's true."

"I was wondering about that. Who was it that referred you to me?"

"My friend Jake Walsh works out here and I told him I was looking for a good personal trainer. He recommended you."

"Jake Walsh," I repeat, "I don't think I know him. Maybe he asked Sergio for someone?"

"Since we give a free session for referrals, I make a mental note to ask Sergio later about Jake. Then I get to work with my new client, who turns out to be not only cute, but really interesting as well. Over the course of the next hour I learn that he has an appreciation for music of all kinds, and I'm impressed to find that he's familiar with some of the more obscure artists, that I love. He's an avid rock climber and kite boarder. Two sports he thinks I'd excel at.

"Rock climbing," I inform him, "is out of the question. I'm so scared of heights that my palms turn to soup even when I'm just looking down from a height in a movie, but kite boarding sounds cool. I like just about anything that has to do with water but my absolute favorite thing is dancing to live music."

"I love dancing," he says. "I just started taking Argentine Tango classes."

"Really? A guy who likes to dance?" I ask, thinking that this man sounds too good to be true. "So what do you do for work, if you don't mind me asking."

He laughs, and the subject changes to art. As he speaks about his work, his whole face becomes animated and focused. He's an artist who survives financially by doing some other entrepreneurial things on the side. What he truly is though, is a sculptor.

"I think the thing I like about dance, is how closely related it is to sculpture in the way that one movement flows into the next. I think a sculpture should have the same effect on the observer as they walk around a piece as it had on the sculptor as the work was being created. I tend to crank up the tunes in my studio and jump around while I'm working. Different music, different jumping around, different outcome with a piece."

I'm a bit mesmerized, as I listen intently to what he's just said. I realize he's waiting for a response, when he asks,

"Did I just sound like a bonehead?"

"Well, I don't know exactly what a bonehead sounds like. I think you sound like someone who's passionate about what he does. It makes me really curious to see you doing this work of yours." I giggle

"Maybe you'll come visit my studio some time."

I smile and feel a flush rise in my face. "So, what are we looking to accomplish with this training?" I say, changing the subject.

C.J. tells me that he'd like to increase his flexibility so we spend a lot of time with the Pilates machines. He's in really good shape, but definitely not what I'd call limber. He's come to realize that his rock climbing skills will be greatly enhanced by becoming more flexible and it's not coming easily to him. I'm trying to give him a lot of encouragement, when he tells me he believes the machine he's on would be an effective tool of torture should the military decide to use it for that purpose. We finish up by heading back to the main floor, where I show him some yoga positions for cooling down, and stretching. As I adjust his body to get him correctly in a pose, his face is just inches from mine and I can feel him studying me with an intensity that makes me blush. I give him a brief glance and his eyes look deeply into mine.

"Keep breathing through this," I remind him and he takes a deep breath.

"Musk and vanilla? You smell great."

"You need to focus and breathe. And no flirting with your trainer." I say, with mock seriousness.

"Yes, Ma'am."

"Good, because there's no flirting with your trainer."

"No. Understood."

I teach him the child pose, which he thinks is hilarious and send him off to shower with the instruction that he stops at the desk before he leaves and fills out a schedule card with Sergio. We set a time to meet again in two days, which is how long I expect it will take for his body to recuperate from today's workout. Before he heads off, he shakes my hand.

"Thanks, Nicola Botticelli," he grins, taking in my face like he's trying to commit it to memory. "It was great meeting you and try to be on time this Friday."

I mockingly cross my heart, "I promise I'll be here ten on the dot. And call me Nicki."

He gives me a look as if I'm cuter than I actually am and says, "I'll see you then, Nicki."

As he walks off I notice Sergio out of the corner of my eye watching the whole scene from behind the front desk. I turn toward him and he raises his eyebrows at me, and shakes his head as I walk up.

"Don't give me that look Sergio."

He does his best to use a stern tone with me and asks, "Are we planning on doing some cradle robbing?"

"No. We are planning no such thing. We are simply being nice to a new client."

He winks at me. "Uh huh."

"Sergio, be serious. Do you know a guy named Jake Walsh?"

"Jake Walsh? Yeah, I know him why?"

"He referred my new client. Can you let him know he has a free session for the referral?"

"Well, I would, but he hasn't been to the club in a few months. I'm pretty sure he didn't renew his membership. In fact, I'm pretty sure he works out at Kipling's."

"Can you check? It would be kind of odd for him to refer his friend to me if he doesn't go here any more."

"I don't know. I wouldn't worry about it though. You know that thing you're always saying, 'never look a gift horse in the mouth.' I'll get your gift horse scheduled when he comes out. Are you going to be here on Friday?"

"Yes, Friday." We give each other a peck on the cheek and then I head out to my car and check my phone for messages. There's one from Kate wondering what I'm doing for lunch. I check my watch and see that it's later than I thought and probably too late for lunch. I give her a call back and find she's home.

"It's not to late," she says, "I've got some chicken salad in the fridge. Come on by and I'll feed and water you."

When she says that, I realize I'm starving and I decide take her up on her offer. On my way there I pass a flower stand and buy a bunch of sunflowers, since they're one of her favorites.

I ring her doorbell and let myself into the kitchen. I'm immediately greeted by Rufus, her energetic, eight-month-old, yellow Lab puppy. Kate comes rushing in to rescue me and we laugh as she struggles to pull him off and shove him outside. Between the two of us, we finally succeed. I breathlessly hand her the flowers, which now look less than pristine.

"For me?" she asks, equally out of breath, and gives me a hug. "Thanks Nicki, who needs men with friends like us? Let's get you fed." I follow her into the kitchen, as Rufus peers longingly through the glass door.

I tell her about my cute, new, client and how he seemed kind of familiar.

"He sounds yummy. I'll bet he was at the club before with that Jake guy, saw you, and just had to have you."

"You've been watching too many soaps." I laugh. "Yeah Kate, I'm sure that's it. Seriously, he's young. He looks about ten years younger than I am."

"So? There's a ten-year difference between Jeff and me. Honestly, it doesn't matter to men. Jeff told me that guys only care if you're hot and interesting and you're both. Go for it," she says, as she makes me a sandwich.

"There's nothing to go for." I reply, "I'm not looking for a playmate, I'm looking for a relationship and one with legs. Besides, I'm feeling very hot for Javier and I want to give that a chance."

I realize as I'm saying it, that I sound defensive. I take a couple more sips of wine and try to chill out. I don't know why Kate's playfulness would make me feel so threatened.

"I'm not trying to give you advice, sweetie." Kate says, " I just think there's no harm in checking it out if the opportunity arises. Javier sounds great, but he's more than a few miles away and that presents some big challenges. I'm not saying that you guys won't overcome those challenges, I'm sure you will if it's meant to be. Just don't be too quick to close the door in some cute guy's face, especially if he's in your own backyard."

I don't know why, but the more she goes on, the more I find what she's saying annoying. I decide to placate her just to change the subject.

"You're right," I say. "You're absolutely right."

She beams at me and lifts her glass to make a toast. "Here's to never passing up a great opportunity, and cute guys in your own backyard." We click glasses and I smile back at her, all the while silently pledging allegiance to Javier.

It just seems so ironic. I've never met anyone I would be remotely interested in at work before. When I first decided to become certified as a personal trainer and I told my girlfriends about my decision, their initial response was, "What a great way to meet hunky guys!" I'd always been a fitness enthusiast. So, meeting burly beefcake as a job perk hadn't been a motivating factor. In fact, the thought hadn't even crossed my mind until they planted it there.

It definitely didn't end up working out that way. The inside of an actual fitness club bears little to no resemblance to those sexy places you see in the television commercials with all those spandex clad, ripped bodies, thinly veiled in Hollywood style sweat, moving with perfect choreography. Sure the machines are there. The music is piping into the room, but the similarity pretty much ends there. With the exception of the stray hard body, you're swimming in a sea of potbellies and cellulite. Instead of meeting hunky men, I'm mainly helping voluptuous moms lose that extra twenty pounds they gained with the last baby. And I've been more than happy with that.

Of course the trainers have the standard six-pack and five percent body fat, but most of them are only pushing twenty-two, or twenty-three and to them I'm an oddity of nature. Their reaction is always the same when they hear that I'm thirty-nine and have two teenage kids. I brace myself, for what is, the most awful compliment a woman can receive. It goes something like this,

"Wow Nicki! You look awesome FOR YOUR AGE!"

With those last three words, they take what starts out as a compliment with so much promise, and turn it into a dagger through my ego. They might as well tell me I look great for an old shoe that's been backed over a dozen times. After a couple of the guys found out my age and about my run in with Boy Scout, they actually hit on me. It was obviously the whole Mrs. Robinson, curiosity factor. I kindly declined the opportunity to be the "older woman," sexual experience some young guys seem to be interested in exploring. It was an ego fluff and barely a temptation for about a microsecond. Then a quick reality check brought to mind that awful joke about how women and dog shit are similar. The punch line is that the older they are, the easier they are to pick up. Dignity always won out over the horny old lady. I was nobody's doggy doo. So, meeting someone as attractive and interesting as C.J. is more than unexpected. In light of my last conversation with Javier, the irony of it can't be missed.

I get home and the kids are already there playing video games, sprawled out on the floor between the dog, a couple of friends and several bags of snacks. Book bags and shoes are strewn everywhere and I'm glad I'm feeling so relaxed from my visit with Kate.

"Hi guys." I say, as I step around and over bodies and things. They murmur their hellos back without their four pairs of eyes leaving the TV screen. I could be walking through buck-naked and they wouldn't even notice. Ren pipes up with a sarcastic tone,

"Mom, you have a message from some person named Javier."

I pretend she's sweet and helpful, and I reply, "Thanks, honey."

I go to check my messages. There's one Kate left this afternoon before she tried my cell phone, one from my mom inviting me for Sunday dinner, and finally one from Javier.

"Bonjour sweetie!" He begins, "I'm sorry I didn't call you back last night. Things with Gabriella took much longer than I thought they would and I didn't want to wake you. She was very emotional. She's missing my kids very much and they are missing her too. It's kind of a mess, but I think things got a little clearer last night. I will try to reach you later. I've got to go do an audition and then I have a meeting with a potential client so I can't call you until about nine your time, okay?

198

Kisses. Email me if that will be a good time for me to call. Oh, by the way, I'm sending you a little present in the mail."

My entire body relaxes. I replay the message three more times just to listen to his voice.

Chapter 32 ~ The Sniff Test

By ten o'clock, I have the kids settled into bed and can barely keep my eyes open. Javier hasn't called. If he did at this point, my ability to converse in coherent English is highly unlikely. No doubt, drinking that glass of wine this afternoon greatly contributed to my now semi-comatose state. Within seconds of my head touching the pillow, I'm deeply asleep and when the phone finally does ring it takes some kind of sixth sense for my hand to find it.

"Hello?" I mumble, trying to swim up from the depths of sleep.

"Oh sweetie, did I wake you?"

"Who? Javier?"

"Yes, baby, it's me! I have good news. I got the part and I got the new client!"

I'm starting to wake up and it's pretty apparent, he's more than a little inebriated.

"Are you drunk?" I ask.

"Yeah," he laughs, "my partner and I went out to dinner with the new client and we had many cocktails. That's a funny word. Cocktails. If I were there with you all cozy in your bed I would give you my cock tail." He makes some suggestive noises and laughs at his play on the word.

"Oh, I'm sure you would, you bad boy." I'm waking up slowly.

"I want to make love to you right now." He purrs.

"I know, sweetie. You're buzzed."

"Yes," he answers, " I'm buzzed and very horny for you, which makes it hard not to be able to kiss your mouth and run my hands over your skin. Do you like to have your neck kissed?"

I'm half asleep, half awake and getting aroused. "Yes, I love that."

"I would gather your hair into my hands and kiss your beautiful, elegant, long neck. And I would kiss your breasts. Soft, slow kisses all over you."

"Mmmmm." I sigh through the phone, "That sounds yummy." I realize as his breathing changes that he's doing more than using his imagination.

"Javier?"

"Yes baby."

"Are you?"

"Yeah, baby." He says it with urgency and the next thing I know I hear him coming at the other end of the line.

"Jesus! Did you just have phone sex with me? Oh, my God Javier!"

He giggles, "Don't be angry with me. You just have such a sexy voice and I am looking at your picture right here next to me. You cannot be blaming me for wanting you. No?"

He's such a cute rascal and so comfortable with himself that I laugh as well.

"I usually like surprises Javier, but I'm not ready to have any kind of sex with you, phone, or otherwise and I'd really like the first time when, and if it happens, to be in the flesh. Okay?"

"In the flesh." He repeats, "I like that word, 'flesh'." He slurs. "So you forgive me?"

"I forgive you." I yawn, feeling myself lapsing back into sleep. "I'm so tired Javier. Can we talk more tomorrow?"

We say goodnight and I awkwardly fumble to hang up the phone as sleep instantly swallows me up. During the night I dream that I'm making intense, passionate love to a man who is whispering to me in French, but when I look into his eyes, the man looking back at me is C.J. He smiles at me, and whispers, "This is where we both belong." And then he kisses me the way I've always longed to be kissed.

I awake the next morning, groggy from a night of fitful sleep and intense dreams. My mind keeps wandering. I just can't seem to stay focused on what I'm doing. My first client finally asks me sharply if I'm okay, after I don't answer her for the third time. I tell her I'm fine, just tired from a bad night's sleep. I don't tell her how I woke repeatedly from dreams of amazing sex with some guy I hardly know and not the guy I would think I'd be dreaming about having sex with. I feel extremely distressed. There were dreams of endless kissing that were so divine I wanted them to go on forever. Apparently, my subconscious has no sense of loyalty. I know that Kate was right when she said I don't owe Javier, or anybody any loyalty. It's just, that after so many years of being faithful to one guy, I don't know how to be any other way and now some cute guy shows up and I start acting like someone I don't even recognize! Driving to my next client I miss my exit from being so lost in a dream-sex fog. Before I head into the gym I look at myself in the rearview mirror, give myself a mental bitch slapping, and the loud order to, "Snap out of it!"

I mutter to myself as I'm walking across the parking lot and get a strange look from a guy passing by me on the way to his car. By lunchtime, I'm feeling like a candidate for meds. I call Paris on my cell phone in an attempt to somehow purge myself.

"Don't you love a good sex dream?" she asks dreamily, obviously not picking up on the upsetting aspect of my story.

"I do, but not with the wrong person!" I sound so distressed, that she finally gets it.

"It's only a dream, Nicki. Don't get so worked up about it. Why are you so upset about a silly dream?"

"It was more like five, or six silly dreams and I have to work with this guy again tomorrow."

She laughs at me, "Well, when you see him try to hold back from saying something like, 'Hi, how are you, I've been having mad sex dreams about you!' and unless he's a very gifted psychic, I think your secret will be safe. I'm pretty sure you can't be held accountable for what goes on in your sleep. You know what I think is really upsetting you?"

I don't ask for her theory, but she continues anyway with absolutely no go ahead from me.

"I think you're upset because this cute young guy got under your skin and you know what else I think?" Again, she barely pauses before she continues expanding on her theory. "I think he's the other guy."

"The other guy? What other guy?" I ask.

"Are you forgetting your reading with Rachel? He's the much younger guy. What's his name?"

"C. J." I answer, suddenly feeling lightheaded.

"You might want to find out what the C stands for. I'll bet you anything his name ends up being four letters long like Rachel said. It's probably Carl, or something. You know I love you dearly, so I say this for your own good. This is freaking you out because you tend to be a control freak and your not feeling in control are you?" There's a long pause before I finally answer her.

"You suck."

"I know." She says, smiling with the self-satisfaction that comes from knowing she's right.

I get home at four. I'm wishing it were my night to have the kids. They would be a welcome distraction from all the crazy noise in my head. I try giving Javier a call and his little girl answers the phone.

"Hello, this is Rae. Who's calling please?"

"Hi, Rae," I answer. "This is Nicola. I'm a friend of your Dad's. May I speak with him?" She doesn't answer me. Instead, she turns toward the room and hollers, "Gabriella, when is Daddy coming home?" I hear a woman's voice in the background answer her, and she relays the information to me. "He'll be home in an hour." I thank her and hang up. Why is Gabriella there? As the minutes pass, I can't stop obsessing about it. I know this is going to be a really long hour if I don't find some way to make it pass more quickly. I grab Aztec's leash and a Frisbee and take her for a brisk walk on the beach. It's a beautiful afternoon and the fresh salt air helps me clear my head a little.

I get home just after five and see that the light is flashing on the phone. The message is from Javier.

"Hi sweetie, Gabriella said you called."

It's reassuring that he's not trying to hide her presence. "I'm sorry about my little escapade last night," he sounds sheepish. "I hope I didn't make you uncomfortable and in case you are wondering why Gabriella is here, and you are a woman so of course you are wondering. She's helping me out with the kids while I'm shooting this part. She's been missing the kids and they've been missing her so it's working out great for everybody. I send you kisses Nicola, nice polite, chaste kisses." He chuckles. "I also wanted to remind you that the TV show I'm on is tonight. Call me if you get a chance afterward. I miss your voice, baby. I've been thinking about you all day."

I feel a sudden twinge of guilt. I've been thinking about someone else all day and not only that, I had forgotten all about the T.V. show, which is on at nine. The girls had asked me to call and remind them since they want to check it out, all except Paris, who already watches the sexy spy drama religiously.

First, I call Lily to see if she wants to come have dinner and watch it here. Kate and Sophia both have their kids during the week so they're planning to watch it at home. Lily's not home, so I leave her a message and head out to the fish market to pick up some salmon. I get back from my errands and find she's left a message saying she'd love to come over and asking if she can bring anything. I give her a call back.

"Summer Designs." She answers brightly.

"Hey Lily, it's me."

"Hi Nicki, this is so cool. Are you excited about seeing Javier?"

"I am. I'm excited and kind of nervous. It's pretty wild isn't? So do you want to come over around seven thirty? I'm grilling some salmon and making a salad. How does that sound?"

"Perfect, so I'll see you in a little while."

I hang up and decide to take a long, hot, relaxing bath before making dinner. It does me a world of good and by the time I've fired up the grill and put some music on, I'm in a relaxed mood. Lily shows up right on time with a bottle of wine and a loaf of French bread.

"I feel like a slob," she apologizes. "I didn't have to meet with any clients today so I got in my sweats and stayed in them. I didn't even put on any make-up. Do I look like shit?"

"No, sweetie, you look gorgeous. I don't think you could look like shit if you tried."

I take the bread from her and put it in the oven to warm.

"Want a glass of wine now?"

"Oh!" She answers dramatically. "Please! What a hectic week this has been. This is the perfect diversion. You know how my business is. It's either really slow, or I'm up to my eyeballs in clients. It's good though. I'm glad things are picking up. So, how are things going with you and Javier?"

Even though I know she'll be horrified, I tell her about Javier's little transgression of the night before. As expected, she covers her mouth with her hand and her eyes get as large as basketballs.

"Oh, my gosh!" She says. Lily is one of the few adult people I know who uses the word gosh, on a regular basis. "What did you do?" her hand is still poised in front of her mouth, as if I had just told her a story that involved the dismemberment of some innocent creature.

"I was too tired to do anything." I laugh. "I just said goodnight and went back to sleep."

Lily joins me in a good laugh as we grab plates, knives and forks and set the table. I light some candles, and giggling, we make a toast to life's surprises as we sit and enjoy the opportunity to catch up with each other.

"So, I understand you and Sophia have been keeping a secret from me and Kate," she says, as we clear the dishes from the table.

"What secret would that be?" I ask her casually.

"The gigs up. Sophia spilled her guts to Kate yesterday and told her she could tell me."

"Oh THAT secret," I say, coyly.

"You realize don't you, that this means everybody has someone, but me." She pouts adorably.

"I wouldn't exactly say I have someone, Lily."

"Okay, so maybe you're not having actual sex, but at least your having phone sex."

I correct her. "Javier is having phone sex, I'm not having any kind of sex. Plus it was more at me, than with me. Don't worry, you'll find someone. You just need to put yourself out there a little more. What do you think about trying the online thing?"

"No, I just can't see myself doing that. I couldn't take all the rejecting and being rejected."

"I didn't think I could either until I realized that it's not personal."

"I'll think about it." She turns to look for the clock. "What time is it?"

I look at my watch. "It's almost time. I've got to find a CD to record this onto. I plan on doing a lot of replaying with pausing and slow motion."

We both giggle and head into the living room. Ten minutes later, there's Javier ruthlessly pursuing the show's heroine, with an automatic weapon in hand. It's surreal watching him running around in this fantasy world within a thirty-seven inch frame in my living room.

"Oooooh," says Lily, leaning back on the sofa and narrowing her eyes at the TV. "He makes an excellent bad guy doesn't he? I said it before, there's something dangerous about the way he looks."

"You're right, and I find it very sexy."

"That man had phone sex with you, Nicki. That's so weird."

I nod my head in agreement. "We're living in a strange, new world Lily."

During the first commercial break, the phone rings. It's Kate. She has Sophia on the other line conference calling me.

"Whoa mamacita!" says Kate, "Pretty hot."

"You think?" I laugh.

Sophia chimes in. "He's a big boy. Honey, you're going to have to climb him like a tree."

"I was always good at climbing trees."

Lily gives me the heads up that it's coming back on. "I'll call you back when it's over."

I hang up and Lily and I watch the rest of the show and even though it's a pretty limited part, Javier is quite good in it.

"That was so cool and so strange." Lily says afterward with a slightly dazed look. "Was that weird for you?

"Definitely, but it was really great too. I feel like I know so much more about him than I did. Just seeing the way he carries himself and how he looks when he speaks and how expressive his face is. I find him even more attractive than I did before."

Just then the phone rings and I see on the ID that it's him.

"Is it Javier?" Lily asks, and I nod. She motions toward the door. "I'll head out and call you in the morning."

I tell her to wait a moment and pick up the phone. "Hi you, can you hold on a minute?"

"Sure, baby." I can hear his smile.

I walk Lily out to the door and give her a big hug. "Thanks for coming over, sweetie."

"Thanks for having me, it was fun. I'll call you tomorrow. Say *hi* to Javier for me."

I get back to the man at the end of the line. "Hi! Lily says 'hi', too. We just watched you on the show."

"Baby! How did I look?" He laughs.

"You looked great in a mean, nasty, sexy kind of way"

"Oh yeah, I'm a real tough guy. I'm very macho. So you liked what you saw?"

"Very much and you also got the thumbs up from my girlfriends!"

"Oh, then I'm in. If the girlfriends approve, I'm all set."

"Hey, don't be so sure of yourself. We still have to do the sniff test."

"The sniff test?" he asks, "and what would that be?"

"We have to see if our pheromones are compatible. You remember how you told me that just the smell of your first wife got you going?"

"Ah, pheromones. The nose knows, eh?"

"Exactly. That's actually kind of a big thing for me. I have to be attracted to a person's smell."

"Well then, let's do it." He says.

We spend the next hour trying to find a way to carry out our sniff test. Since we both have the responsibility of parenting and the constraints of being for the most part, self-employed, this isn't going to be easy. We discuss the idea of meeting somewhere in between shores, but where? Then we realize that in addition to the expense of traveling we would now have the added expense of lodging. I could fly to L.A., but since Javier has the kids twenty-four seven I would have to still find a hotel.

We finally conclude that the thing that makes the most sense is for Javier to come here on a weekend when I don't have the kids. Deep down, I'm hoping that once he sees what a great place this is, he'll picture himself happily raising his kids in this cozy little town. I offer to split the cost of airfare with him. I don't think he should take this gamble and shoulder all the expense to see it through and I tell him so. He argues with me at first, but I put my foot down and insist. In the end, I win. After we check our calendars to come up with some potential weekends, we have the beginning of a plan in place. I feel excited and terrified at the same time.

"So," I ask him, "we're really going to do this?"

"Do you want to?" He asks.

"I do. I guess that after writing to you for four months it's hard to believe that this surreal thing is going to become real."

"It's a strange feeling, but a good one. Yes?"

"Yes, a good one."

"You know what I'm most looking forward to?" He asks me.

"What?"

"Being able to look in your eyes when I talk to you."

I smile and sigh. "Yes, that will be wonderful."

We talk a little more before he has to go and get the kids to bed. After we say goodnight, I sit at my desk looking at the dates I've circled on the calendar. In about a month Javier will be here beside me. I will finally know if my life is going to

change in ways I hardly dare to imagine. I'm
excited and terrified.

Chapter 34 ~ Mr. G.Q.

I wake up with my neck in a spasm and blasting it with hot water in the shower barely helps. I take two ibuprophen, do some stretching and a half hour later and I can turn to the left, just slightly. I'm wishing I had time for a quick massage, but I'm meeting C. J. at the club at ten, which doesn't leave room for one. I'll just have to tough it out. Getting to the club a little early gives me time to find Sergio and his bag of goodies for injuries. It includes these great little heat pads. He pops one open and holds it on my neck while he dishes all the latest gossip.

"I almost forgot," he says, "I looked up Jake Walsh's records on the computer and he hasn't been here in four months. Josh heard he's been working out at Kipling's. You'd think his friend would have gone with a trainer there. So, you're right about the strange referral. Can you hold this? I've got to go train a new guy."

I put my hand up to hold the heat pad in place, gingerly stretching my neck and breathing through the pain.

"Thanks, Sergio. I thank you and my neck thanks you." He kisses the top of my head and goes trotting off toward a ridiculously buff looking guy waiting out on the main floor.

By the time C.J. arrives, I have a headache to go with the spasm and I guess I'm looking a little beat up because the first thing that comes out of his mouth when he sees me is, "Are you okay?"

"Neck spasm," I say, pointing to the impaired part. "I must have slept on it wrong, but I'm okay."

"I don't think so. Come sit down over here," he says. "Let me see if I can loosen that up." He smiles at me with those incredibly warm eyes and I'm thinking he looks damn good and wondering why I'm feeling so annoyed by that fact.

"Oh no," I wave off the offer, feeling the color rise in my face. "I'm fine. It's just a little tight, but no big deal."

"Good," he says, and leads me by the arm to the mats, "then it should be easy to take care of. Here, sit down."

I sit obediently and he moves close behind me. He slides his hand up the back of my neck and gently eases my head forward so that my chin moves down toward my chest and then he begins working on the muscle.

"Is that to hard?" he asks.

"No, it's just right."

He has amazing hands. They're strong, gentle and sensuous and they move with the kind of intuitive knowledge that only a talented massage therapist has.

"You're really good at this." I murmur.

"I studied body work for about a year and thought about possibly doing it for a living, but I think I like it best when I'm just using it on people I like. I'm pretty tactile and touch is important to me. Boy, you're tight little lady. You might want to try some yoga." He teases me.

After about fifteen minutes I feel the muscle loosening up and my headache has disappeared.

"How's that?" he asks.

"Much better. You're a miracle worker. Really, I think you may have missed your calling." We get to our feet.

"Not really, I just add it to my list of many talents." He grins. "Are you up for this today because, if you're not, that's okay. We can reschedule."

"No, no I'm completely up for it, but after that great massage, this is a freebie."

He starts to protest and I put up my hands to silence him. "I insist and I'm more stubborn about this sort of thing than you can ever be, so just give in now."

He laughs. "Alright, you win." He reaches into his backpack and starts fishing around.

"Before I forget, I made something for you." He pulls out a CD case and hands it to me.

"You know how we were talking about music the other day? I burned you a compilation of some songs I think you'll like. I put a bunch of my favorites on there too. I hope you like it."

I take it shyly, not sure what to think about him making me a compilation CD.

"Thanks, I'm sure I will. That was really nice of you." I smile at him and it's his turn to act shy. He gestures toward the locker room. "I'll go put my stuff away and then we can get started."

"I'll meet you back here then."

We spend the next forty-five minutes working out and talking between sets about

215

everything from art and philosophy to movies with John Cusack, which we both love.

"So, what's your favorite?" I ask.

"If I have to pick one it would be *High Fidelity,* but I also love *Grosse Point Blank*." He says.

"Oh yeah, with Minnie Driver. I love those two together. She doesn't sound like a Brit at all in it. For some reason, that impresses the hell out of me. I love *Runaway Jury,* but my favorite would have to be, *Say Anything*."

"Aw, yeah, that definitely has my favorite romantic moment in a film," he smiles, "that scene with him holding the boom-box over his head playing that Peter Gabriel song." He trails off and I pick up.

"That look on his face," I sigh.

"Yeah," C.J. sighs back nodding his head in agreement and looking into my eyes. For a moment we just stand there smiling at each other. I laugh, and look out across the room suddenly feeling an uneasiness creep in. I realize I'm putting off asking him what his initials stand for. I decide that when he comes back from the shower, I'm going to ask the question. The one that's been dogging my mind since my conversation with Paris, and her belief that he's the other guy.

When he returns to set up his next workout, I begin awkwardly. "I was wondering about something." I ask hesitantly.

He looks as if he senses that I'm feeling uncomfortable and he tries to put me at ease as he slings his backpack onto his shoulder.

"Shoot. Ask me anything. Really."

"It's not anything big," I lie to him and myself. "I was just curious what the C.J. stands for?" I tilt my head to the side, just slightly, trying to look extra casual.

Perhaps it's my imagination, but he seems to hesitate for a second.

"Cole Joon-Yung." He says.

"Cole?" I ask, "Is that short for something?"

"No," he replies. "Just Cole and Joon-Yung is a family name on my mother's side. She's Asian."

It's Cole. Not short for anything, four letter, Cole. Damn. I swallow hard. Something else about this whole exchange is ringing bells for me, but I can't quite identify what it is. I'm trying hard to look nonchalant, but my face has this frozen, freaked-out feeling. I work my eyebrows back down to what feels like a fairly neutral position on my face. He looks down at his watch.

"I'm sorry, Nicki, but I've got to run. I'm meeting with a gallery owner in twenty-five minutes. So, we're scheduled same time on Monday?"

"Yeah." I reply, and nod my head like a bobble doll. It's the only word I can manage to come up with in my confused state. As he turns to go, he waves and I get a visual that triggers my memory. Now I remember why Cole, a.k.a. C.J., seemed so familiar on that first day.

It all comes flooding back to me. I don't know how he did it, but Mr. G.Q. tracked me down.

Cole Joon-Yung McCarthy had emailed me right after the Slater Gray fiasco. He had had a somewhat generic ad with a gazillion photos. I had written him back saying, "No, thanks," and cited our age difference, plus his desire for having children as my reasons for not pursuing things any further. Now, here he is rubbing my neck, burning me CDs, being so interesting, and smiling at me with those eyes, and that gorgeous mouth. WHAT THE HELL! I'm feeling a disturbing combination of being turned on and intruded upon.

Should I be flattered or freaked out? It's as if the cyber world has broken out of its safe constraints and is now running rampant through my very real life. It hadn't occurred to me that this was a possibility and now that it's happened, I'm more than a little creeped out. Is he stalking me, this guy who didn't take no for an answer? What makes him think he had a right to totally disregard what I wanted? And, how did he do it? I'm searching my memory trying to remember where he was from.

As I get into my car, I cautiously look around to see if anybody's watching me. This is great. Now I'm feeling paranoid. I lock my doors and with both hands firmly wrapped around the steering wheel I take a deep breath.

Chapter 35 ~ Stalker Boy

Kate is the first person I decide to call. I can't call Paris. She'll mega gloat and I'm definitely not in any kind of mood to tolerate that. I run the whole story by Kate and ask her,

"Do you believe this?"

"That is so hot, Nic!"

"What? You think this is hot? You don't find it kind of creepy?"

"Well," she begins, way too calmly, "does he seem like serial killer material?"

"How the hell would I know? What do serial killers seem like? Remember that Ted Bundy guy. He was kind of cute and supposedly charming. I think the really good ones must be, otherwise how could they get so many women to put themselves in harm's way?" I realize panic is making my voice sound like Minnie Mouse on speed.

"Take it easy. I'm sure this guy is safe and if he's not, it can be dealt with. He doesn't know where you live, right?"

"Right." I say, and begin fishing through my bag for my anxiety medication.

"Did you say you have his phone number?"

"Yeah, it's on his file."

"When you get home call him and let him know that you know. Be sure to block your number."

"Then what? Do I tell him to fuck off?"

"If you feel like it. I think you should just see what he has to say for himself."

"I hate this, but I think you're right. I need to do this right away. If I don't it's just going to make me crazy."

"Call me later," she says, "and let me know how it goes. If I'm not home leave a message and I'll call you back when I get in. Jeff and I are going out to dinner."

"I will. So how are things going with you two?" I ask, happy to change the subject.

"You've been kind of quiet about him lately."

"I honestly don't know," she answers with a sigh. "Maybe next time we get together I'll tell you the whole frustrating story."

"Why wait until we get together? Can you talk now?"

"Well, you know how I've mentioned before that he wants to have kids and I really don't want to have more?"

"Yeah."

"It keeps coming up and each time it seems to become a bigger issue. We had a huge blowout fight about it a month ago. The reason you haven't heard me saying anything about him lately is because we went our separate ways a few weeks ago. I just felt it wasn't fair for me to expect him to give up something he wants so much and it also wasn't right to give in to doing something that I don't want to do. We were at this horrible impasse. So we talked about it and cried about it and decided that ending it now would probably be the best thing for both of us."

"I can't believe you were going through this and you didn't mention anything. Why did you keep all of this to yourself?"

"I don't know. It felt to painful to talk about, if that makes any sense."

"Oh, sweetie, I'm so sorry. What's happening with you two now?"

"We can't stand being apart. He sent me flowers with a really sweet card a couple of days ago saying how much he missed me and then I called him and told him I missed him too. The frustrating thing is, we have such a great relationship in so many ways. We have wonderful talks for hours and so many things in common, not to mention, amazing sex." We both laugh.

"Ah yes," I giggle. "Amazing sex, that's nothing to sneeze at."

"Hell, no," she agrees. "So tonight we're going to go out to dinner and talk."

I don't tell her that it will all work out for the best. That isn't what she needs to hear from me right now. It brings to mind that same bizarre theory about God being an addict who gets off on our pain and how often it seems like a reasonable belief. At the very least, He's got to be a big fan of irony. Why else would it be such a challenge for so many people to find a love that fits? Shouldn't such a basic need, be a simple thing to fill? I tell her I'll call later that evening and we'll talk. I tell her I love her and I hope it all works out. Right now I'm feeling like I don't know anything and that I'm the last person with any worthwhile advice to give in the area of romantic love. I feel as deflated as a slashed tire.

I give Sergio a call to get Cole's phone number from his file and he takes the opportunity to tease me once more, this time asking me if I've decided to become a child molester. Of course he has no idea how bad his timing is. At this moment I'm so tense that I read him the riot act and in the silence that follows my outburst, I imagine him feeling the space on his neck where his head used to be. I apologize immediately and fill him in on the psychodrama that's just unfolded.

"Whoa! That's pretty hot!"

I can't believe I'm hearing this for the second time in less than an hour.

"Is there something wrong with me, Sergio, because I'm not seeing it that way at all? How is some questionable guy, who is possibly stalking me, hot? I said no thank you, and he didn't take no for an answer and then he tracked me down. It's creepy."

"Don't be such a drama queen. You want my take on it? He's a really nice, resourceful, young man and for some strange reason he's hot for your old bones."

"Thanks for the evaluation, Dr. Phil, but seriously, I don't know this guy or what his motivation is and until I find out what's going on I think I have every right to be a little freaked out."

"You go girl." Sergio deadpans. "Here's his number, the poor guy."

"Are you siding with him? I don't believe you. Yeah, I'll call you later, Judas."

"I love it when you call me names," he says, hanging up.

I stop off at the liquor store on my way home and pick up a bottle of wine and a nip of Baileys. Normally, I think don't use alcohol this way, but due to the unusual nature of the situation I'm giving myself some leeway with the possible option of a lot of leeway should the need arise. I have the feeling tonight is going to be one of those nights.

I park my car in the garage and before I get out I down the bottle of Baileys. I toss the empty container into the trashcan next to my back door, marveling that something so small could affect the way I feel, this quickly and dramatically. It dawns on me that not eating anything since breakfast probably has a lot to do with my lightweight buzz.

I get in the door, kick off my shoes and open the refrigerator. Scanning for something that appeals to me, I pull out a bowl of tuna pate', grab some crackers, and pour a glass of wine. After a few minutes of nibbling and sipping, I'm in a much calmer frame of mind. The crisis of an hour ago has softened around the edges. I'm now wondering if it's possible that Kate and Sergio are right. Maybe Cole McCarthy is just a sweet guy with a crush who got creative, but how the hell did he find me? The more I sip and nibble, the more my panic is softening into simple curiosity. I rummage through my bag in search of the scrap of paper I scribbled his number onto, and sit for a couple of minutes just staring at it as I try to formulate something relatively intelligent to begin the conversation with. When nothing inspired comes to mind, I decide to wing it.

"Who the hell is he, that I should give a shit?" I loudly ask the air around me with my recently acquired, liquid bravado. I finish my glass of wine and energetically dial his number.

Each time I hear his phone ring I take a deep breath and refocus myself. On the fourth ring his answering machine picks up. I listen to his voice on the outgoing announcement and quickly try to come up with some kind of reasonable message to leave. I end up hanging up at the beep. This isn't the kind of thing you can leave a message for.

"Oh, hey, stalker boy, could you call me back? I'd like to talk with you about the way you've been scamming me. Thanks!"

No. This is a conversation that needs to be had in a real time, back and forth, kind of way. I sink back into the sofa feeling frustrated that I can't use the pumped up courage I have at this moment and I realize I'll have to get myself psyched up all over again to do the deed later. Alcohol, and the stressful events of the day have left me feeling as though I could use a transfusion. I pull the throw off the back of the sofa, wrap it around me and curl up with a yawn. Within seconds, I'm deeply asleep.

It takes a Herculean effort to rouse myself when the phone begins ringing. I clumsily feel for the phone and mumble "Hello?" with my eyes still closed.

"Hi, Nicki, you called?" the voice at the other end asks.

I don't recognize the voice and I sit up and rub my eyes. "I did?"

"I think so," the voice continues, "Its C.J."

Instantly, I'm wide-awake and on my feet. "How did you get my number?"

He hears the tension in my voice and answers defensively. "It was on my Caller ID."

Damn! In my pumped up, inebriated state I forgot to block my number. I feel like an idiot for several obvious reasons.

"Oh, of course." I mumble, trying to sound casual.

"Are you okay?"

"Yes, I'm fine Cole." I say his name in a deliberate way. "I called because there's something I wanted to ask you."

I'm fumbling in my mind with how to begin. I begin pacing nervously.

"You know how you told me that your friend referred you? Well, Sergio told me that he goes to a different club now. Wouldn't your friend want you to work out at the same club he does? I'm just wondering about that. Why didn't you go to the same club as your friend?"

Cole is silent for a moment before answering. "You're right. He did want me to work out with him, but he's a really good friend and he understood where I was coming from."

"And where were you coming from?" I ask. I stop in the middle of the room and exhale as quietly as I can.

There's a long pause. I hear him let out a sigh.

"Look, I'm just going to level with you. I saw your ad a few months ago on an online dating site and I wrote to you. You totally blew me off for a couple of reasons, our age difference being one and in the questionnaire I said that I didn't have kids, but I wanted them. I felt frustrated that I was being reduced to some random stats especially, when it seemed to me that we had a lot in common. I couldn't care less about the difference in our ages and it's much more important to me to have a great relationship with the kind of woman I want, than to have kids. I wanted the opportunity to tell you that and it didn't seem like email was going to be a way in with you. Jake was at my house the day you wrote back. I showed him your ad and he immediately recognized you from your photo. He told me you worked as a personal trainer out of Sergio's place and I saw that as a way for me to meet you. I just waited a few months and hoped you wouldn't remember me from my ad and that you wouldn't meet someone in the meantime," he pauses, "you didn't meet anybody, did you?"

I'm momentarily stunned by his straightforward confession and it takes me a few seconds to realize he's waiting for an answer from me.

"Nicola?" he asks the silence.

"Yes," I answer. "Yes, Cole, I have met someone and I did end up remembering you. The C.J. nickname threw me off at first, but I had a feeling I had seen you before and when you told me your first name was Cole, I remembered it from the email you sent me." I drop down on the couch,

226

resting my forehead in my hand. "I can't believe you did this."

"You can't believe I did what? All I did was take advantage of a great opportunity. Would you have passed up a chance like that? I doubt it, Nicki. That night at my house, when Jake recognized you, I felt like someone had handed me a gift and all I had to do was take it. I'm a strong believer that if nothing's ventured, nothing's gained. If I hadn't tried to meet you, I'd still be regretting it." He paused. "I'm a little flattered that you didn't find me completely forgettable by the way. I thought for sure I was busted that first day when you were checking me out. So, who's the lucky guy?"

"His name is Javier. It was kind of hard to forget a guy with an ad that looked like a GQ layout and I wasn't checking you out. I was trying to place you."

"So, did you meet this guy online? Wait; did you just say you thought my ad looked like a GQ layout? Thanks."

"Yes, I met him online right around the same time you wrote. I only found your ad GQ-like in its sheer volume of photos." I don't try to mask my sarcasm.

"So, Javier, let me guess. He's old and doesn't want kids."

"He's *my* age and he already has kids."

"So how long have you been seeing Javier? If you don't mind my asking."

"I do mind. We haven't actually met yet, he lives in L.A." As soon as the words leave my mouth, I regret saying them.

227

There's a long pause until Cole quietly asks, "If you haven't met yet, then maybe you shouldn't be so sure you've found someone, if you don't mind my saying."

"Again, Cole, I do mind."

"Sorry," he says, not sounding sorry at all. "I'm just savoring a renewed sense of optimism. Didn't I see your profile still up on the site a day ago?"

"There really isn't anything to feel optimistic about and my profile status is none of your business." I say, feeling rattled and flustered by his nerve to ask me all these questions. I really don't like how confident he seems. I'm glad I'm not talking to him face to face because I have this intense urge to kiss him and walk off, just to show him what he'll be missing.

"I hope you'll understand that I no longer feel comfortable working with you as your trainer," I pause, "but I'll be glad to help you find someone really good."

"Come on, Nicki, don't be mad. I don't want someone good. I want you." He laughs.

"That didn't come out right. I think you're the best. Look, I'm sorry you feel this way, but don't worry about it. I'll go workout with my friend Jake, and if you change your mind, call me. I want you to know I think you're an incredible woman and I'm glad I got to meet you. It far exceeded my expectations. You've got to admit Nicki, we have a pretty good time together."

I'm feeling awful in this moment. I'm horribly confused. Am I doing the right thing in sending Cole on his way? He's right. We do have a great time together. Maybe we could be friends? Just at that moment I visualize his face in front of me, his warm intense eyes and that incredibly sensual mouth and my resolve returns. How can I be friends with this man? Knowing how he feels about me? Especially with Javier's visit quickly approaching?

"I'm sorry Cole, I just don't feel comfortable doing things any other way. Please try to understand."

"Yeah, it's okay. I'm wondering though, if you hadn't connected with this guy and we had met, do you think you would you have considered going out with me?"

Before I can answer, he stops me, "You know what? Don't answer that. I'm sorry for putting you on the spot. Well, take care of yourself and if you ever feel like talking, call me. I hope I see you around, Nicola Botticelli."

For the first time I hear sadness in his voice. I hear him giving up.

"Good-bye, Cole." I say, and hang up. I stare up at the ceiling and blink back tears. His last question to me hangs in the air around me as new ones begin forming in my mind.

Chapter 36 ~ The Missing Letter

I'm twenty minutes late. I abruptly pull up in front of Ren's school. I can tell by the way she's standing with her hip cocked and fist planted firmly upon it, that she's pissed. She slings her book bag onto her shoulder and ambles sullenly over to the car without looking at me. Her face is a dark storm cloud.

"Sorry I'm late." I say, without sounding terribly repentant since she usually interprets that as weakness and an opportunity to rip me up one side and down the other.

"Traffic was horrendous. How was your day?" I ask.

She has her face turned toward the window and her arms folded tightly across her chest.

"Fine."

Ah, I think, the joy of parenting a fifteen-year-old girl. I give it one more shot. "You seem upset. Were you waiting a long time, or is it something else?"

"I'm FINE. Please just leave me alone."

I don't say it, but I think, "You've got it!" After the day I've had, a quiet ride home is just what I need. I pull out into traffic and head for home, relishing the silence. In the days since I last spoke with Cole, my life has quietly returned to its predictable patterns, complete with teenage issues and I find myself relaxing into all of it. Even Javier's presence, in the form of his nightly phone calls, has become another familiar ritual in the picture that is now my life.

My first day back at the gym after the phone call with Cole, found me furtively looking over my shoulder, expecting to see him at any moment. By the fourth day I began to stop anticipating him there. A couple of days later, as I was working out a new client, I felt a hand on the back of my arm. I turned, with a strange rush of fear and excitement to find Sergio with a question and my heart fell with disappointment. Part of me misses Cole and part of me vehemently dismisses the absurdity of that. I mean we hardly spent any time together at all. What's there to miss, really?

The day of Javier's arrival is fast approaching and I'm busily running around buying little things for the house to make it even more warm and inviting. Each day I come home with something different, scented candles, beautiful flowering plants, thick bath towels and sexy lingerie. I'm cleaning out closets and organizing every nook and corner. Javier had mentioned that one of the things he disliked most about his last girlfriend were her pack-rat tendencies. He's a lover of cleanliness and order, qualities that I admire and, in my better moments, I try to emulate. So I'm exterminating any evidence that could incriminate me as a member of that other sub-species. In so many ways this will be the most high-pressured, first date I've ever had.

I pull into the driveway and Ren can't seem to get out the car fast enough. Slamming the door hard behind her, she storms up to the front door.

She pulls out her key, lets herself in and disappears into her room before I even set my bundles down on the floor. It's just as well. At the moment I'm feeling less than enthused about working through another teenage crises with her. She's been unusually moody lately and I'm feeling tapped out by her constant negative drama.

Max comes exuberantly bounding in the door a few minutes later with his friend Tommy in tow. I recruit the two of them in bringing in the remaining bags from the car, which they immediately begin foraging through for snacks. As I'm packing things away I notice a letter out on the counter and pick it up to check it out more closely. I see from the return address it's from Javier. Another first, I think to myself, as I look at his interesting handwriting and enjoy the feeling of holding something that was in his hands only a couple of days ago. It's then that I notice how crumpled it is and the postmark is several days old. Where has this letter been and why is it the only piece of mail sitting on the counter? I go out to my mailbox and it's full of the usual catalogs, bills and flyers. As I look at Javier's letter in my hand, I get a sneaking suspicion that one of my children has been its custodian for the past few days and judging from the way they're both behaving at this moment, it's not Max. I wave the letter and ask him. "Max, do you know anything about this?" He squints from across the room at the letter in my hand.

"What is it?"

"It's a letter from Javier," I say.

He shrugs and shakes his head. "Ren said something about it the other day when I brought the mail in."

I'm wondering if this may be part of the reason my petulant daughter is being a bitch on wheels. I go and knock on Renoir's door. When she doesn't answer, I realize she's probably wearing her headphones and I cautiously peak my head in the door. She gives me a disinterested glance from where she's lounging on her bed, cocooned within her many throw pillows. I walk over and sit down on the edge, waiting a moment before leaning over and lifting one side of her headphones from her ear.

"I need to talk to you for a moment."

She rolls her eyes and takes off the headphones. I see her glance at the letter and I can tell by the way her body immediately tenses that she's the one with the answers I'm looking for.

"Do you know where this letter has been?" I ask simply.

She flies off the bed with her fists clenched, her eyes welling up with angry tears. "I'm NOT moving to California!"

"Whoa, Ren, what are you talking about? Who said anything about moving to California?"

"Don't think I don't know what's happening, Mom! You really like this guy! He calls you all the time and I see how you act all happy and shit. I'm not going! Dad said I could stay with him, because I'm not leaving my friends."

"Slow down sweetie. We're not going anywhere, and I wouldn't ask you to give up anything for me. You've got to believe that. I wouldn't do that to you. I do like this guy, but I haven't even met Javier yet. If anything comes of it, it's going to have to be something that works for you and Max too. I love you both too much to not take you into consideration. I wish you had come to me right away with these questions. So," I ask gently, "you've been talking about this with Dad?"

She looks sheepish and relieved at the same time, but that look quickly transforms into guilt.

"Yeah, Dad thinks you're crazy with this whole online dating thing and he said if you tried to take me and Max to California he'd let us stay with him."

"What! I wish I had known that this whole drama was going on behind my back. I wish your dad had come to me about this. I could have saved you all a lot of anguish. I can't believe your brother never said anything about this."

"He was getting kind of psyched about being a surfer." She mutters under her breath.

We both sit there silently for a few minutes.

"Can I give you a hug?" I ask, holding my arms open. Reluctantly, she allows herself to be folded into them and then relaxes into that place of comfort, resting her head against my shoulder and for a moment she's five again. I stroke her hair, talking to her softly. "There are no two people in this whole world as important to me as you and Max." As I tell her this I know that I've learned, somewhat painfully, that those places where we find the most comfort are sometimes the same places that bring us the most pain. Sitting there with my arms around her I find myself wishing I could keep those hard lessons from her. I know eventually we all experience these truths. And as the saying goes, what doesn't kill us does indeed make us stronger.

I wait until after the kids are in bed to take the letter out of my bureau drawer and open it. It's hand written on yellow, legal pad paper. It reads:

Hello Sweetie,

I'm calling you this, because I have a strong thing going with my feelings and I have not yet found a good pet name for you.

O.K. I have to tell, or at least write the truth about what is happening with me and I thought a letter would be the best way to do that. Do you remember in my last email when I said that I felt so strange? Right? Anyway, I had to go to another meeting so here I am waiting in the lobby of the Hilton near where I live and I have a "pulsion viewing"... I'll explain.

I am thinking about you with what I know of you; your photos, your writing, and your voice. It pulses in my consciousness with each wave of blood reaching my brain....

WHAT is THIS? Reality, or infatuation? I have NO idea.

I have been wrong before, so now I am kind of scared, or at least, very careful. It is curiosity mixed with fear. I am afraid that I may be disappointed to know you and that I also might not be up to par with what you expect from a man.

Now look at me: Mr. Baggage, two ex-wives, two kids, not yet a rock star (LOL!) financially still trying to make my way up. Am I living in a fantasy? Is it reality and if it is, where

and how do we start? Where is it going to go?
Hmmmmm.

What am I saying? I am blabbering. I am
laughing at myself. My appointment just paged me.
They are going to be late, so back to us. I can't wait
to talk to you again because this is the only thing
that links me to you in a real, live way.

Here are the questions in my mind:
Q. Do I know what I want?
A. I think so
Q. Do I have friends?
A. YES!
Q. Do I need another friend?
A. Not really, my kids and I are doing just
fine as we are.

Q. Do I really NEED a woman in my life?
A. Hmmm?
Q. Are you a potential trouble source?
A. You could be
Q. Are you together, but still cool?
A. You seem to be
Q. Are you so cool that you can feel secure
within yourself without needing to be
manipulative?
A. God I hope so!
Q. Do you know how to respect a man, his
emotions, tastes and space?
A. At almost 40, you've run around the block
a couple of times, hopefully that has
taught you a lot
Q. Are you this "coolest woman" that every
man hopes to someday meet?
A. Dunno, maybe

Q. Are you just that, or am I imagining it?
That's the whole thing.

AHHHHHHHHH! I'm so confused, and so
dramatic. There goes my beeper. Hold on, I've got
to go to my meeting.
Okay, I'm back. I just got a small thing in
the next Gwyneth Paltrow movie (cash, just cash).
I have to go. I'm glad I will see you soon,
even though I am scared. We both need to know. I'll
call you later.
Kisses, Javi

I put the letter down after reading it a second
time. It seems Ren isn't alone in needing to voice
concerns over this situation. I open the nightstand
drawer next to my bed and stuff it in the back,
unplug the phone, and close my bedroom door. As I
lay in my bed with the covers pulled up around my
neck, doubt and fear seep under my closed door and
spread out, thick as ink in a deep, menacing pool
across the floor. I pull the covers over my head and
close my eyes tightly.

Chapter 37 ~ Diversions and Collisions

My birthday falls on December 22 and every year, when I was a kid, my parents would tell me, "We didn't get you a whole lot this year, since Christmas is only a few days away."

By the time I was ten I didn't know why they even bothered to continue saying it. My expectations had been permanently lowered. As a result, any little thing I got was seen as a major victory for my side. I have, over the years, never completely stopped having low expectations when it comes to surprises. I still love them. I just don't expect very much. Nathan definitely added his own personal stamp to that whole thing. The up side to that is, I'm rarely disappointed. Again, the key word is *rarely*. When you don't expect much, it's pretty hard to be let down. Lately, I've begun wondering how this penchant for low expectations has found its way into the other areas of my life.

Take the arrival of Javier, who will be here in just eight days. On a minute-by-minute basis, my excitement is competing with my certainty that it's just going to be a big let down. The way I manage myself, is with an ongoing reminder that it doesn't really matter. I find myself able to buy that line for maybe an hour, or so and then the whole convincing process begins again. I feel like I'm wearing myself out. I need to get away from it for an evening with a major distraction, so I call Kate to see if a night out can be put together at the last minute.

"I was just thinking about the same thing," she says. "How's that my psychic friend? I'll call Sophia and Lily. I've been dying to check out this new jazz club. They have an excellent woman singing there tonight. How does that sound?"

"It sounds perfect. I'll call you right back."

A few phone calls later and Kate and I have rounded up the whole posse. We've got Lily, Paris, Terrence, and Sophia with Theo in tow. Even Jeff, Kate's new boyfriend, is going to come along.

I take a quick shower, and put on an Angelique Kidjo CD and I do my hair and makeup. It's a casual place so I throw on jeans and a white shirt with some simple silver jewelry. A quick spray of perfume, and I head out the door.

When we get there at nine the place is already pretty packed. The singer is an up and coming artist, who's been getting a lot of airplay on a couple of the local college radio stations. The publicity has paid off and the place is filled with mostly twenty-somethings and few of us stray, *older* folks. We make our way to a table that's toward the back of the room in the corner where we can still talk over the music. Theo orders a round of drinks with trendy names. This place is known for its great martinis. Half way through my Chocola-tini, I'm feeling pretty good. I notice Lily and Paris with their heads together talking and looking over at me with huge grins on their faces. I'm about to ask them what gives, when Lily sits down next to me, leans over, and in a conspiratorial tone says,

"Don't turn around. Just to your left, standing against the back wall there's a really cute guy who hasn't stopped staring at you."

Paris is looking at me with her eyebrows up and a smirk. Kate's impeccable radar catches that something's up and Lily immediately fills her in. She casually looks around and turns back to the table.

"Ay, Mamacita!" she says, and smacks the table as Jeff shakes his head at her.

I want to see what the big to do is about and Paris and Lily coach me as to when to look. I have two false starts before they say,

"Okay he's looking away. He's standing next to a woman with the long dark hair and he has dark hair and a light blue shirt."

I look over quickly scanning the sea of people and my eye instantly catches sight of him. He's like a beacon in the midst of all those people as he listens intently to the woman in front of him. As if he feels my gaze on him, his head turns and our eyes meet. He smiles and waves. I limply wave back turning my attention to my drink as my friends try to decipher what just happened. As usual it's shrewd Kate who solves it in a matter of seconds.

"Don't tell me," she says, as she dramatically puts her hands up to her head. "It's the stalker, isn't it? C.J.? It's Cole? It *is* Cole." She doesn't wait for me to answer, as my pained expression says it all. "Of all the freakin' luck girl."

"Oh my gosh!" Lily says, as she follows what Kate is saying. She's in my face with eyes the size of dinner plates, "He's gorgeous!"

At this point the whole table is buzzing. I watch the story make its way over to Theo and Sophia,

What I want to know is, who's the attractive woman? She seems to be getting Cole's rapt attention.

Theo looks over at me as I squirm in my chair and with his head, gestures toward the dance floor. I nod back at him. It's not the first time he's rescued me. He gets up and makes his way around the table to where I'm sitting. He takes me by the hand, leading me past the dance floor, and out the back door onto the deck overlooking the harbor. It's a warm, beautiful night and I deeply breathe in the salt air.

"Are you okay?" He asks, grinning broadly.

"Don't I seem okay?" I answer, and playfully whack him on his broad chest.

He shakes his head and narrows his eyes. "Not really. You look kind of freaked out little lady. So, what's the story with this guy?"

I fill Theo in on all the recent events in my life as he listens, quietly attentive, and when I'm through he smiles and says,

"I'm kind of bummed that I didn't know about this. We used to talk all the time. A year ago, I would have already known all of this already. It's not your fault either. It's mine. I guess that's one of the pitfalls of my business taking off." He pauses. "So, let me see if I have this right. You've got the L.A. Frenchmen about to arrive on the scene and things with him are pretty hot and heavy albeit in a virtual kind of way. Behind door number two you have tenacious Young Guy ready, more than willing and from the looks of him tonight, completely able. He's practically sitting in your own backyard. However, there are obstacles with Young Guy. The first, he's ten years younger than you and the second; he's expressed the desire to be a parent at some point in his life. Now I could be crazy, but I see way more obstacles with Frenchie. He's twice married, twice divorced, a father of two, living on the other side of the country with ex-wives living there and you said his nearest blood relations are in Paris. And you're telling me he has an ex-girlfriend who won't go away?"

I start to protest and Theo stops me, raising his palm in front of my face. "I'm not through little lady. Now, I think this is the heart of it. We both know that obstacles aren't the issue. Look at Sophia and me. Her father is on the verge of disowning her for dating a black man, but I'm determined to win that man over. It's just a matter of time before I wear the guy down. I love her and I'm going to make this work. Her father just needs to get to know me because as we both know, to know me is to love me." He flashes me his perfect smile. "You have issues with both of these guys. I think it's a question of who is worth the effort of working them through. Can I assume that Cole doesn't appeal to you in that whole man/woman kind of way?"

I roll my eyes. "It's not as simple as that."

"So, he does appeal to you?" He smirks.

"I think Cole would appeal to any straight woman with five senses and a pulse."

"Then why won't you give him a chance?"

"There are two very good reasons. First, Javier will be here in about a week and I want to be clear-headed about that and second, I can't imagine how Cole and I could have a relationship that would last."

"Nicola Botticelli, if this about your age, that's just bullshit. You are the youngest, most vivacious woman I know. You're ageless. And if this man loves you, he's always going to see that. Besides, charisma doesn't age." Theo says this with such adamant sincerity, that I give him a big kiss on the cheek.

"One last thing," he says, holding on to me, "Since when did life come with any guarantees? Just because your marriage ended can you honestly say you wish it never happened? Just because love doesn't always last forever doesn't mean it wasn't worthwhile."

"Jesus, Theo, when did you start sounding like a greeting card?" I give his arm a tug.

"I can't take any more of this heavy emotional crap. I came out tonight to get away from it. I need some mindless fun. So, what do you say we head on in and do some serious dancing?" I ask, bouncing up and down and tugging on his arm like an impatient child.

Theo shakes his head at me.

"See, that's what I'm talking about. I think you're actually too young for him."

Once I'm back in the club, my challenge becomes figuring out how to be in the same room with Cole and pretend he isn't here. I'm doing a great job until there's a tap on my shoulder and I turn to find him only inches away from my face. "Hi, how are you?" he asks, with his eyes and mouth melting into an incredibly warm smile. "You look great, Nicki."

I can't respond. I just stand there looking like someone just shot me with a gun and I can't fall down. I don't understand why I feel this flustered. What's wrong with me?

The pretty, dark haired woman comes up on Cole's left, and as she reaches her hand forward, he introduces her as his sister Janet. I immediately notice the family resemblance, from the coloring and high cheekbones, to the sensuous mouth and playful eyes.

"It's nice to meet you. Cole has told me so much about you." She says, as she pumps my hand enthusiastically.

I manage to compose my features even though the thought of what Cole might have shared with her makes me feel more than a little uncomfortable. I decide to match her warm greeting. We fall into a conversation that soon has the same kind of ease that I had had with Cole before I found out he was a cyber-stalker. In only a few minutes, she feels like someone I've known for years. I can tell how pleased Cole is, as he watches us interacting. I'm even feeling almost at ease with the fact that Cole is standing only two feet away from me until Janet notices that my glass is empty and offers to get me another drink. "No, I'll go get them," I offer, my stomach making a panicky drop.

It seems she didn't hear me. She holds up her empty glass with her back to me and looks at

Cole to see if he wants another. He shakes his head no. Just as she's heading off to the bar, she turns and calls back at us, "Why don't you two dance while I'm gone?"

As I helplessly watch her retreating back, Cole's hand lightly touches my shoulder and reluctantly, I turn back toward him. He smiles and holds his hands out to me.

"Would you like to dance?"

My eyes quickly scan the room for some kind of way out, and I realize that there isn't one. It occurs to me that his sister deliberately set us up. It's a slow song and couples are cozying up to one another on the dance floor. I decide to make the most of this awkward situation.

Without looking directly at his face I say, "sure," as lightheartedly as possible. We move out to the dance floor. He gracefully gathers me up in his hands. One curves along the small of my back and the other hand enfolds mine, drawing it against his chest close to his heart, which I imagine beating beneath my fingers. My face is only inches away from the little hollow at the base of his throat. I'm so close that I can see the texture of his skin and breathe in his clean, warm smell. He's wearing a scent that's subtle. Perhaps it's only the chocolate martini that I just drank quickly, but I find my body relaxing into how good this feels. Cole moves like a dancer. I'm intrigued by how aware he is, of his body and the more subtle aspects of touch and movement. When I look up into his face, instead of his usual smile, his face is quietly serious. I'm about to ask if he's okay, but the look in his eyes stops me and we hold each other's gaze too long. His eyes look intently into mine. I look away to the other couples as I feel the color rising in my face.

"I've missed you." He whispers softly into my hair. "I know that probably sounds crazy, but I've missed you." I concentrate on slowing my breathing. When I look back up at him, he looks intently into my eyes. He delicately brushes a few strands of hair away from my face. His finger trails along the side of my cheek. He looks away and I feel him inhale deeply then slowly let the breath out. I continue looking at his face, as he seems to be contemplating something. When he turns his gaze back to me, it's with his trademark warm smile.

"So, how are things going with your man from California?"

"Good," I answer uncomfortably. "He's going to be here for a meet and greet next weekend."

I'm not sure why I volunteer this information and I immediately regret saying it.

He nods his head.

"Next weekend. You must both be pretty excited about it." He's smiling, but his eyes look sad.

"Yeah." I look away and focus on a couple just beyond his shoulder.

The song ends and Janet walks over and hands me my drink. I thank her and tell her it was nice to meet her and then I tell Cole it was great to see him. I nod toward the table of my friends and I try to graciously excuse myself. The whole way across the floor I fight back tears. When I find

Sophia, I hand her my drink and ask her if she and Theo can give Lily a ride home. I have to get out of there. I grab my bag and make a quick exit to my car fumbling in my bag for my keys as my eyes fill up. I'm having trouble seeing clearly enough to get the key in the door. I hear someone come up behind me and turn to find Cole standing there.

"Are you okay?"

"No Cole," I shake my head, "I'm not okay."

I can't hold back any longer and the tears pour down my face. He moves toward me enveloping me in his arms, drawing me close him. I let myself lean against all that strength and kindness with my face against his chest, as he softly strokes my back and whispers into my hair, "It's okay."

He kisses my forehead and when I look back up into his face I kiss him without any hesitation. He kisses me back until my limbs feel so weak I can barely stand without hanging on to him. I feel him pouring himself into me and I pour myself back into him, as we fill each other up. Lightning shoots through every limb in my body and it takes all I have to let go of him and get into my car. As I drive off, I look into my rearview mirror with my heart still pounding. Cole stands there alone, watching me pull away.

Chapter 38 ~ Sleepless in Sandyport

The next day I stay in bed and turn the ringer off on the phone. Nathan has the kids and I selfishly claim this day to indulge in my sadness and confusion. I let it own me in a way that is eerily reminiscent of those first days after Nathan left me. The floor of my bedroom is liberally littered with mounds of soggy tissues. I wade through them, as I make my way into the bathroom to pee. When I venture a look at myself, the face in the mirror peering back looks grossly swollen and haggard, like a boxer who lost the fight.

Each thought of Cole brings me to tears, as do my thoughts of Javier who will be here in less than a week. My heart longs for both of them, but in different ways. My feelings for Cole are completely tangible, like an electrical current along the surface of my skin. While my feelings for Javier, have an almost ethereal quality. In spite of never having met him face-to-face, I have strong feelings for Javier, a deep affection, and because of that I feel guilty. Part of me thinks that it's silly for me to feel this way and part of me knows that this is just the way I'm made. Even behind the swollen ravages of hours of crying, the face in the mirror seems alien to me. Who is she? Who is this woman? I've never been the kind of person who could have strong feelings for two people at the same time. Why can't I let go of this attraction that draws me to Cole?

I burrow under the covers creating a fortress of pillows around me, sinking into this self-made womb. I flip through the channels on TV, searching aimlessly. *Sleepless in Seattle* is on and like a sucker for punishment I watch it for the millionth time. There they are, two people on opposite sides of the country who find their way to each other in spite of all the obstacles along the way.

"If they can do it, why can't we?" I loudly shout at the TV with no reply. I give my chafed nose a long hard blow and shuffle out to the linen closet for another box of tissues. At the rate I'm going, the pile on the floor is going to swallow the entire bed by the time the movie ends.

A few days ago, while rummaging through my glove compartment, looking for an extra pair of sunglasses, I came across the tape of my reading with the psychic in Salem. I stuffed it in my purse and took it into the house where I dropped it ever so casually on the nightstand next to my bed. Now, as the commercials come on, I periodically give it a sneaky sidelong glance as if I didn't want it to catch me looking. When the movie ends, I prop myself up in the bed and slowly pick the tape up as carefully, as I would a vial of nitro-glycerin. It takes me a few moments to realize that I'm holding my breath. Jesus, what am I so afraid of? Why am I such a wuss? I need to grow a set. I look back and forth from the tape to the tape deck. Tape. Tape deck. Finally, I summon the courage to put it in and push play.

As Rachel's voice fills the air around me, I burrow back under the covers pulling them up snug under my chin in much the same way I did when, as a child, I would protect myself from the boogey

249

man. I listen as she talks about the two men that I will feel strong feelings for at the same time and how things will not be what they seem. What does that mean? Maybe Cole is not the wonderful man I think he is? Maybe I'm afraid of committing myself to the idea of being with Javier because of the ways it could complicate my life and I'm just using Cole as a way to sabotage the possibility?

I try to decipher what seems to be a very cryptic message. She says something about the least likely answer being the right one and after what Theo said last night perhaps it's true that with all the obstacles between us, Javier seems like the least likely. Then again, it could be Cole. She goes on to say that I won't find the answer until I start choosing with my heart, which is presently only pumping equal parts of blood and pain and delivering nothing in the way of answers. I'm so exhausted from trying to figure it out that I fall asleep.

I wake up hours later. I can tell by the light that it's mid-afternoon. Several windows are open and the salty smell of the ocean fills my room. It's a smell that has always made me feel inexplicably happy and I breathe it deeply into my lungs. A wonderful saying that an old friend of mine used to tell me comes to my mind.

"Life is not a problem to be solved, it's a mystery to be lived."

She would remind me of this whenever I would be trying to find an answer to a problem that didn't necessarily have one. I know she would be saying it to me now if she were here.

I get up, turn the phone's ringer back on, and check my caller ID to see who's called. There are five calls. Two are from Javier. One is from Paris, one from Sophia and, the last one from Cole. I decide to take a shower and eat something before I listen to any of them. I feel strangely calm, as if something inside of me has let go.

I sit down at my desk and listen to my messages. Javier's first one comes at nine-thirty. He asks if had a good time with my friends and wonders if I'm still sleeping off all that good fun. His next message comes at noon and he's now trying to mask his uneasiness at still not finding me home. He doesn't ask the question directly, but I can tell he's wondering if I made it home at all and also wondering if I didn't, where did I end up? Paris leaves a message a little after his. Sophia told her the state I was in last night when I bolted from the club. Little did I know, she had followed me on the heels of Cole out of the club to see if I was okay and ended up catching our kiss in the parking lot. So, of course she's wondering what the hell is going on. Sophia's is basically the same. Lastly, there's a message from Cole.

"Hey, it's me." He begins softly. "I was up half the night thinking about you and worrying about you. I need to know you made it home okay. I hope you're not beating yourself up for that kiss. It happened and I don't know what it was for you, but for me it was amazing. I respect what you feel you need to do and I'll leave you alone, but if you change your mind, I'm here. I'm waiting. I dropped off something I've been making for you and I left it outside your door."

I throw on my robe, slide into my slippers, and head down the stairs. There inside my gate on the walkway is a beautiful piece of sculpture. It has an organic fluid quality and as I'm studying it I realize that it's a fountain. There's a card inside and I open it. In Cole's interesting script he has written a bit of Shakespeare from A Midsummer Night's Dream.

> *Things growing are not ripe until their season:*
> *So I being young, till now not ripe to reason;*
> *And touching now the point of human skill,*
> *Reason becomes the marshal to my will*
> *And leads me to your eyes.*

To say I'm blown away would only diminish how I feel. I sit down right there on the steps in my robe and fuzzy slippers and read his note again. I wipe the tears from my face on my sleeve and awkwardly gather up the fountain, which is over three feet high and heavy. I lug it in stages, stopping for a few minutes to catch my breath before I attempt the stairs to my bedroom. Cole has put instructions inside the envelope and I spend more than a half hour getting it going. With enormous satisfaction, I lie back on my bed and listen to the water flowing through it. What a smart man he is, to give me a gift that would remind me of him every time I hear it. Did he know I would put it in my bedroom where it would murmur to me every morning and evening?

I go back downstairs, make myself a cup of tea and dial Javier's number. Rae answers the phone in her sweet little six-year-old, baby doll voice. After all the phone calls, she now recognizes my voice right away.

"Hi, Nicola, Papa's giving Vaughn a bath and he's being really bad. Can he call you back?"

I laugh as I imagine Javier struggling with a slippery, wet, and willful three-year-old. Rae hollers to her dad without moving away from the phone and practically blows out my eardrum. I hear him asking her if I'm at home.

"Yes, Rae, tell him I'm at home and he can call me when he gets a chance."

I go open up my email to reread some of what he's written to me recently and I find myself quickly reconnecting with my feelings for him. I'm baffled by what seems to be my new, fickle nature. The confusion is much painful. I feel I must push all thoughts of Cole out of my mind whenever they try to creep in at the edges of my consciousness. Like a border patrol guard, I struggle vigilantly keep out the tenacious intruder.

About a half hour later Javier calls.

"Whoa babe, you had me worried. I am thinking, what if something happened to you? I would have no way of knowing. That's pretty weird, huh? And if something happened to me how would you know? I want to give you a couple of phone numbers you can call if you ever can't get a hold of me. One is my friend George who is just the coolest guy and knows everything that is going on with me and the other is my ex-wife who would know if I was dead, or something."

"Jesus, Javier, that's pretty gruesome."

"But it's realistic. Oui?"

"I guess so. So I should give you a couple of numbers too."

I give him Paris and Lily's numbers since I figure that they are the most likely to think of him should something ever happen.

"You have a friend named Paris and I am from Paris. I think this is a very good sign. Now tell me, did you have a fun night out with your friends?"

I fill him in on all the details of the evening minus the parts that involve Cole and then I ask him about his night and he tells me about it with so much energy and animation that I feel as though I was there.

"In six more days," he says, "I will be with you there and I will finally be able to look into your eyes and hold your hands when I talk to you."

I imagine that. Any fear, or trepidation I had felt earlier has been banished to the outskirts of my mind along with those pesky thoughts of Cole. My mental patrol guard is not only on duty; it's armed to the teeth.

Before saying goodnight after more than an hour on the phone we decide to hire a limo from the airport to get Javier to my house. When we hang up, I'm feeling really excited about his arrival.

I collapse onto my bed, completely exhausted, only to climb back out a couple of minutes later. As I stand in front of the fountain, listening to its peaceful bubbling, Cole's presence quietly asserts itself. I lean down and pull the plug.

Chapter 39 ~ The Three Date Rule

The day before Javier's arrival Lily calls all excited about a blind date she's going on that evening. Ordinarily, a blind date is something Lily avoids as much as a highly allergic person avoids a patch of poison ivy, but this time it's different. Her neighbors, Rob and Lori, are fixing her up with Rob's older brother, James. She's going on some assumptions. Rob is a good-looking, smart, seemingly wonderful husband and dad. Lily is hoping that these are dominant genetic traits that she can depend on being present in Rob's brother. And finally, since she's been going through a serious man drought, she figures it couldn't hurt. Too much.

She asks me to come over after work for some all important wardrobe advice. After I finish up with my last client of the day I and pick up some wine, with cheese and crackers for nibbling. I don't want to send Lily off on her date half lit.

She answers the door with a breathless excitement I haven't seen in her for quite some time.

"Oh good, you brought wine. I need to calm down a little. I'm so excited."

"Really? I hadn't noticed." I say, handing the bottle over. "I thought we might need a little fashion lubricant."

We head into her bedroom where we spend the next hour pulling things out of the drawers and the closet before finally deciding on a simple halter top dress in an incredible shade of light violet that hits just above the knee. It showcases all of Lily's best physical attributes from her showgirl legs to her buff arms and shoulders.

"You don't think it looks like I'm showing off?" She asks, as she checks out her reflection in the mirror.

"Oh, it definitely looks like your showing off, but in a way that I don't think he's going to mind."

I give her a final pep talk along with a big hug, as I head out the door.

"Remember, he's just a guy and not the only guy. Wear crappy underwear so you won't be tempted to get naked if you somehow forget the third date rule."

Her eyes widen.

"I would never sleep with a guy on the first date!"

"Neither would I sweetie, but I never say never. Do you know what he has planned?"

"He's picking me up and we're going to dinner and then maybe dancing. Why am I so nervous?"

"Probably because it's been a while. Relax; it's going to be fun. Just enjoy yourself and for God's sake, breathe."

I feel like my instructions are as much for me as they are for Lily. I'm going to be face to face with Javier in less than twenty-four hours. I check my watch and realize I have to head out for a waxing appointment. I'm preparing for every possible contingency. In our last few phone calls,

Javier and I talked about the issue of sex and our meeting. We both agreed that if it didn't feel right for either of us it wouldn't happen and that that was not going to be a problem. We decided we're going to value this meeting regardless of the outcome. Addressing the sex question relieved a lot of the pressure and also made me feel even better about the kind of man he is.

My appointment is at Eliza's spa and she ushers me into one of the private rooms like a gossipy teenager.

"So, Kate tells me your Frenchman will be here tomorrow. It's so romantic." She puts both hands on her cheeks and opens her eyes widely. "Tell me all about it."

And even though I know that sharing any information with Eliza is like putting out an all points bulletin, I tell her what she wants to know as she waxes. When she gets to my bikini area she says,

"You should do a Brazilian. Men love it. I know that you might not sleep with him," she says this sarcastically, "but if you do it will be fabulous!"

She pauses, looking at me expectantly with her fingers forming a steeple in front of her chin.

"A Brazilian?" I ask, unconvinced.

Eliza nods silently, a Mona Lisa smile on her lips.

I leave Eliza's feeling like a new designer breed of hairless critter, and I'm glad it's summer since one cold draft could do me in. I was a little horrified when I got the first glimpse of my new look. It was almost pre-pubescent with barely any remaining evidence of my adulthood.

On the way home, I stop for some Thai take-out, pick up a bottle of champagne for Javier's arrival. I also buy some cut flowers for the house. Aztec greets me at the door with her leash in her mouth. I stuff a Thai roll in my mouth and take her for a much needed walk to the park.

It's a warm evening. The air has a soft thickness that feels like I'm somewhere tropical and the mosquitoes are out in full force causing Aztec and me to move faster than either of us has the energy for. By the time we get back to the house, we're both ravenous. I feed the dog and then fill a plate for myself with Pad Thai, Drunken Chicken, and a spring roll. I pour myself a glass of wine and by the time I've finished my meal I'm so sleepy the only thing I have energy for is arranging the flowers in a vase and climbing the stairs to my room. The phone rings as I'm brushing my teeth and I say hello through a mouthful of toothpaste. It's Javier. We go over the last details for tomorrow.

"So, if you want to change your mind, do it now," he teases.

"Hmmm," I say, as if I'm mulling it over, "No, I think I'm still up for it."

"I'm definitely up for it." He laughs at his innuendo.

"Down boy." I say, going with his double entendre.

When we say our goodnights to each other we're as excited as a couple of little kids anticipating Christmas morning.

259

I wash my face and scrutinize my skin in the mirror searching for any tell tale sign of the volcanic type of zit, which only seems to appear when I really don't want one. My skin is auspiciously clear. Things are coming together perfectly.

The steady humming of the ceiling fan coupled with my exhaustion help to override my excitement and I'm deeply asleep in just minutes. So when the phone rings an hour later it startles me so badly, when I finally locate it, I sit up and scream into the receiver.

"HELLO!"

"HELLO!" the voice at the other end screams back apparently as startled by me as I was, by them. "Nicki! It's me, Lily."

"Lily? Oh my God! Are you okay?"

"I'm sorry for calling you so late, but I'm so upset I had to talk to you."

I lean over and turn on the light by my bed.

"What is it? Was he a jerk? Was the date awful?"

"No, it was great. He was wonderful, but I did the stupidest thing."

Lily is famous for being hard on no one, but herself.

"What did you do, sweetie?"

"I completely forgot about the three date rule." She wails pitifully. "I slept with him."

I laugh. "It's okay. I don't think it's a huge deal these days. Lots of women sleep with guys on the first date. In fact, Kate does it all the time."

"Yeah, for sex! But she would never do it with a guy she really likes. A guy she thinks she could have an actual relationship with. Oh my God, I can't believe I did that and now he probably thinks I'm just the biggest SLUT!" She sounds like she's on the verge of tears.

"Oh, sweetie I can't imagine anyone thinking you're a slut. Kate, maybe, but you, never."

"This isn't funny, Nic. I just met the most incredible man. He's smart, and interesting and he's a great listener and he's so cute. He has these amazing blue eyes and dark curls." She trails off wistfully. "And I blew it."

"Now don't be so quick to declare it a disaster area. I think you should get some sleep and see what happens tomorrow. Maybe he has a thing for sluts."

"Nicola!"

"Only kidding."

Late night phone calls have always gotten my adrenaline pumping and it ends up taking me the better part of an hour to fall back to sleep, so I have plenty of time to worry about my own impending, high-pressure date and the deep, dark circles that will be forming under my eyes if I don't get to sleep soon.

Chapter 40 ~ The Sniff Test. Part 2

In spite of an interrupted and restless night, I wake with energy coursing through me in mega watts. Of course it's the nervous variety, but I use it for running errands, walking the dog, and taking care of any last minute details I can think of. I write up an ambitious to do list, which includes doing a workout, getting a massage, stocking the refrigerator, and vacuuming. I make a reservation at a very sexy local restaurant, with a fabulous raw bar. I'm so OCD about this meeting, I've even planned a strategy regarding outfits for the next few days, allowing for every possible weather variation. Being a New Englander, I'm well aware that it could run the full gamut from sunshine to snow. Nothing has been left to chance.

By the time the car pulls up with Javier, I'm so pumped I can hardly keep from screaming and jumping up and down like a crazed contestant on a game show. I've spent the last hour going back and forth to the window every few minutes trying to catch him pulling up. When I finally spot the limo, I bolt down the stairs, out the gate and to the street. I just stand there grinning and taking him in as he thanks the driver and gathers up his bags. I knew he was a big man, but somehow seeing him in person he seems huge. As the car pulls away, he sets his bags down on the sidewalk and raises both of his hands to his head all the while smiling at me broadly.

"Look at you!" he says dramatically, raising both arms in the air, "You are so beautiful! This is crazy!"

I laugh and move toward him as he opens his arms and draws me in for a hug. He smells of stale cologne and strong sweat. I'm hoping that the old cliché about earthy-scented French people isn't true and it occurs to me that he's probably been feeling as anxious and stressed about this meeting as I have.

We pick up his things and make our way upstairs with Javier making exited comments about the condo.

"This is fantastic. Look at that view! You know, this area reminds me quite a bit of Brittany. Except for the houses being made of wood here, and made of brick and stone there, it has a very similar look and feeling." He sets his things down, still smiling at me, and I suddenly feel shy and self-conscious.

"How was your flight?"

"It was fine." He smiles as he takes me in and I feel the color rising in my face.

"Can I get you something to eat, or drink?" I offer turning toward the cabinets to regain my composure. I feel his eyes following me.

"A glass of water would be great and then I'd like to shower and freshen up."

I smile, and hand him the glass of water as his eyes continue to drink me in.

While he showers, I prepare a tray of cheese and crackers and open the bottle of champagne. French of course. I don't know about him, but I'm certain a few sips will help me to relax. I set it on the table out on the back deck feeling pleased with the gorgeous picture this place paints. It looks like something out of a magazine.

The phone rings and I can see by the Caller ID that it's Lily. She probably needs a little more reassurance. I take it out to the deck.

"Hi, Lily. Are you okay?"

"I'm great. James sent me a dozen red roses and a note that says, 'Thanks for last night. It was wonderful.' A guy wouldn't do that if he thought you were a slut right?"

I can't resist the opportunity to tease her and answer her in as serious a tone as possible. "Probably not, unless he thought it would guarantee him some more great nookie."

She pauses a moment as she mulls that over and I have to interrupt her thought process before she starts freaking out. "Lily, I'm joking. A man would definitely not send a woman a dozen red roses the day after a date unless he thought she was pretty amazing."

"I should call him and thank him for the flowers. Right?"

I agree with her. "You should and that will be a good chance to feel him out. No pun intended."

"You're so bad. Hey, is Javier there yet?"

"Uh huh, he's in my shower as we speak."

"Oooooh, in your shower," she says, suggestively.

"Yeah, I did him as soon as he got here."

"You did?"

I can hear through the phone how big her eyes are.

"God, no! It's actually a little weird having him here in the living, breathing, flesh." I say this under my breath in case he's lurking around. "He smelled pretty funky when he got here. I'm hoping the shower will take care of that."

"Oh yeah, you and the sniff test."

"Exactly, the sniff test."

Just then I hear Javier making his way across the living room and I tell Lily I have to go. I hang up just as he comes through the French doors and out to the deck rubbing the towel over his damp hair. He drapes it around his bare shoulders and I take a moment to appreciate his shirtless state. Not bad.

He leans over and kisses me on the cheek and I get a whiff of the same cologne he was wearing when he got here. Turns out it wasn't stale. It was just cheap smelling. I find that interesting since I thought the other cliché about the French and great fragrance was true. It seems that Javier is a fan of things more American. I find myself planning how to get him into a more appealing scent.

"This looks great," he says, as I hand him a glass of champagne. "Thank you. How about a toast?"

I hold up my glass, smiling at him over the top of it.

He leans forward looking into my eyes, with his full of mischief. "To my beautiful hostess and to a beautiful new beginning."

We click glasses and sip with our eyes locked. He is one big, very sexy boy.

The wine and cheese have the desired effect of easing us into a great conversation. Javier, being a gifted storyteller, takes advantage of this opportunity of not being restricted by different time zones, and children's schedules. He tells me many tales of his adventures since he got to the US. As he tells me each story, he holds my hands as he had said he would do, and only lets go of them for a momentary gesture. At one point he pauses and just looks at them turning them in his own hands.

"You have very beautiful hands. I've imagined holding and kissing them many times." He gives me a melting look and raises my hands to his lips, sensuously kissing my fingertips. The sensation is ridiculously arousing. I'm grateful that he stops there and continues with his storytelling. In what feels like no time at all, it's time for us to get ready to go out to dinner. I take a quick shower and fix my face. Then I slip into a slinky, little black dress with spaghetti straps. With a light spray of perfume, some long silver earrings, and silver high-heeled sandals, I'm ready to go.

When I walk back out to the deck, Javier looks at me appreciatively. He stands and says,

"Wow, that dress, it is very Audrey Hepburn. You look beautiful."

I beam. "You look pretty handsome yourself."

He's wearing a white, raw silk shirt with the sleeves rolled up to show his muscular, tanned forearms, and a pair of beige linen trousers. A chunky silver watch and some other tasteful pieces of jewelry complete the look. In Javier's case, the cliché about French style is definitely true.

The restaurant is only a fifteen-minute walk from my condo, so I suggest we take a stroll. It's another softly warm night and as we make our way along the waterfront his story telling continues. He takes my hand and it feels natural that he would. We stop briefly, peeking into the windows of the many little shops and art galleries. A shop with a display of silver jewelry catches his eye and he asks if we have time to go in for a moment. I've given us plenty of time to make our reservation with allowance for a few possible stops along the way, but I teasingly peek at his watch.

"You'll have to make it fast." I sigh.

"I promise." He teases, crossing his heart with mock seriousness.

He asks the salesperson to show him a piece in the window. It's a silver necklace with fresh water pearls, rose quartz and blue-green tourmaline stones.

"Isn't this exquisite?"

"It's gorgeous." I agree.

"I'll take it," he says to the clerk and just as I'm wondering who he's buying jewelry for, he walks behind me and puts it around my neck.

"It looks great with that dress and the blue-green stones match your eyes." He stands back looking very pleased with himself and winks at me.

I put my hand up to it not sure what to say. "Thank you, Javier it's really beautiful, but you don't have to give me anything."

"But you are giving me something wonderful by having me here in your home and when I saw it I wanted you to have it." He leans over and kisses me softly on the cheek.

We arrive at the restaurant a little early for our reservation so we let them know we'll be sitting at the bar having drinks. We order some oysters and wine.

"I love oysters," he says, "but you must know that they have a strong aphrodisiac effect on me. I'll try to control myself, but the combination of oysters and your body in that dress may be more than I can bear." He groans and I laugh at the pitiful face he's making.

"Maybe you shouldn't have any then." I suggest as the waiter sets them down in front of us.

"Maybe you will take pity on me," He neatly downs two of them, takes a sip of his wine, and sits back smiling at me broadly.

I shake my head and try not to laugh. He's as mischievous here in person as he's been on the phone for the past few months.

Our table opens up just as we're finishing our oysters and Javier has started a second glass of wine. I'm still nursing the first one. I want to be sure that I'm doing things for the right reasons and with as much clarity as the unusual circumstances will allow. With the second glass of wine Javier's already exuberant personality is practically bursting at the seams and as if he senses my reluctance, he says,

"We are here in this beautiful place, in this beautiful moment. May I make a suggestion? Let's just have a great time together and really enjoy ourselves and each other without worrying about what will become of tonight. Okay?"

I hesitate a moment. I'm not sure if I'm comfortable with that, or what I want to do. As I look across the table at the playful, open look on his face, I decide that perhaps now is the time to throw my fears to the wind, and go wherever this night takes me. I nod my head and smile, "Okay."

Over the next couple of hours, we enjoy a great dinner of seafood delicacies and then head down the street to a funky little club on the water with live music. I'm glad we're on foot and have no need for a designated driver. Javier is more than a little lit and I'm feeling less than sober myself. There's an uninspiring blues band playing, but the lively crowd makes up for it. Javier wastes no time dragging me out onto the dance floor for some highly suggestive gyrating. His past experience as a stripper is screamingly apparent and I catch more than a couple of women checking out his moves. I do my best to match his outrageousness and become aware that we're turning heads all over the room, which only seems to fuel Javier further. With his hands very low on the back of my waist, he leans into me and purrs in my ear.

"I see you're not shy." He kisses my neck and I feel the blood rush to my face.

We only make it through a few more songs before this musical foreplay reaches an incendiary level and we have to leave and make, what now feels like a painfully long journey back home. Javier keeps stopping to kiss me furiously and I'm grateful that it's so late and there aren't many people driving by to witness this spectacle. I'm partly horrified that I'm doing this and partly oblivious to what's going on around me. We barely push through my tall gate and into the courtyard outside my door when he backs me up against the house pressing into me and kissing my neck and my mouth.

Somehow, I manage to locate my keys without looking into my bag and I awkwardly get them into the door, giggling through Javier's kisses the whole time. As we enter the foyer I slide my hand along the wall blindly groping for the light switch as Javier gropes me. I'm really not quite sure how we do it, but somehow we make it up the stairs, into the living room, and onto the sofa. Javier sensuously kisses my neck, and sliding the strap of my dress down, continues kissing along my shoulder, teasingly stopping above my breast.

"Do you want to make love?" He pauses, to look at my face as if the answer wasn't obvious. I nod my head and he smiles broadly.

"I'll be back in a minute." I say, kissing the end of his nose.

I turn on the light in the bathroom blinking from its sudden brightness. It takes my eyes a moment to adjust. I brush my teeth, as I search through the bag that I stashed at the back of the linen closet with a supply of condoms should the need for them arise, so to speak. I've got two different sizes and if my sense of feeling is any good the larger one is going to be needed. I head back to the living room stopping in the kitchen for matches to light some candles and when I get back, Javier isn't there. I turn up the dimmer on the light just to be sure and as I do, he calls me from upstairs.

"I'm ready for you baby."

When I walk into my room I find that he's already lit the candles and placed a bottle of wine with two glasses on the nightstand. He's propped up with pillows against the back of the headboard and he's completely naked. I also realize in that moment, that the large size condom I'm holding in my hand probably isn't going to do it. Not by a mile. Javier has the largest erect penis I've ever seen. It's a porn star dick. I stare at it with my jaw dropped and my eyebrows raised, involuntarily saying the only two words that come to my awestruck mind.

"Holy shit."

He smiles, and proudly gazes down at his enormous package oblivious to the fact that my response wasn't an appreciative one, but one that was the result of simple fear of possible bodily injury. He gets up and comes over to me; his dick reaches me a moment before the rest of him does. He kisses me and takes the inadequate condom out of my hand, tossing in onto the floor. He holds up a packet with the right size. I didn't know such a thing existed. The packet is the size of a snack bag. He puts my hand on his erection. I say it again.

"Holy shit!"

This time, he hears the trepidation in my voice and he laughs as he undresses me planting soft kisses on each place he exposes. "Don't worry little, Nicola. I will be very gentle."

He lays me back on the bed. When he discovers Eliza's handiwork, it's his turn to react.

"Wow!"

It would seem that Javier and I have different ideas regarding what gentle is. Sex with Javier is like running off and joining an X-rated version of Cirque du Soleil. There's a lot of acrobatic flipping and twirling with a serious amount of contorting involved. It requires a degree of athleticism and endurance that under normal circumstances, I definitely don't possess. Even in my aerobics class I don't work up this kind of sweat and I find my body suddenly capable of doing things that I never thought possible. With this heightened level of adrenaline, I'm like one of those one hundred and fifteen pound women we've heard of who, in a crisis, manage to lift an automobile off of their trapped child. Javier's extra inches make a whole other level of sexual creativity and versatility possible.

After several heated hours we collapse, utterly spent. It was definitely fun and sexy, but it wasn't what I would call making love. Within what seems like only seconds, Javier is snoring loudly beside me. After several minutes it gets even louder. I try rolling him over with no success. He's out cold. Across the room, the dark silhouette of the fountain silently offers salvation. When I can't stand another second, I get up and plug it back in. I blow out the candles, climb back into bed and stare up at the ceiling. The first time with someone is always a little strange. Cole's fountain eventually sends me bubbling off to sleep.

Chapter 41 ~ The Morning After

I wake the next morning with a head that feels like someone pored hot nickels into my skull while I was asleep. I moan involuntarily, as I slowly sit up. Javier is standing by the window with his back to me looking out at the view. He turns when he hears me.

"Bon jour!" He says, brightly, in a voice that sounds a hundred decibels too loud.

"Ooooooh." I cradle my forehead.

"Is my sweetie not feeling well?" He sits down on the bed next to me and kisses my head gently.

I don't answer him, but my pained expression as I look up at him through barely opened eyes, makes it clear.

"Do you have orange juice and bananas?" He asks softly.

"Uh huh." I murmur, without moving my lips.

"I'll be right back with something that will make you feel much better."

I watch his bare butt head out of my room and carefully lay back down. Far off I can hear the blender whirring. As I hear him coming back up the stairs, I pull myself up slowly. He walks into the room and hands me a smoothie and a couple of vitamins, which I take. Even though my stomach feels like it's on a rollercoaster, I finish it.

"By the way," he says, casually, "there's a little boy downstairs."

"What!" I gasp. "Did he see you?"

He gestures with his hand along the length of his naked body like a game-show spokes-model, presenting a high-end refrigerator. "All of me."

I gasp again and shoot out of bed grabbing my robe and wrapping it around me as I make a swift decent down my spiral staircase. My mind is the only thing racing faster than my feet. Why is Max here? I thought that he was miles away with Nathan and Ren on a camping trip. Isn't this just the sort of thing Nathan was trying to avoid? He knew Javier was here for the weekend. Poor Max, a trauma like this could have him in therapy for years. What do you say to a twelve-year-old boy who just came face to face in his own kitchen with a strange naked man who has a cartoon dick between his legs?

As I make my way to his room I can hear him opening and closing drawers. He's not slamming them. Maybe that's a good sign.

"Max?" I say, as I round the doorway.

He doesn't look up from his search.

"Yeah?"

I'm at a loss for words, so I blurt out the obvious.

"Are you looking for something?"

"One of my games."

"One of your games? I thought you guys were off camping."

"We were. We came back early. Ren got bad cramps."

"Oh, can I help you find it?"

He still hasn't looked me in the eyes once and I'm not so sure if he did that my guilt and embarrassment would allow me to look back. He pulls what he was looking for out of the drawer and raises it in the air above his head all the while looking straight ahead.

"Got it," he says, quickly moving past me in the doorway. He heads straight toward the door.

I call after his retreating back. "I'm sorry about Javier, honey. I wasn't expecting you here."

"It's ok, Mom." He answers half-heartedly. Without looking back he closes the door behind him too softly. I feel numb. It's the first time Max has gone out without giving me a hug goodbye. I feel sick. I go into the bathroom, close the door behind me, and kneel in front of the toilet waiting for the wave of nausea to pass. After a few minutes Javier taps on the door.

"Are you okay?"

"Yeah, I'm alright. I just need to take a shower. I'll be out in a little while. The coffee maker is ready to go. Just push the button. There are muffins and fruit. Help yourself, okay."

I climb into the shower and under the masked sound of running water; I have a good hard cry for Max. How am I going to fix this? Nothing like this has ever happened and I feel ill equipped to handle it. As I put on my make-up, I feel like I'm trying to hide what a bad mother I am. What have I done? What am I doing?

I find Javier out on the deck in a robe that I wish he'd had on earlier. He's set the table and created a delicious looking spread of fresh fruit and muffins. He gets up and pulls out a chair for me.

"Here, sit and have a cup of coffee. I'll take a quick shower and be right back." He plants a kiss on the top of my head. "Don't worry. Everything is going to be okay."

I pull my feet up onto the chair and sip my coffee with my knees tucked under my chin. My chair faces the sea. Watching the sailboats do their waltz across the shimmering water calms me. I reassure myself that Max and I will work through this. We're tight. We can do this. It could have been a lot worse. It could have been Renoir who walked in on a naked Javier in the kitchen. Knowing Ren, that sight could have damaged her for life either turning her into a nympho-maniac, or a nun. All she needed was one more good reason to crucify me and I'm sure she would have wasted no time running to Nathan with all the gory details. Who knows what the outcome of that would have been? I tuck my knees closer to my chest. A shiver runs through me.

Javier comes out to the deck with the coffee pot in hand.

"Refill?"

I hold out my cup and nod. He fills my cup and sets the pot down, takes the towel from around his neck and dries his arms. By the time I've finished my coffee and watched Javier dry his very strong looking chest, he's convinced me that Max will be fine. He even thinks that it's possible that Max didn't see as much as he first thought. I find myself trusting more in Max's resilience and our good relationship to see us through this.

"You Americans are too uptight about bodies and sex," he slowly runs the towel down his chest in a sensual way. "It's a natural thing. Oui? You just present it to him that way and I think he will see it that way."

I wish I could share his optimism.

While I clear the table and fill the dishwasher, Javier gets dressed for the day I've planned for us. I'm going to show him the local sites and if time and energy allow, we'll make a visit to Salem to see Rachel for a reading. I could use some confirmation since I'm finding this whole weekend more than a little surreal.

I pack us a picnic for a late lunch on the Headlands. It's a spot with a panoramic view of the sea and the town. It's one of my favorite places. I've already picked up things so we can make dinner in tonight, since this will be our last night together. Javier is catching a flight back to L.A. in the morning and I need to make the most of this time to find out what this thing is between us.

Before we head out, I go get the necklace that he gave me. I still can't believe he gave me such an expensive gift and I want to show him how much I appreciate his generous gesture.

As I pass the bathroom on my way upstairs, I hear Javier behind the door speaking to someone on his cell phone in muffled tones. When I come back downstairs, he's pacing in the living room. He stops short when he sees me.

"Can I use your computer for a few minutes? I forgot to bring my laptop and I need to check my email."

"Of course, it's right over in the corner at my desk."

He scrutinizes my laptop for a moment.

"Do you mind if I take it out to the deck?"

"Not at all. Is everything okay?"

"Yeah, fine. It's just a minor business thing."

He picks up the laptop and heads out to the deck, closing the door behind him. He positions himself facing the living room. It's probably paranoia on my part, but it feels as if something is up. I quietly open the door to get the empty coffee pot and he looks up abruptly.

"Could I have some privacy please?" He snaps, realizing as the words leave his mouth that he sounds irritated and he quickly covers for it by smiling at me sweetly.

I stop short at his reaction. I haven't seen this side of him before and it really takes me by surprise. I'm not sure what to make of it. I attempt to be gracious.

"Oh, I'm sorry. I was going to get the coffee pot, but I can get it later." I close the door softly and decide to take Aztec for a walk while he's taking care of business. I leave him a note saying where I am.

By the time Aztec and I have returned from the beach he's put the laptop back on my desk and is ready and waiting to go.

"I'm sorry for being a grouch to you," he apologizes, pulling me in toward him and hugging me.

"I've been really stressed about this business deal. I just needed to concentrate and get this thing taken care of or my partner will be on my ass."

"It's alright. I understand." I say, but I really don't. I'm not sure what to chalk his strange reaction up to. He takes my hand and kisses it.

We get to my car and Javier asks if he can drive and I toss him the keys. His driving is as exuberant as every other aspect of him as I direct him down the road to one of my favorite beaches. By the time we've finished our exploring and settled down atop the headlands with our lunch, the effects of the night before are catching up with me. The sun and food have a sedative effect and as Javier tells another one of his tales, I drift off to sleep curled up on the blanket like a cat basking in the sun. I don't know how long I'm asleep before I'm aware of his hands under my clothes traveling like heat seeking missiles in search of their target.

"What are you doing?" I ask, half asleep.

"You look so beautiful sleeping there, I want to make love to you."

"Right here?" I ask, pivoting my head around to find that we are alone for the moment.

"No one will see anything. We have this blanket we can wrap around us and if someone finds this spot they will realize they're intruding and go away."

"Oh really. You seem to have this all figured out."

He kisses me like a man who will be crushed by the word "no" as he deftly unhooks my bra.

"I love bras that unhook in the front." He murmurs and kisses my neck.

"Me too." I giggle as his hands explore.

"I want to hear you come." He sighs in my ear.

And even though I'm not at all comfortable with this, there under the clear blue sky with the gulls circling aimlessly I forget who I am, and where I am, and Javier gets his way.

The sound of voices rouses me out of my stupor and I shake Javier roughly to quickly wake him, while straightening my clothes as fast as I can. I barely manage to restore a somewhat respectable presentation, when a group of five Asian tourists with cameras appear. Javier subtly reaches over and smoothes my hair, which is sticking out in several directions. They're only about ten feet away from us as they pass by speaking in their native language. From the corner of my eye I can see them giving us suspicious, sidelong, glances. It doesn't take a translator to tell that they don't approve of the scene that Javier and I present. Giggling under our breath we pack up our picnic and blanket and head back to the car.

By the time we arrive at The New Moon Boutique in Salem, we find out that Rachel has left for the day. I tell Javier about my reading with her and her predictions, editing out the part about the other guy. I don't want to complicate things in his head any more than they probably already are. He finds it all fascinating and seems open to such things. When we leave Salem to head home, I'm exhausted and only too happy to hand him the car keys again.

We get back to my house, and Javier pulls a bottle of wine out of his suitcase. It comes from the vineyard that his family owns in France and he proudly opens it letting it breathe before he pours me a glass.

We sip wine and listen to music while we cook dinner, which amounts to me doing most of the cooking while Javier regales me with stories of what might be called his glory days. He rips off pieces of garlic bread and dips it into the red sauce I'm making for pasta. He moans his approval, rolling his eyes in ecstasy.

"Oh! That is delicious baby. Look at you. You're a beautiful, sexy, smart, woman who can cook like this! How lucky am I?" He comes from behind me encircling my waist and kisses the side of my neck in an impromptu dance.

We carry everything out to the deck and light several lanterns for light, as the sun sinks low in the sky. The waves whisper in to shore and a couple of brazen gulls light on the railing of the deck to see what smells so good. Javier tosses a few pieces of bread over the rail and they noisily dive in a competition to retrieve them.

After a couple of glasses of wine and a belly full of food we sleepily stretch out together on the chaise. Javier goes back into the living room and brings back the blanket that was on the couch. It's a little cooler than it's been lately and the light throw feels good. I snuggle in with my head on his shoulder and he tilts my face up to his and kisses me, softly at first, but with increasing intensity and after a few minutes he guides my hand downward. There it is again and larger than life. I stop kissing him and pull back slightly to look at him with mock terror. He grins and says,

"The beast has awakened."

"When, exactly was he asleep?"

"He naps," he says, sliding his hand up under my shirt.

"I see." I answer playfully in spite of another feeling creeping in along the edges. My body responds to the physical attention, but my heart feels removed and seems to be observing from somewhere outside of me. I feel like something is missing.

He pulls his pants off under the cover of the blanket and starts unzipping mine.

"Hey!" I swing my head around. "The neighbors can see us."

He gets up and with the blanket covering him and quickly extinguishes the lanterns. He returns to the chaise and begins removing my clothes with the focused determination of a man unburying treasure he's been anxious to find. We put the chaise to work as a creative prop in our play and in spite of the cool evening in a matter of minutes, I'm covered in beads of sweat. We fall asleep there on the deck and it's not until the temperature drops, that we wake enough to groggily drag ourselves upstairs to bed.

Chapter 42 ~ Au Revoir!

I wake the next morning at about seven and look over at Javier who is fast asleep on the pillow next to me. He has to leave to catch his plane at eleven so I should wake him up, I just want to lie there and look at him. I need to look at his face and ask myself, "Is this the face of the man I want to wake up to everyday? Is this the man I want to be with?" It's as if I'm looking at a jigsaw puzzle with so many pieces missing that I'm not sure what I'm looking at. The only thing I do know is that he's leaving in a couple of short hours and I need more time for all my many unanswered questions.

As if he feels my eyes on him he slowly opens his and smiles as he rolls onto me.

"What do you say? One last one to send me on my way."

"Jesus Javier, you've got to take it easy with that thing. I may never walk again."

"We can do other things. You just lay back and I'll take care of everything.

The next thing I know he's pulling toys and oils from his bag. We get so caught up in playing, that we completely lose track of time and getting him out the door ends up being a mad scramble.

When the limo driver shows up he rings the bell and I follow Javier down the stairs dragging ones of his bags with one hand and holding my robe closed with the other. We kiss, knowing it might be the last one for a long time. Out of the corner of my eye, I can see the limo driver pretending not to look.

"I'll call you tonight, sweetie," he says, stroking my cheek as I feel tears welling up in my eyes. He gives me a hug. "It's okay, baby. We'll figure it out."

He waves from the back window as the car pulls away. When it takes the corner and I can no longer see it, I go back into the house, slowly climbing the stairs. I wipe my face on the sleeve of my robe. I don't feel like they're tears of sadness. They're tears of frustrated confusion.

I crawl back into bed and bury my face in his pillow. I can still smell him on the sheets. I breathe in his scent and ask myself all the questions that come to my mind. What if I never see him again? Am I sad about that possibility? I feel like I have an emotional hangover. I'm not sure what just happened. I have to get some kind of perspective so I pick up the phone and call Paris.

"Is he still there?" she asks.

"No. He left a little while ago."

"So, how was it?"

"Well I don't think I'd ever be sexually bored. He's a little overwhelming. It's going to take me a while to physically recover."

"I had a feeling. You could tell from his photos that he was full of the devil. So, give me all the juicy details."

I walk around the room with the phone telling Paris about my weekend with Javier from start to finish. I mention the necklace and she perks up and asks me for a detailed description. I go over to my nightstand to pick it up so I can do it justice.

"Where did I put it? I thought I took it off before I went to sleep, but it could have come off when we were out on the deck if you know what I mean."

"Well that seems pretty serious honey. The man bought you an expensive piece of jewelry. That's very classy."

"Yeah, he's a pretty classy guy except in bed. In bed, he's an animal; a very big animal."

"Sounds like the perfect man to me." She laughs.

I wander downstairs and out to the deck looking for the necklace with no success.

"I can't find it anywhere. I'll be sick if I lost it."

"It'll turn up. I've got to run out to meet with a new client. Can I call you in a little while?"

After I hang up with Paris, I do a more in-depth search for the missing necklace checking under the chaise cushions and under the nightstand but it's still not turning up. I tell myself that if I stop trying so hard, I'll find it. I decide to send Javier an e-card for his arrival home.

I sit down to the computer, and go to my email account. I have a lot of new mail in my inbox and as I'm scanning down the list it's as if I've walked into my house, but none of the furniture is mine. I'm not sure what I'm looking at. There are several emails that are supposed to be responses to my emails on a dating site that I don't belong to. Perplexed, I open one up. It begins.

*Hi Javier... You sound as hot as you look.
I'm glad you liked my ad and I agree that we have a
LOT in common!*

It goes on and is dated as arriving today. I
can't seem to take it in. I don't know how it's
possible, but I'm in Javier's mailbox. I'm about to
click out of it when I notice there are several emails
from Gabriella. I'm suddenly feeling queasy, but I
want to know what's going on. I open the most
recent one and take a steadying breath.

Javier,
*I keep looking at this beautiful ring you gave
me and remembering your proposal to me only a
month ago and I can't believe that it's all been a lie.
How could you ask me to be your wife and make all
these plans for our future together while writing to
all these other women online and dating them?
Yeah, Javi, that's right I found out the truth and I
know what your little trip to the east coast is all
about. Business trip huh? I hope the sex is really
worth it. I just feel sorry for the poor bitch who
thinks you're going to move anywhere for anybody.
I thought you had changed. I thought that you had
learned your lesson from your last two marriages.
That was a very touching story you told me, by the
way. Too bad it was all a manipulative lie! I won't
be here when you get back. I'm packing all my stuff
and moving out. I've called George and told him
everything and he's offered to watch the kids till
you get back. It might be my imagination, but he
didn't seem at all surprised. Fuck you.*

P.S. I'm pawning the ring

I sit back so hard in my chair I feel like someone shoved me. I'm grasping the edges of the desk as if I'm hanging onto a ledge ten stories above a busy street. Instead of the usual hyperventilating I do under this kind of stressful situation, I'm holding my breath.

"Breathe." I order myself out loud and as soon as I let that first exhalation out, the tears come with it. Part of me wants to read more, but what would that do except tell me more of the same. He must have forgotten to close his mailbox when he used my laptop. Gabriella's message had come early yesterday morning. The phone call I'd overheard him having in the bathroom must have been an attempt on his part to placate her.

When I think about this drama that was going on in his life yesterday, the things we did together horrify me. I feel nauseous. How could I have been this clueless? I was fooled by a Class A manipulator. I'm pissed. I'm hurt. I'm pissed.

I refuse to feel like a victim. I'm not going to curl up in a ball and keep crying even though it would be easy to do that. All of this feels a little too eerily reminiscent of Nathan's cheating. Why did this happen? Is it something I'm doing? I get in the shower and play things over in my head. It's no longer surprising to me that I had felt disconnected to him in some inexplicable way. My gut had known something was wrong. I have to fight the feeling to beat up on myself for ignoring that wise voice within me. Why did I do that? I vow to myself in this moment, *never again.*

I get dressed, find my sunglasses, so it won't be so obvious that I've been crying, and grab Aztec's leash. She's only too happy to head out. I make my way downtown to the shop where Javier and I had stopped on our way to dinner and there in the window, prominently displayed is the same tourmaline and pearl necklace. I loop Aztec's leash around a bench outside the door and walk in. There's a young woman behind the counter and I ask her if I can see the piece. She takes it out of the window for me.

"This is beautiful," I say, when she hands it to me. My hands are shaking. She nods at my response. "Do you have more of these?" I ask.

She shakes her head. "That's the only one we have and it was actually returned just this morning by a man who had bought it as a gift for his girlfriend. He said she broke up with him before he got a chance to give it to her."

"She didn't time that very well did she?" I manage to feign a laugh as I hand it back to her. "I hope she had a good reason for kicking him to the curb."

"I don't know. He seemed pretty nice, cute and he had a great accent."

I thank her and head back home. I go straight to my computer and print out several of his emails so I have a tangible record of the transgression just in case I try to romanticize what happened. I think about what the girl in the shop had said. He did seem nice, but people and things are not always what they seem. After Nathan's lies, Cole's deception and now this, it would seem that I have a talent for attracting dishonest men.

I'm not going to get sad. I'm going to get even. For what it's worth, Javier is going to have to deal with some more fallout. I open Gabriella's email and I begin composing an email back to her.

Hi Gabriella,

My name is Nicola. I'm the "business trip" here in the east. Javier left a little while ago to catch his flight back home and I just read your email to him. He totally screwed up and left his mailbox open on my computer so, like you, I now know the truth. I wanted you to know that I had no idea Javier was in a relationship with anyone. If I had any idea that he was with someone, I never would have pursued something with him. I feel awful that he lied to you and awful that he lied to me. The picture he painted was that he was looking for someone to be in a serious relationship with and he had given me every indication that he thought I might be that person, but here you are living with him with a ring on your finger. He's been emailing and phoning me for months. It felt real

Nicola

After I hit send, I sit here thinking about that last line. It had felt real, but it hadn't been real. I had been caught up in a faux-mance. In the world of online, virtual love, it was so easy to mistake this new form of connecting as real intimacy. But none of it had been true or real. This man had gone from my computer, to my home, to my bed, and out of my life in one short weekend.

Chapter 43 ~ The Opposite of Gravity

Almost a month later, an apologetic email arrives from Javier. I don't know why he even bothered except perhaps, to appease his guilt. He says he's sorry if he hurt me and that it wasn't his intention. He says he was confused about marrying Gabriella and he needed to know that he wasn't settling. He says his kids love her and that she's a big help with them. He says it would be impossible for him to move his kids across the country even though he has custody. Blah, blah, blah. He says a lot of things he should have said way before he ever decided to get on a plane, fly here, and mess with my life. The bullshit is so deep, I consider climbing up on my desk to escape its rising tide. I don't bother to respond.

As much as I feel betrayed by Javier, I can honestly say my heart doesn't feel broken, only slightly bruised. It surprises me that after the daily routine of speaking with him on the phone every day for the past four months, I barely miss his presence. Paradoxically, the person I find, that I do miss is Cole.

I wouldn't say I'm in a state of depression. It's more like feeling profoundly discouraged. I take care of my clients and my kids with an almost robotic precision. Meals are always on time. I never miss an appointment. The house is always clean. My life is TV with the volume and color turned down.

As bland as my waking hours are, my dreams are the polar opposite. It's a world of intense drama, noise and riotous color, populated with mythical looking creatures and places. I start telling them to Paris who is a big believer in signs.

One night I have dream with Cole in it. In it, I'm at home and he comes to the door and asks me to go with him. He tells me he had something to show me. I'm intrigued. We walk to this huge open meadow and he says,

"I want you to run and then jump into the air." I hesitate and look at him, a perplexed expression on my face. He simply gestures with his head as if to say, "Away you go." So I run and jump.

To my amazement, I rise into the air and soar at least thirty feet. I land softly and turn around. I look at him with my eyes wide and my mouth agape. He lowers his eyes and grins at me, then gestures for me to do it again, coming back toward him. I do. This time I go even higher and I begin laughing uncontrollably. I land at least ten feet past him, laughing so hard, I'm crying. It feels amazing. Breathlessly, I turn to him and ask,

"What is this?"

He smiles at me slyly and quietly says, "it's the opposite of gravity."

I do it again and again and I can't believe how good I feel and when I'm too tired to do it anymore he takes me home and says, with his eyes warmly melting, "I wanted to show you that." We stand there, inches apart, and I have the urge to kiss him, but he turns and walks away before I get a chance

The next morning I tell Paris the dream.

"Tell me again," she says.

So I tell her again and she laughs. "What did you eat before you went to sleep?" She teases. "I think I know what it means. You know what I think the opposite of gravity is?

It sounds like a trick question and I answer her slowly. "No."

"It's levity!"

"Levity?"

"Yes, levity! That boy wanted to show you how to lighten up, honey. Lighten up and have some fun. Levity is the opposite of gravity!" I hear her laughing at the other end.

Levity. Fun. They're two words that haven't been a part of my recent reality, or vocabulary. The dream with Cole is the first time I've had those feelings since finding out the truth about Javier. I've noticed Renoir and Max watching me anxiously, looking for signs that I'm returning to the abyss I inhabited when their father left. I've walked to its edge several times and stared into its familiar depths, but I keep backing away. I don't ever want to be that person again. It's a struggle, and in a way more than ever, because of what is going on around me. Sophia and Theo are deeply in love and her father's bigoted heart is opening. Jeff has moved in with Kate and for the time being they are at peace with their differing needs. Lily and James completely hit it off and for the past few weeks, have been commuting back and forth on weekends between Rhode Island and Massachusetts. I'm so happy for all of them. Happy and desperately envious, I'm a barren island in the midst of a sea of love with nothing but rocky coastline, a few scrub pines, and windblown gulls to claim as my own.

"So," she says, "you wanted to kiss him."

"It was a dream and we had just had a great time and he had those lips."

"Yeah, he does have good lips for a white guy," she teases. "You should call him."

"I'm not going to call him. Why would I call him?"

"To get yourself some of that good levity."

"He's a con artist."

"Well," she drawls, "I don't know if he's a con artist, but he is an artist and I just so happen to have an invitation to his opening at the Acacia Gallery in three weeks. It's going to be a very chic affair and I need a date. Don't say no, say maybe."

I pause. "Maybe."

"That's a good girl," she says, patronizingly and I imagine kicking her in the shins.

After I hang up I go up to my room and lay down on my bed. I close my eyes and play the dream over in my mind trying to recapture the feeling of bliss. After a few frustrating minutes, I quit trying and sit up. Cole's fountain is on the opposite wall. I go over, plug it in, and return to my bed where I sit contemplating it, and the possibility of seeing him again.

Chapter 44 ~ Love and Envy

Lily calls me the next morning, just as I'm getting out of the shower. I hold the phone between my ear and my shoulder awkwardly drying off. Her voice has the same excited quality that it's seemed to have had every since she met James.

"What are you doing tonight? Do you have the kids?" She asks.

"No, I have them this weekend. I'm not doing anything after work."

"Great, Sophia and Kate aren't doing anything either. I want to have you all over for dinner. Would seven be okay? It seems like we haven't just hung out for a while and I have a surprise."

"A surprise?" I ask.

"Yes, it's a good one."

"It sounds like fun. Can I bring something?"

"Just you. I can't talk right now. I've got to meet a client at nine and I'm not even dressed yet." She giggles, as if even running behind schedule is a new source of fun.

After we hang up, I begin to look forward to getting out of the house and spending some time with the girls. Except for going to work, I've been a bit of a recluse lately and I'm feeling like its time to start venturing out again.

Just before I leave work Sophia calls asking if I can pick her up at her house since her car is in the shop again. There's something oddly comforting about the familiar ritual of pulling into her driveway, flashing my high beams at her kitchen windows, and seeing her hand wave with one finger up to let me know she needs a minute. When she climbs into the car and begins dramatically recounting her day with her arms broadly gesturing, I feel more peaceful than I have in weeks. This is the world I know and love. I find a parking space almost directly in front of Lily's building and we spot Kate a few yards up the street pulling in. As Sophia and I wait on the sidewalk for Kate to catch up with us, she continues her rant temporarily snapping out of it to give Kate a hug and then resuming where she left off without missing a beat. She starts to wind down as I knock on Lily's door. Lily answers the door with a smile that almost needs more cheek area to spread out on. She dishes out hugs and kisses all around as she gently herds us into her white on white living room. There's soft jazz playing in the background and lots of candles illuminate the room. Kate makes the first wisecrack of the evening.

"Well, isn't this romantic. I should have worn better underwear."

Lily strikes a pose with both hands on hers hips. "That's because I was feeling romantic. She cocks her head to the side and slowly rolls her eyes toward the ceiling.

"Notice anything different?" she asks, and we begin scanning, starting at the top of her head. Kate continues to be the quickest. She discovers the sparkler flashing on Lily's finger and I hear her inhale sharply just as Sophia and I spot it. There's an instantaneous three-part chorus of, "OH MY GAWD!" Kate reaches out, grabbing Lily by the hand and we all lean in to check it out.

"Wow!"

"When?"

"WOW!"

Lily beams. "I know. I can't believe it either. We went to the movies last night and even though the place was almost empty, he wanted to sit on an aisle seat, which I thought was weird cause he usually loves to sit in the middle. He said his stomach was bothering him and honestly, he didn't seem like he was feeling well. He looked a little sweaty. I asked him if he wanted to go home and he said no he'd be fine. So, the previews are on and he goes out to get me popcorn and soda and he hands it to me and I'm scarfing my popcorn down and he's looking at me funny like I'm eating like a pig, or something. Then that message comes on the screen about shutting off your cell phone and then this screen comes up and it says in big letters "LILY, WILL YOU MARRY ME?" And just as I'm reading that my fingers hit something in the popcorn. So, I pull out this little box and open it, and there's a ring, and I realize he's on his knee in the aisle. He takes the box out of my hand and takes the ring out and says, 'Lily Summer, will you be my wife?' It all happened so fast. I was laughing and crying at the same time and as you can see, I said yes. The five people who were there were clapping and cheering. It was so sweet."

There's a collective, "OH" from all of us, that sounds like the same one that people make when they see a new baby.

Lily has her coffee table set with plates, silver, and champagne glasses. Kate does the honors and pops the cork. While she pours, Lily goes to the kitchen and comes back with a huge platter of sushi and condiments. She pulls out a bunch of floor pillows and we sprawl out lounging, sipping, and nibbling.

"Have you guys talked about a date?" Sophia asks, between bites.

"We're thinking about the first week in December."

"That's only three months away. How are you ever going to plan a wedding in only three months?" asks Kate.

"We're going to keep it very simple. His birthday is on the eleventh of December and we'd like to have it close to that."

"What's the rush?" I ask, hoping my envy isn't completely transparent. I'm so happy for Lily. The irony of the situation is a little much for me. Lily met James for the first time only hours before I met Javier and look what she got compared to what I got. I feel like the heavens opened up and rained Rose petals on Lily, and sharp rocks on me.

Lily's face goes softer than a bale of cotton. "There's a big rush. I don't want to wait one minute longer than I have to, to be his wife."

It's so heartfelt that even I can't help joining the others in an involuntary chorus of, "OH, sweetie."

With that, the conversation turns to talk of bridal gowns, food, places for the reception, and the band. We're in unanimous agreement that if it were at all possible, Terrence's band would be the perfect choice.

"James hasn't heard them yet. We'll have to find out when they're playing so I can take him to see them. Could you find out from Paris?" Lily asks me.

"Sure, sweetie I'll talk to her about the whole thing."

By about nine the food, the champagne, and the big news have left me feeling really drained. I call it a night, with the plan to go out with them the next time Terrence's band is playing out.

When I drop Sophia off at her house she gives me a big hug and asks,

"How are you doing?"

"I'm fine." I muster an unimpressive smile.

She just sits there looking at me. "Really?"

"Really." I insist.

"If it was me, I think I would be pretty bummed," she says. "There's just no way to know when someone is going to be a lying asshole, or when they're going to turn out to be the man of your dreams. I'm the first one to admit I can't judge at all. If you had told me a year ago that I was going to find the best love of my life with a black man and it was going to all work out fine with my bigoted father, I'd have peed my pants laughing at you."

I nod my head in silent agreement. Sophia's right. There is no way to know and right now I feel like I could be *the* least knowing person in the world. I try to swallow the hard lump in my throat.

The next morning I call Paris and tell her Lily's news. She too, doesn't miss the irony of the situation and she feels the need to console me.

"I'm okay." I tell her. "I'm really happy for Lily. I just want to be happy for me too."

"I know, sweetie."

"So, I'm on a mission to find the best band I can for this wedding. Can you help me?"

Paris pulls Terrence's schedule of gigs up on her computer. "She wants to have it on the Saturday after the eleventh? Let's see, he has a tentative Christmas party booked, but we haven't received a deposit yet, so you're in luck."

I call Lily after I hang up with Paris to give her the good news and I get her machine, where I leave a message. I almost feel relieved that I don't have to talk to her.

The phone rings and I check the Caller ID to make sure it isn't her and I see that it's Kate. I brace myself for more possible consoling.

"Hi, Nic. Are you upset about this? You seemed a little off last night."

"I guess I suck at hiding my feelings."

"Yeah, I'd love to play poker with you. Talk about easy money."

"Do you think Lily noticed my less than enthusiastic reaction?" I ask.

"Lily's in such a state of bliss she wouldn't notice if you pulled a monkey out of your ass and sat it down next to her. Listen, I want to throw them an engagement party and I need your help. Are you in?"

"It sounds kind of therapeutic. What can I do to help you, Ms. Winslow?"

The kids get dropped off just before lunch and they're a wonderful diversion with their usual demands and noise. Getting caught up in our normal Saturday routine of laundry and chores takes my mind off of everything else. Since the disappearance of Javier and online dating, both of the kids have seemed more relaxed, especially Renoir.

She seems to like this new Stepford-mom version of me.

I drop Max off at Kate's to hang out with Homer and then I take Ren and her boyfriend Tyler, a surprisingly sweet, patient boy, to the mall to see a movie with their friends. I decide to go shopping for a wedding gift for Lily and James. One of the places they're registered at is Williams and Sonoma. Since it's a list with things like a pasta maker and other tools, nothing out of the ordinary, I decide to wait for something more inspiring. I want to give them something special. I think I know just the thing and where to find it.

Chapter 45 ~ The Opening

With so much going on, it seems as though Lily's wedding day is rushing to meet us. I've been so busy helping Kate plan the engagement party and Lily plan the wedding, that I've pretty much forgotten about my date with Paris to go see Cole's opening at the Acacia Gallery. She calls to remind me and let me know that there will be no backing out for any reason other than an extreme act of God.

She's smart. She's waited until only two days before, so I won't have enough time to concoct a good excuse, or scheme. She even called Nathan to arrange for him to take the kids for the night, since it's my weekend to have them. So, rather than throwing myself down my stairs and breaking a leg, I opt to be her reluctant date. Even though the thought of being in the same building with Cole still send a tremor through me.

The reception starts at seven thirty with cocktails. When Paris shows up at my house at seven twenty to pick me up, I haven't even showered yet. You could say that I'm trying to delay the inevitable. It's an old strategy that I used to use as a child to put off something I preferred not to do. It didn't work well then, and it isn't working well now.

"Get your ass in the shower now, or I'm going to make you go looking like that." She says, in her no nonsense mom voice. I obey, like the naughty child I know I'm being.

As I'm putting on makeup, she comes through the door with several possible outfits, which I give the ax to before going with a slinky black skirt with a ruffled hem and a deep red, off the shoulder sweater. By the time I zip up my boots, my creative foot-dragging keeps us from heading out the door until eight forty-five.

We arrive a little after nine-thirty. The party is in high gear and we're able to walk in completely under the radar. Acacia is a large gallery with three levels. It's so packed that we're there for almost another fifteen minutes before we spot Cole with a gorgeous, chic looking woman hanging on his arm. She looks a little older than him. Maybe that's his thing. Older women. Seeing him sends an ache through me. Seeing him with another woman makes my heart feel like it's been dropped off a cliff. Paris turns to me.

"Do you want to go say *Hi*?"

I shake my head. "Not yet. I want to look around first. It looks like he's found someone very attentive."

Paris doesn't respond to my comment as she watches a waitress walk by with a tray just out of her reach. "They just brought out some great looking food and I need to get me some. I'm starving."

"Champagne?" a waitress asks at my elbow and I hand her my empty glass trading it for a full flute.

"You might not want to get drunk." Paris suggests, in an overly casual tone.

"I don't plan to, Mom. This is my second and I'm going to stop there, FYI"

"I'm just saying." She's pretending it's no big deal, but I can tell she's going to be keeping an eye on me.

"I hear ya." I reply and walk away.

I enter a room with several tall clocks that look like Cole consulted with Dr. Seuss after time traveling back here from the medieval days. There are two beautiful fountains that remind me of mine except they're both about ten feet tall and not as sensual in their shape. As I'm standing there contemplating them, a question materializes in the air next to my ear.

"Would you prefer one of these bigger ones?"

I turn at the sound of Cole's voice. "No," I answer slowly, collecting myself, "haven't you heard that size doesn't matter. I love my fountain. Besides, I don't think I've got the muscle to lug one of these puppies up all those stairs."

"Well, if that's the issue, I could take care of that for you."

Since I don't know what to say to his generous offer, I just smile back at him. We stand there smiling at each other for what feels like an absurd amount of time. I'm trying to remember why I was so angry with him. Finally, my brain snaps to, long enough for me to formulate a reasonably intelligent comment.

"Your work is like nothing I've ever seen before."

"But do you like it?" he jokes, tipping his head to the side and running a hand through his hair. He momentarily looks awkward and shy as he points to my empty glass. "Can I get you another?"

I wave off his offer. "No, thank you. It's my second and I haven't eaten anything yet so it went straight to my head."

"You haven't eaten anything? Well, let's get you some food, okay?" He extends his hand and smiles.

I shyly take it and he gently begins towing me into the next room, weaving us in and out of the crowd like fish swimming against the current. Heads turn as we pass and hands reach out from the sea of people, touching him as he flows by. With his free hand he touches them back without pausing, moving across the room gracefully distributing love. The pulse of dance music and the noise of conversation are much louder in this room. The lighting is dramatic, accenting some large pieces. Trailing close behind him in my inebriated state is a surreal journey. A door materializes in front of him and as his hand reaches to open it, the chic woman materializes out of the ethers, instantly placing herself between Cole and the door. She looks down at his hand holding mine and then at me over his shoulder. I see her quickly arrange her features in a big smile that doesn't involve her eyes. She extends her hand toward me.

"Hello, I'm Chantal Tousseau. I'm Cole's agent." She says, laying her other hand on his chest and sliding him a sideways glance that implies more.

I let go of Cole's hand and shake her hand. "I'm Nicki Botticelli. It's nice to meet you. The show is fantastic."

She continues looking at me with her flat, shark eyes. Her perfect teeth flash like trophies. "Botticelli, like the artist? How perfect." She looks me up and down.

Cole gestures toward the door. "I'm getting Nicki something to eat. I'll talk to you in a minute." He reaches for my hand again, She opens her mouth to speak and he pulls me through the door closing it behind us and shutting out that other world.

The light is so bright in here. I blink for a few seconds as my eyes adjust. It's a kitchen area with the catering staff buzzing about. Cole grabs a plate and begins heaping it with hors d'oeuvres. He fills another plate with cheese and crackers and hands it to me. He reaches into the refrigerator and pulls out a bottle of champagne.

"Follow me." He says.

I tentatively follow behind him. My trepidation is trumped by my curiosity.

We pass through the maze of catering people moving like choreographed ants, through a door on the other end of the kitchen, and enter an instantly quiet space. Cole brings up the dimmer switch and I see that the walls are covered with large abstract paintings.

"What is this room?" I ask, slowly pivoting around.

"This gallery has a section that they devote to paintings only. They're getting ready for a show for this artist. That's why it isn't completely hung."

He sets the plate of food down on a long upholstered viewing bench and pats the spot next to him for me to sit down. He pops the cork on the champagne, pours some in the cups and hands me one.

"I think I need to eat something before any more alcohol passes my lips."

"Just a toast," he says.

"Okay." I say. I hold my cup to his. We sit looking at each other for a moment. His eyes study my face. I think he's going to kiss me. I hold my breath. His face melts into a grin,

"To unexpected dinner companions."

I laugh and take a small sip following it with some salmon puffs. I'm so hungry that each bite of food that enters my mouth is met with focused rapture. It's not until I've woofed down an entire plateful of food, that I look up from my Hoovering and realize he's been watching me.

"Geez, I'm sorry. I'm like Pig Girl here."

"Is she some new super-hero? Because, I think Pig Girl kicks butt. I don't believe I've ever seen a woman eat that much food in front of me ever. Except my mom and that shouldn't count."

"Great," I grimace, "now, there's something I want to be memorable about me."

"There are a lot of things that are memorable about you. It's just one more thing to add to the list."

"There's a list?" I ask, nervously.

"Oh, yeah."

"Geez." I exhale under my breath and look around at the canvases leaning against the walls.

309

"I don't really get this stuff, do you?" I ask, changing the subject.

He answers, "The way I understand it, it's free to interpretation. Take this one in front of us. I see a women lying on her side and her head is tilted back. She's gazing up into the branches of the tree above her, which is full of exotic birds."

I squint at it and tilt my head to the side. "Really? You can see that?"

He points to the one behind him over his shoulder. "Go ahead, you try one."

I ponder it a moment and then begin making up my analysis. "Okay, I see two people, they're traveling down a road and there are wild animals hiding in the woods that line the road. The people are afraid that the wild animals are going to eat them."

He's watching my face as I study the painting. He turns to look at it when I finish.

"What do you see?" I ask.

He takes a deep breath, squints slightly and purses his lips.

"I also see a man and a woman. There's a chasm between them separating them. It's deep, but it's not wide." He turns back to me, looking into my eyes. "They're closer to each other than they realize. It's just a matter of stepping over the chasm and those are people hiding in the woods. They're waiting to see what they'll do. Some are hoping that they'll keep to their side of the chasm and some are hoping that they'll take that step."

I'm barely breathing. "That's what you see?" I ask softly.

"Yeah," he holds my gaze. "That's what I see."

The door we came through flies open and Chantal strides in. Her stilettos click loudly on the tiled floor.

"Cole, sweetheart, there are people out there buying some major pieces and they'd love to meet the artist and here you are, hiding out with your little friend." She makes no attempt to hide her condescension.

He turns back to me. "Duty calls, little friend. I've got to go pimp my ass. I'm glad you came and that we got to talk."

"Me too."

He leans forward and kisses my forehead. "Be good, Nicki Botticelli." He whispers into my ear.

Chantal stands at the open door with her arms folded across her chest. I see her skin flexing along her jaw. As Cole passes her, she gives me a quick look that seems to say, "Back off!"

I sit there on the bench and sip the champagne in my cup, contemplating the painting we just looked at. Now that he's pointed out the chasm to me I see it clearly. Now I see it all.

Chapter 47 ~ Channeling John Cusak

On the car ride home, Paris fills me in on all
the gossip she managed to get out of Alexa, one of
the Gallery's owners. Chantal, it seems has a
penchant for young, attractive, promising, male
artists. With her background in PR, she can market
almost anything, so talent isn't always part of the
equation. Sex is. She has a short-term fling with her
talented flavor of the moment and then moves on to
the next flavor. Presently, her taste is for Cole and
according to Alexa, Chantal feels it's just a matter
of time, and little time at that, before he becomes
her next conquest.

Alexa isn't so sure. Cole, she feels, is a little
older and wiser than the usual neophyte. And
although she has noted a definite chemistry between
them, she's not sure if that is going to work for
Chantal this time. Chantal seems to be enjoying this
more challenging prey and has stepped up her game
of seduction. A man would have to be missing a
pulse not to appreciate the dazzlingly long legs
perched on stilettos and perfectly framed, perfumed
décolletage. I listen to all of this with an
accelerating level of discomfort that's only reduced
when I picture dumping a bucket of fish bait over
her head.

"So, what are you going to do about this,
girlie?" Paris asks me gruffly. "Are you going to let
some nasty wolf bimbo in expensive designer sheep
suits steal your man?"

"He's not my man, Paris."

"And whose fault is that?" She snaps.

"Mine?" I ask. My voice is barely audible.

"Damn straight!" She whacks the dashboard of her car.

It bothers me. I can't stop obsessing about it. The thought of Cole and that woman makes me feel like crying and throwing up at the same time. I keep picturing how territorial she was. Hell, she did everything, but pee in a circle around him. After several mostly sleepless nights, I have a plan. It's a plan that scares the shit out of me. When it occurs to me, it seems so perfect, that I know I have to do it. My fear is so strong, that it takes me two days to psych myself up to follow through on it. I call Paris to tell her that I Googled his address.

"Finally! You go get that man!"

"We'll see."

"That's the wrong attitude. You're going to get nothing with an attitude like that. Honey, that man is yours for the taking. I've seen the way he looks at you."

"You think so?" I ask, with complete uncertainty.

"I know it and you have to know it too. Say it, girl. Say, 'I know it!"

"I know it."

"Louder!"

"IKNOWIT!"

"That's better."

The next night I buy a bottle of Baileys to bring to Cole as a gift. I shower and put on jeans and a pullover shirt. I don't want to look like I'm trying too hard and I hope dressing casually will mask how desperate I feel inside. I take the directions and my old boom box and get into my car. Even though I've put on a thick layer of antiperspirant my armpits feel soggy. I practice breathing deeply for the thirty minutes it takes me to get there. All that breathing doesn't make me feel relaxed, but I do feel lightheaded.

I find Raven Lane and make my way along this tiny back road. It's quiet and wooded and through the trees I glimpse the river, or the occasional home. I come around a bend and I see a sign made of a mix of found objects, for the Cole McCarthy Studio. I stop, straining to peer down the long drive. It's twilight and I can make out what looks like a house to the left and down closer to the water a smaller building that must be his studio. Lights are on in this building and I imagine he must be working. I have the sudden awful thought that Chantal may be here and I look for another car beside Cole's pickup. From this vantage point I can't be certain. I pull the car over as much as I possibly can on this little road and try to think. I hadn't anticipated this possibility and panic is setting in. I try talking my way through it with no luck and ultimately decide to have a little of the Bailey's to calm my nerves. After about twenty minutes and a considerable amount of sipping, I decide that I need to investigate before it gets too dark. Slowly, I make my way down the long driveway.

I feel like I'm traveling through an enchanted forest. Pieces of Cole's work dot the landscape. Some of the pieces are draped with climbing and flowering plants. It's all a little wild, slightly overgrown, mysterious, and fairytale-like.

I shut off my headlights and kill the engine, as I roll up next to Cole's truck. There aren't any other vehicles. I sit for a few minutes swigging Bailey's, and try to catch a glimpse of him in his studio. He has to be here. I pick up the boom box, load the CD in, and cue it to the song. Awkwardly, I climb out of my car and that's when I realize how drunk I am. I wobble my way to the end of the driveway until I'm less than twenty feet from the door of the studio. All the windows are open and I catch a glimpse of him with his back to me. He appears to be staring out at the river.

It's a beautiful night and I feel like this is one of those moments that no matter what happens, I will remember it for the rest of my life. I hear the sound of the river and the wind in the trees. I smell the sweetness of the pine needles beneath my feet. My fingers fumble as I push play, turn the volume up, and lift the boom box above my head sending the sound of Peter Gabriel's voice out across the space between us.

At first it seems that he can't hear it and just as I'm about to turn it up, he turns. I can't see the look on his face clearly and I'm so nervous a strong shudder passes through me. A moment later he appears at the door and slowly pushes it open. The

315

look in his eyes makes my fear float up and off into the night sky. I continue to hold it above my head as he walks toward me. His eyes are shining. As the song comes to an end, I shut it off and set it down on the ground. We stand there looking at each other. Neither of us speaks. A breeze caresses the silence between us.

"I love that song," he says, stuffing his hands deep into his pockets.

"Yeah." I agree.

"I love that movie"

"I know. Me too."

"So, you're John Cusack."

"I guess I am."

"Then that would make me Ione Skye?"

I start to giggle and cover my mouth with my hand "I guess so," I say, rocking on my feet just slightly. He catches it and his eyes narrow slightly.

"Are you drunk?"

I nod my head and look down at his shoes.

"You didn't drive here like that?"

"God. No. I sat in my car up the road trying to get up the guts to do this and I brought you a bottle of Bailey's." I gesture toward my car. "Sorry, but I drank some of it. Most of it."

He shakes his head and a huge grin spreads across his face.

"Nicola Botticelli, this is one of the craziest, most romantic things that's ever happened to me and I don't think you're in any condition to go anywhere. You look like you're going to tip over."

"I don't feel so good." I say, putting my hand up to my head.

"You need some food, and to lay down."

He takes me by the hand and moves toward the house. It's then that he realizes how wobbly I am on my feet.

"I think you need a lift." He scoops me up and I wrap my arms around his neck, and lay my forehead against his cheek.

"Thank you." I murmur.

He kisses my forehead and carries me into his house. Gently, he lays me down on the sofa, propping a throw pillow under my head.

"I'm going to get you some water and bread. I think we need to dilute the alcohol in your stomach."

I nod my head and he goes to the refrigerator. His home is cozy and has a garage sale, grandma's hand-me-downs, eclectic quality. It's orderly, and comfortably unkempt at the same time. He sees me looking around and as if he's reading my mind he says,

"I wasn't expecting company."

I draw my knees up and hug them. "I like it. It's very homey." The room seems to tip a little and I grab the arm of the couch to steady myself.

He hands me the glass of water and sits down next to me. Then he slips my shoes off and puts my feet on his lap. He picks one up and begins massaging it.

"Cute feet."

I'm immediately thankful that I got a recent pedicure.

"Thank you," I eye him over the rim of my glass.

"How about an omelet and some toasted French bread?"

"That sounds delicious, but if I hurl please don't take it personally."

"I won't," he laughs and pauses, "and I understand that you felt scared out there. When we were at the gallery I wanted to kiss you, but the last time I did that you left in a hurry so I didn't."

"You wanted to kiss me?" I slur and lean toward him.

He looks at me like I'm adorably stupid and I give him a bleary-eyed smile.

"Right now I need to make you something to eat. You lay back and relax."

He puts on some soft music and starts cooking, filling the room with wonderful smells.

"How do you like your toast, light, or dark?"

"Medium, please."

"You have nice manners."

"Thank you." I giggle.

He fills a tray with plates of food and sets it down on the ottoman next to me. He helps me to sit up, drapes a large cloth napkin across my lap and sets a plateful of food on top of it.

"This looks wonderful, thank you, Cole."

As we eat I start to feel a little less drunk, but sleepier by the mouthful.

"This is so good. What did you put in the omelet?"

"It's Boursin cheese."

"You're a good cook."

"I have a very limited repertoire, so don't get any unrealistic expectations."

"You could just be the omelet guy and I would be perfectly happy with that."

"Omelet Guy. I like that. I could get a shirt with a big O on it."

I make a face and shake my head. "Yeah, maybe not." He laughs.

When I've finished eating I set my plate down on the tray. "I feel much better now." I yawn and shiver at the same time. Cole doesn't miss a thing. He disappears into the bedroom and emerges with a blanket, and drapes it over me. He moves over to the fireplace like someone who has done it many times before, and quickly builds a fire. Once it gets going he shuts off the floor lamp and joins me on the couch. The room is bathed in firelight, which dances on the walls and across Cole's handsome features.

"Is that better?" He asks.

"This is wonderful, thank you."

He finds one of my feet again and begins rubbing it. I'm so relaxed and warm I can barely keep my eyes open. I yawn.

"Stay here tonight. I won't make any moves on you." He takes his hand and raises two fingers. "Scout's honor. You can even have my bed."

"Thank you, but I'm okay right here." I say, and with heavy eyes I drift off.

Chapter 48 ~ Secrets, Clues and Answers

Something in these unfamiliar surroundings wakes me, and it takes me a few moments to orient myself and figure out where I am. The fire has burned down to a few glowing embers and provides little light. I can barely make out Cole, who has fallen asleep at the other end of the sofa and doesn't look at all comfortable. I gently shake him awake.

"Hey you," he says, rubbing his face. "Did I nod off?"

"We both did. I have no idea what time it is. You should go climb into your bed and get some real sleep."

"Come with me." He puts his hand out to me. I look down at his hand and back up at his face before taking it. He carefully leads me through the dark from the living room to his bedroom. He turns down the covers and sits me down on the edge of the bed. I slip out of my jeans and climb under the sheets. Even though the light is low I can see that Cole has stripped down to his underwear before he climbs in beside me. I shiver against the coolness of the sheets. He leans over and lights a candle on the bedside table before he moves next to me.

"Is this okay?" he asks, brushing my hair back off my forehead.

"Yes," I answer, looking into his face. His eyes shine in the dim candlelight. We lay there looking into each other's eyes. He kisses my forehead and when he looks back at me, I kiss his mouth.

We kiss, and it's a dance with a partner who moves in time with you. We kiss, and he draws me closer to him. We kiss, and I melt into him. I feel him hard against me. I want to be as close to him as possible and I struggle to pull my shirt up over my head. When I get stuck, we both laugh as he works to free me. He undoes my bra and softly kisses my skin. We lay back down, naked against each other. We're both smiling and he says what I'm thinking.

"This isn't where I thought I'd be when I got up this morning."

"Life is surprising."

"Indeed." He chuckles, and trails his fingertips along my skin.

"Are you nervous?" I ask him.

"No, not at all. I'm just happy." He says it so calmly.

"I am." My heart is pounding. I take his hand and press it against my chest so he can feel it.

He strokes my hair and kisses my face and mouth. "Don't be, sweet girl." He whispers between kisses, "I want to take care of you. I just want you to feel good and safe."

He delicately moves his fingertips across my skin, sending a current through me. He's a man in search of secrets and clues. I can feel him listening to my body like a thief listening to the tumblers of a safe. I surrender every answer his hands, lips, and eyes seek.

We explore each other's bodies, touching, tasting and breathing in each other's scent, until the sun begins to warm this edge of the world and we are completely spent from giving and receiving so much pleasure. We fall asleep tangled in each other.

When I finally wake hours later, I can tell by the angle of the light entering the room that it's around noon. I haven't slept this late in a long time. Across from my pillow is Cole's sleeping face. He looks peaceful and beautiful. His breathing is deep and even. I move closer to him, kissing the tip of his nose lightly and waiting for a reaction. He stirs slightly and then settles back down. I do it again. This time I kiss his mouth. He makes a sound like someone who just tasted something delicious and without opening his eyes he wraps himself around me like an octopus.

"So, it wasn't just a really great dream," he says, trapping me in a full-body bear hug, and kissing my neck. I half-heartedly struggle to free myself.

He gets up to make a trip to the bathroom and I get a good look at him in all his naked glory. I find myself thinking, *God, he's young and gorgeous*! As he walks back into the room, he notices me checking him out and looks pleased. He climbs into bed and starts to peel the covers back off of me. I grab at them to cover myself, suddenly feeling self-conscious.

"Hey, you just saw mine," he teases.

"Noooooo." I whine.

"Come on." He coaxes, gently pulling the covers out of my grip and slowly peeling them back exposing me little by little. I lay there with both hands over my face, my eyes tightly closed.

"Now why would anyone want to hide all this beauty?" he asks, distributing light kisses on my skin as he moves down my tummy. "This body is too beautiful for clothes. You should be naked all the time."

I peer out at him from under my hands and he looks back up at me with a grin.

"So, tell me, Ms. Botticelli, how is it that you happen to be naked in my bed?"

"What do you mean?"

"I'm wondering what caused this remarkable change of heart."

"Oh." I falter, "Well, mostly I missed you and when I saw you at the Acacia Gallery it really hit me how much I missed you."

He seems to like that answer and plants several more kisses on my tummy.

"And then there was Chantal." I add.

"Chantal?" He looks up from my tummy.

"She really freaked me out with the way she kept touching you and looking at you and the thought of you being with her was too upsetting."

He props himself up on his elbows. "Whoa, wait a minute, me with Chantal? That would *never* happen. I think that woman wears those stilts she calls shoes so she has room for putting notches on the heels. She's a sexual predator in skirts."

"She's a beautiful sexual predator."

"Maybe according to some guys, but not this guy. You know, if my attention hadn't been someplace else it might have been something to do, but I had someone else on my mind."

323

I try not to smile too much, but I can't hide how happy I feel. He slides back up next to me and I take his face in my hands and I kiss him long and slowly. He's an amazing kisser.

"Do you remember waking up in the middle of the night and asking where you were?" He asks.

"Yes. Did I say that out loud?"

"Uh, huh."

"Did you say something to me? I think you said something."

"I did. I said you're where you belong."

I smile, and lay my face against his shoulder.

"Yeah, now I remember, that was so nice." I murmur.

"Are you hungry?"

"Uh huh."

"There's a great little place that makes a killer breakfast just a short walk from here. I want to take you out for breakfast."

" I'm a mess. I don't have any clean clothes."

"You look beautiful. All you need is a shower and put on what you were wearing last night. I promise, you won't run into anyone you know.

Cole is right. We don't run into anyone I know, but we do run into about half the people he knows including: aunts, cousins, friends, and even his cat's vet. It's obvious Cole's a regular from the way the waitress comes over to our table, fills his coffee mug without asking, and hands him a copy of the paper.

"Hey Cole, who's your friend?" She asks, eyeing me up and down.

"Linda, this is Nicki Botticelli."

"Oh, Nicki, I've heard a lot about you." She sets down the coffee pot and shakes my hand enthusiastically after she wipes it off on her apron. She gives Cole a big smile and he looks a little sheepish.

"Nice to meet you." I smile at her and massage my hand back to life under the table. I'm wondering what Cole said about me to her, or to any of the other friendly faces smiling at us from different spots in the room.

After she hands us a couple of menus, Cole leans over and kisses me. I've never been terribly comfortable with public displays of affection and in this type of fish bowl environment, in broad daylight, I feel even less so. With so many of his family and friends in the same room, sneaking peeks at us. I find myself worrying what they're all thinking. I focus hard on my menu, hoping he won't do it again.

While we're waiting for our breakfast to arrive, he leans across my plate for another kiss, I playfully bop him on the nose with my finger and look down into my cup of tea as if I'm reading the leaves in the bottom and getting a very important message. I can feel him looking at me and I'm reluctant to look up at him. I pick up the paper sitting next to my tea and intently check the headlines. He reaches over it and lowers it from my face.

"Are you okay?" he asks.

"Uh huh," I smile, "I'm great."

He doesn't look convinced. The waitress brings our food just in time and I put the paper down to attack my Belgian waffles with over the top enthusiasm.

"Oh my God, these are delicious. How are your eggs?"

"They're good, but a kiss would be even more delicious."

I pause with my fork in mid-air. My eyes quickly scan the room counting the pairs of eyes looking in our direction. I lean forward giving him a quick peck on the lips and then refocus on the plate of food in front of me.

"What was that?" He asks.

I look at his questioning eyes. I'm afraid to answer him.

"Come here." He says it so sweetly, gesturing me forward with a hopeful look in his eyes.

I bite my lower lip searching for a way out that won't hurt his feelings.

"Cole, there are all these people around that know you. I'm a little uncomfortable."

I can see his mind working behind his eyes.

"It's ok, they're all my friends."

"Yeah, I know, but I'm not really comfortable with being affectionate in public. Don't you think they might think this is weird?"

A quizzical look passes across his face. "What would they think is weird? We're two people with feelings for each other."

I take a deep breath and look down at my waffles wishing they contained an escape hatch.

"What do you think is weird about that?" He asks.

I don't answer him and my silence changes his whole demeanor. I can't tell him that I'm wondering if they're looking at me and thinking *older woman, younger man*. He looks like he's possibly reading my mind.

"If people are looking at us, maybe it's because we look happy and they wish us well, or maybe it's because we look happy and they're jealous. There could be a lot of reasons people are looking at us. The bottom line is, do we really care? I know I don't."

He sits there looking at me, waiting for a response of some kind, but I don't know what to say. He runs a hand through his hair and stares hard at his plate of half eaten food.

"Then, what was that last night? Why did you come to me? Was that a one night stand?"

I open my mouth to speak and nothing comes out as my mind gropes for something to say to him.

"No. I. I." I fumble for words and lean my forehead onto my hand.

"I want to be with you Nicki, and I don't care who knows it, or who has an opinion about it good, or bad. If you don't feel the same way, then I don't know what I'm doing here. I'm not doing this any other way. You know, I wouldn't have taken you for someone who gave a shit about what other people think. Maybe you need to lighten up."

He stands, and takes his wallet out of his jeans, pulls some money out, and drops it onto the table. I watch his face close up. He doesn't even glance at me. Wordlessly, he turns and walks out the door.

I sit there blinking back tears. If people weren't watching before, they certainly are now.

Chapter 49 ~ December

The Holiday season is fast approaching along with Lily and James' wedding, and my fortieth birthday. It's a rollercoaster of emotions, and I'm riding it, white knuckled all the way.

The engagement party was beyond wonderful. Lily's family flew in from the West and James' drove up from the South. Kate and I hired amazing people and orchestrated the whole thing. The florist created beautiful table settings. The caterer did an amazing raw bar and seafood chowder. The D.J., and the two bartenders kept the drinks and music flowing. It was an evening of eating, dancing, laughing, crying and lots of hugging and kissing. I left feeling as if I had known these lovely people all of my life.

Since I knew it was going to be non-stop for the next two weeks until Christmas, I decided to get a tree early this year instead of right before my birthday like I usually do. The kids helped me haul in the ten-foot beauty, which we plan to finish decorating before my birthday arrives.

The smell of the pine greets me when I walk in the door of my house. I drop my bags and rush to catch the phone before it goes to voicemail.

"Hello?" I ask out of breath.

"Hi, sweetie, it's me." Lily's voice chirps at the other end. "I'm calling to remind you that we're going for our final fitting tonight."

"Oh God, I completely forgot. What time?"

"I'm heading there now. Can you be there by seven?"

I glance at my watch. "I'll be there." I move to the freezer and begin hunting for something quick to whip up for the kids before I have to head out. Again. I just have to get through the next forty-eight hours and then it will all be manageable. Somewhat.

I pop frozen lasagna in the oven, tear open a bag of salad with my teeth, and shake it out into a bowl wondering when I'll get a chance to eat. I munch on a couple of baby carrots, and head to the kids' rooms to let them know that I have to go out for a little while. Max is playing a game on his computer and acknowledges my presence with a barely perceptible nod of his head and a grunt.

After the whole naked Javier fiasco, I took Max to a therapist. It wasn't easy, but I knew I had to do it for the sake of my great kid. The two of us did a few uncomfortable sessions together, where I was assured that I hadn't scarred my child for life. I'm glad I did it. If I hadn't, I would have been paranoid when he started acting like the teenager he's becoming.

"Did you hear me Max?"

"Mom! I'm going to die if I stop!"

"That's a lovely thought." I mutter under my breath as I make my way to Ren's room.

With her sweet boyfriend Tyler around, Ren has been transformed into a girl who smiles a lot. I find myself doing double takes. It's as if aliens abducted my surly daughter and left this obvious counterfeit version in her place. I'm not complaining. I'm just confused.

I poke my head into her room. Tyler is strumming on her acoustic guitar and Renoir is sprawled out all over the floor with her schoolbooks, doing her homework with Tyler's patient assistance.

"Hi guys, I've got to go out for a little bit. There's dinner in the oven. The timer's set to go off and there's salad on the table. I should be back by nine at the latest. Please make sure that Max stops playing long enough to eat and do his homework. Call my cell if you need me."

The imitation Ren smiles at me and simply says, "Okay, Mom," and gets back to the math problems she's doing. It's mysterious as hell.

I holler in to Max's room as I head back to the kitchen. "Max, I'm going to check your homework when I get home so finish up that game ASAP!"

He hollers back,
"MOM!"

It's as if he and his sister have switched bodies. Damn aliens.

I rush into Yolanda's Dress Shop, peeling off my coat as I come through the door. It's snowing lightly and I shake it out of my hair before it gets a chance to melt.

"Wow, it's cold!"

"But isn't it beautiful?" Lily asks, with the same dreamy response she seems to have about everything lately. The stress of her upcoming nuptials, which turns most women into Bride-zilla hasn't really affected her. She seems to just float around the rest of us on her extra fluffy love cloud.

Beth, of Yolanda's assistants ushers me into a dressing room and helps me into my dress as Kate and Sophia come rushing in.

"It's like a freakin' blizzard out there!" Kate exaggerates, stamping the snow off her boots. Sophia comes over and gives me and Lily hugs and kisses, as Beth zips me up. I stand back to check myself out in the three-way mirror. The dresses are gorgeous. Since it's a winter wedding and at night, Lily has gone with a very dramatic look. Our dresses are velvet, cut on the bias, fitted through the torso with a fishtail hem and a low, wide ballet neck. The color, according to Yolanda, is claret. It fits me like a glove.

"No need for alterations." Sharon smiles at my reflection.

"You look gorgeous," says Sophia, "I hate you."

"Don't be a bitch, Soph," says Kate, climbing into her dress. As Beth zips her up she takes a deep breath. "I think this is going to be tight squeeze."

"I don't even dare to put mine on." Sophia moans, "Theo's been cooking for the past week. I could kill him."

"Was he force feeding you again? I'll kick his ass." Kate deadpans.

"Shut up." Sophia growls at Kate.

"This fabric has a little stretch to it," says Beth, as Kate relaxes into her dress. She drapes her hands on her hips and admires herself in the mirror.

"I look hot."

"So am I the only one who got fatter. I'm going to need two sets of Spanx." Sophia pouts, as she reluctantly pulls her dress on, only to find as Beth zips her up, that it fits.

"It fits?" She asks, a confused look on her face.

"It fits!" We both answer.

We're standing together in front of the mirror, admiring our bad selves, when Lily comes in from the back fitting room with Yolanda behind her, carrying her train. We seem to say it in unison.

"Wow!"

Lily beams at us. "You think so?"

She walks toward us and we move her in front of the huge mirror. Her dress is a rich ivory satin, strapless and simple, with a fitted, beaded bodice, and a slightly full skirt that ends with an understated train.

"Look at us." Lily says.

We stop staring at her and all turn together to face the mirror. Even without the finishing touches, it has a lot of impact and I immediately start welling up.

"Oh, Jesus, there she goes again," says Kate, making fun of my recently heightened emotional state.

"Our little Lily's getting married," I sniffle.

As soon as my water works start, it sets Lily off and Beth quickly stuffs a tissue in her hand to keep her from dripping on the satin.

"Oh, man." Kate whines, when Sophia joins in.

"You look so beautiful," Sophia sniffles, putting her arms around Lily, "and I'm so happy for you."

"Thank you, sweetie," says Lily, dabbing at Sophia's cheeks with her tissue.

"Okay, give me some of this action." Kate relents, joining in the group hug.

We finish up with our dresses ready to go and every detail prepared for. Tomorrow will be the rehearsal and dinner with friends and family. Lily goes over her checklist for the umpteenth time, and we reassure her that everything will be perfect, as kisses are given out all around.

We pull on boots, gloves and hats, wrap our faces in scarves, and head out into the snowy December night. In less than forty-eight hours, Lily will be married.

Chapter 50 ~ Going to the Chapel

Lily has hired two limos for the wedding. There's one for her to arrive in and one for the maids of honor, James' best man, and the groomsmen. We're each getting picked up at our homes. It's Lily's plan that we will have a built in designated driver for the ride home in case any of us party a little to hard. I'm the next to the last person on the list, with Sophia being our last stop before we head to the church and I'm hurrying to be ready on time.

The kids have opted to stay home even though Lily invited them. At this stage in their lives, dressing up in formal clothing and eating what they refer to as *freaky food*, is not their idea of a good time. I'm leaving them with specific instructions, pizza, and several DVDs. Nathan has offered to stop by later to check on them and make sure that they don't throw a party in my absence.

I'm so excited as I rush around getting ready, you'd think I was the one getting married. I stop in front of my full-length mirror to give myself the once over, when my phone rings and I'm informed that my chariot has arrived.

"I'll be right down."

I sashay into the living room in my dress to give the kids some quick final instructions, and the opportunity to check me out.

"Mom, you look so pretty," says my newly, non-sarcastic, daughter.

"Yeah, Nicki, you look awesome." Adds, Tyler.

"Nice dress." My son mutters in an obligatory tone.

I step out my door into the chill of the December air and I'm glad a warm limo is waiting for me. A Groomsman is holding the door open for me, and as I pass him, I stop and give him a long kiss on the mouth.

"Thank you." I say.

"No, thank YOU." He smiles at me.

I arrange myself on the seat and he climbs in next to me.

"You look beautiful," he says, taking my hand and kissing my fingertips. I smile coyly.

"You look pretty beautiful yourself."

"Jesus, you guys. Should we climb in the front with the driver and put up the privacy window?" Kate teases, as I kiss him again.

"I love you, Cole McCarthy."

"I love you, Nicola Botticelli."

"I now pronounce you horny and horny," mocks Kate, making a strange version of the sign of the cross in the air between us.

When we stop for Sophia and Theo, Sophia asks Kate, "So, have they been doing that annoying pawing each other thing?"

"Pretty much the whole time," answers Kate, in her most disgusted tone.

"Sounds good to me." Theo winks at me, and turns to kiss Sophia.

"I thought this was a limo, not the love train." Kate rolls her eyes and turns to James' best man, his brother John.

"Do you want to make out?"

"My wife wouldn't be happy about it. Otherwise, it's a great offer."

Kate nods her head. "That was very diplomatic of you."

I snuggle in next to Cole thanking the powers that be for giving me the sense that day more than two months ago, to get up and go after him when he walked out of the Café.

I had sat there for a couple of minutes with my heart pounding, and my thoughts racing. His last words, that I needed to lighten up, were eerily familiar and I thought about the dream and Paris' interpretation. Using those very words, she had said Cole was the man who was going to teach me how to do that. The agonizing thought that I could lose him got me up out of my seat. When I got out the door I could see him walking more than a hundred yards down the road with his head down, and his hands stuffed into his pockets. I sprinted after him. In spite of my aerobic classes I was so winded when I caught up with him, that I had to lean forward with my hands on my thighs to catch my breath.

"Are you okay?" He asked.

"I want to be with you." I struggled to get it out.

"What was that?"

"I want to be with you." I huffed.

"No matter what people think, or say?"

"No matter what people think, or say. You're right. I need to lighten up."

He didn't look convinced. So I grabbed him, and kissed him long and hard right there in broad daylight as people drove and walked by. A couple of guys in an old Ford pick-up beeped their horn and yelled something unintelligible out the window at us. I held onto him as tightly as I could.

"You're freakishly strong for such a small woman. Ease up before you crack one of my ribs." I looked up into his smiling face.

"I'm sorry Cole. I'm a silly insecure woman sometimes. This isn't easy for me, but I want to try."

"Try? I think it was Yoda who said, there is no try, there is only do."

"Then I want to do!" I answered him emphatically.

He took me by the hand and we headed back to his house.

Sitting next to him in the limo, I look down at his fingers entwined through mine. I realize he's been taking me by the hand ever since.

Lily hired Kate's boyfriend, Jeff, to photograph the wedding. After she saw his beautiful black and white shots around Kate's house, she knew he could give her the look she was going for. He greets us as we open the door of the limo, and clicks off several candid shots before we climb out. Then he directs us all onto the front steps of the church taking more candid photos along the way. We assemble quickly in the cold as he checks his light meter. He takes a few more and sends the guys into the church to wait for him just as Lily's limo pulls up. I carefully make my way down the stairs to help her with her train. Jeff hurries us as we're losing the light and takes more candid shots of the two of us coming up the stairs.

"Kate, you and Sophia on this side and Nicki move in close on Lily's other side." He directs us, as he snaps shot after shot.

When our teeth start chattering too hard for us to smile, and the light fades, we move into the vestibule waiting for the sound of Somewhere Over the Rainbow to send us on our journey down the aisle with Lily. Jeff makes his way to the front of the church to take more pictures from that angle.

As the first bars of the piece are played, Lily looks at us with big eyes and says,

"Here we go." She takes an audible, steadying breath. I fix her train and kiss her cheek. She gives Kate and Sophia quick hugs and as we line up in front of her, I blink back happy tears.

Following Kate in step, I pass Paris and Terrence who are beaming at us. Everywhere I look smiling faces surround us. Love swirls over the pews, spilling over us and onto the floor. I glide across its glistening surface. When I look up, I see Cole's smiling face. His eyes never leave mine.

I've thought many times of going back to Rachel, the psychic in Salem. I want to tell her she was right. I did find love and just as she said, it wasn't what I thought it would be. It didn't come easily, because my fear made me fight it. It came to me only after I let go of the fear, trusted in my heart, and in a man who showed me just how high and far love could take me. Paris says she probably already knows.

Epilogue ~

The following summer Lily and James welcomed a beautiful, eight-pound, baby boy into their family. It turned out that when Lily said 'I do,' to James, she was pregnant. She was the only one who knew. Two days before the wedding she did a home pregnancy test because she was a couple of weeks late. It came up positive. James got the happy news on their honeymoon. The rest of us had to wait to get the news when they came home. Little baby Sean has a lot of doting, honorary aunties.

Sophia and Theo moved in together in the spring and are crazy in love. Sophia's twins really like him and the feeling is definitely mutual. Her dad finally came around and has even invited Theo to go fishing with him. So that's a done deal. The two of them have been house hunting and between you and me, Theo's also been ring shopping.

Kate and Jeff broke up not long after the wedding and she was so torn up about it, she buried herself in her work. That ended up winning her top honors as Real Estate Broker of the region. At a huge luncheon in her honor, she was introduced to another hotshot broker named David Stelton, and it was Real love at first sight. There's been some talk of them uniting the kingdoms. We'll have to wait and see.

Paris and her brood are doing well. Terrence started to do a lot of gigs in Europe, which developed into a huge following in a short amount of time. They're talking about moving to France. I don't know what I'll do without my Bestie. I guess we'll both have to rely on Skype.

My business has continued to grow. Cole helped me to create a bunch of instructional videos and I've developed a little following on YouTube. Renoir and Max are both wonderful, for teenagers. Under Cole's tutelage, we've all taken up Kite-boarding and love it. We're planning a Kiting vacation to Costa Rica for my birthday. Cole had wanted to surprise me, but I told him I'm not a big fan of birthday surprises.

Most days you can find me at Cole's little house on the river. For now, it's perfection. Hell, my mom even likes him. Pinch me.